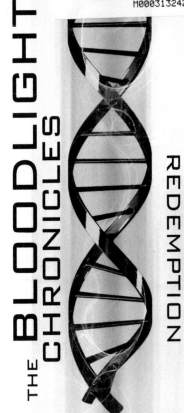

THE **BLOODLIGHT** CHRONICLES

REDEMPTION

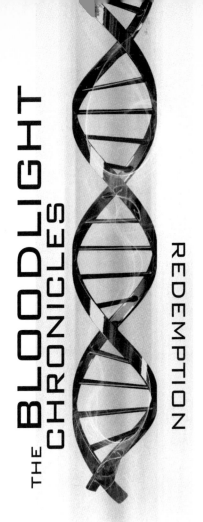

THE **BLOODLIGHT** **CHRONICLES**

REDEMPTION

STEVE STANTON

ECW PRESS

Published by ECW Press
2120 Queen Street East, Suite 200, Toronto, Ontario, Canada M4E 1E2
416-694-3348 / info@ecwpress.com

LIBRARY AND ARCHIVES CANADA CATALOGUING IN PUBLICATION

Stanton, Steve, 1956–
Redemption / Steve Stanton.

(Bloodlight chronicles)
ISBN 978-1-55022-989-9
ALSO ISSUED AS: 978-1-77090-101-8 (PDF); 978-1-77090-100-1 (EPUB)

I. Title. II. Series: Stanton, Steve, 1956– . Bloodlight chronicles.

PS8587.T3237R44 2012   C813'.54   C2012-902695-6

Design and Artwork: Juliana Kolesova
Editor: Chris Szego
Development: David Caron
Printing: Trigraphik l LBF 5 4 3 2 1

This book is set in Garamond 3.

This is a work of fiction. Names, characters, places, and incidents either are the product of the author's imagination or are used fictitiously, and any resemblance to actual persons, living or dead, business establishments, events, or locales is entirely coincidental.

The publication of *The Bloodlight Chronicles: Redemption* has been generously supported by the Canada Council for the Arts which last year invested $20.1 million in writing and publishing throughout Canada, by the Ontario Arts Council, by the Government of Ontario through the Ontario Media Development Corporation and the Ontario Book Publishing Tax Credit, and the Government of Canada through the Canada Book Fund.

 Canada Council   Conseil des Arts
for the Arts   du Canada
 Canada
 ONTARIO ARTS COUNCIL
CONSEIL DES ARTS DE L'ONTARIO

PRINTED AND BOUND IN CANADA

"I did not come to bring peace, but a sword."

—Yeshua bar Yosef

ONE

Jimmy Kay frowned when he first saw the girl. Her background harmonics sounded like a symphony to his highly trained senses, a holy aura of speed and potency. She should have been way up Prime with logistics like that, not cruising Main Street like a tourist. Very odd. Jimmy Kay edged away from this exotic young avatar. She was out of place yet seemed an integral part of the landscape, at home and connected to the heart of the digital city. A couple of greysuits ambled near, checking for vagrant users and bad buzz on the boulevard, but gave her nary a glance as they passed. Very odd. Jimmy seized the moment to drop Sublevel through a back-door conduit. He had business downstairs, not illegal exactly, but not licit enough for Main Street.

He pushed some arbitrage buttons and slid some data, massaging the white market for his daily bread, but when he turned to exit he saw the girl again, watching him from a careful distance. Not good. He was supposed to be invisible in this avatar; this was his best outfit, the one he always relied on for anonymity. He wondered if she was a regent hunter or government gestapo. Why else would she follow him down to Sublevel Zero?

"Who are you?" he said, preparing to flee at the first perturbation.

The young avatar approached him without hesitation, making eye contact with familiarity, sucking his source code into an infinite vortex of power. "I have another job for you, Jimmy."

In a flash he recognized the persona—an echo of a deal gone sour. "Phillip?"

"Hardly appropriate now. Call me Philomena in this form."

"The virgin martyr?"

"Well, I know you have a penchant for the pretty girls." The avatar smiled to show no offense. Her harmonics were impeccable, deep and placid like a black lake. She blended seamlessly into the terrain, comfortable even here in the underground.

"I thought you were dead," Jimmy said.

"I was."

"How long have you been following me?"

"All your life."

Jimmy Kay winced and turned away. Philomena appeared in front of him again, faster than a blink. Jimmy shook his head, feeling weak and weary of existence. "I'm just washing some money, clipping data, nothing for you to worry about."

"I like you, Jimmy."

He inspected the young avatar with greater care, now that his future hung in a delicate balance. Asian, almond-shaped eyes, black hair cut short and spiky, designer body somewhere in that sweet spot between twenty-five and thirty-five—just another perfect girl off the digital shelf. "You're not even real."

"None of us are real," she said. "You know that better than most."

"What do you want, Phillip? Sorry, Phil-o-men-a." He stretched out the syllables with sarcasm.

"I'm looking for a business partner."

"I'm retired."

"You keep saying that, but you don't mean it."

"This time I'm serious. It's nothing but blue-zone livin' for me now. Get lost." He turned away again, but the girl blocked his path. She moved without effort. She was already everywhere.

"Don't underestimate me, old friend." Philomena winked at him and Jimmy heard a pop in the back of his head like a bubble bursting, felt a warm glow seep down his spine, some direct-connect devil hack. His eyesight went fuzzy for a moment, then quickly cleared again, more focused than ever, as though he was seeing everything for the first time with a brilliant lucidity.

Jimmy felt a whisper of fear. Phillip had been burned by the Beast. His brain had been obliterated for manifold sins against the V-net. He had died, that much was certain. Now this powerful girl was impersonating him. She had probably hacked into his system as his spark faded, stolen his access logarithms, some *otaku* genius from out east.

"You're wasting your talent on me, kid," he said.

"I'm spinning a web on the V-net, Jimmy, fixing things. Everybody wants a better world."

"I'm kind of busy today," he said. "Can we talk later?"

Philomena flashed a toothy grin. "After all these years, you still won't believe your own eyes, your own ears. Why do you doubt the truth?" She took a step back and began to metamorphose. Her body expanded. She grew taller, wider. Hair sprouted from her skin as her face took the snouted shape of a bear, her teeth long and pointed like daggers. Her bandwidth went off the scale as data cartwheeled around her like spinning whorls of light, a direct connection to Prime Eight or higher, into unfathomable reaches. Her eyes became red demonic beacons as she stretched out her hands and her fingers elongated and intertwined into the walls and ceiling, into the fabric of Sublevel

Zero. She laughed and the sound came from everywhere, even inside his own avatar, in the very core of his being.

Jimmy turned and ran in blind panic from the Beast unleashed, holding both hands up to his skull as he stumbled forward, his neurons overclocking in the upper registers, his cerebrum beginning to cook. Holy ghost, his synapses were at stake, his life! He was too vulnerable, caught in a snare like a vagrant animal. The Beast could flense his brain to the bone in a flash. Who was this mystery girl? He jumped in a public zoomtube and quickly willed himself back home to Main Street. He dove into the milling V-net crowd for safety, spread his parameters wide, submerged into the digital underground to hide from the AI monster, just another anonym in the mix, transient code, a digital gypsy from nowhere, no ripples, no traces.

But infinite eyes followed him even there.

In desperation, he pulled his plug.

He felt pain like a hammer blow to his temple.

God, what happened? Jimmy sat up from his launch couch and blinked his eyes a few times for surety. He had a fearsome headache from his overclock—could almost smell the fried dendrites—and he reached up to massage his bald pate, trying to think. Was Phillip back and more psychotic than ever? Was he impersonating the Beast? How could that be?

He stumbled to the kitchen like a zombie burn-out, parched and thirsty. A security chime sounded from street level as Jimmy downed a glass of cold water from the communal tap. He checked the webcam and saw Helena's face looking up at the camera, grim and tired. Helena Sharp, Chairman of the ERI, power broker extraordinaire. He hadn't seen her in two years and had a bad feeling. They had been lovers once and had never broken it off officially. Weeks had drifted to months. He touched his finger to the sensor pad, feeling spacey and vacuous at the twisted turn of events. "Helena?"

"Hi, Jimmy. Can I come up?"

"Sure." He pressed the lobby unlock and heard a click. "Take the elevator to the top and go up one flight of stairs to the penthouse. Never mind the gridwork. It's a Faraday cage." He watched the top of her head turn and disappear from view as vacancy gnawed at him. He should have kept in touch. He tried to remember back to the last time they had met in V-space. She had been busy running the Eternal Research Institute, getting younger every day thanks to the regenerative virus in her veins. She had been throwing money at a public inoculation program, a black hole of interminable and expensive research, and resources had been growing tight. He had granted her a small loan of a few million and never expected repayment.

Jimmy stood in the doorway to watch her come down the hall, recognizing her walk like a welcome vision from the past, her royal stance with determined and magnificent gait a potent memory. But on close inspection, he could see a hint of dejection in the slump of her shoulders, something amiss. Her blond hair was cut short, businesslike, and she wore her usual dark skirtsuit and stockings. She carried an oversize handbag but no luggage. She was a long way from home.

"Welcome to Canada," he said when she came within earshot.

"Thanks."

"Any trouble at the border?"

She smiled. "What border?"

Jimmy ducked his head and chuckled. "Well, it will be a different story on the way back."

"I'm not going back," she said.

Helena held out her hand on approach, businesslike again, no hug, no running into his outstretched arms. He should have kept in touch. She was young and beautiful, always had been, always would be, thanks to the Eternal virus.

He gripped her hand firmly and felt equal strength in return. They lingered with this one tactile gesture, testing the years until Jimmy dropped his arm with reluctance. "So, did I miss your birthday, or do you still bother with anachronisms?"

"I turned ninety just last week, but I didn't bother with a party. I went for a med check instead."

"Sounds like fun. How did that go?"

"Not good." She pressed her lips and looked down, chose not to elaborate just yet.

"Well, you look forty-five if a day, Helena. The virus has been good to you."

"Thanks."

Jimmy swayed a gallant arm to invite her inside, and she stepped in with wonder at the architecture, the Roman columns sunk into the walls and ornate arches between rooms. He had a series of exotic alien landscapes on display, oil paintings from an artist who had travelled through the Macpherson Doorway to Cromeus Sigma on an eccentric and expensive journey of discovery. Helena paused before one dark and haunting canvas, a twilight scene with the rogue planet Babylon rising over a craggy horizon. She tilted her head momentarily in study, or perhaps recognition, then continued on into the wide expanse of his main living area. With a clinical eye Jimmy noticed shirts and shoes lying on or under the furniture, his pyjamas draped over a chair, and felt bachelorhood full force, a self-conscious dismay.

Helena seemed not to notice. She wandered around, quietly touching things, examining his collection of rare artifacts and curios, taking it all in. She seemed somnambulant, dream-walking. Something had gone terribly wrong. Helena had been the strong shoulder as long as Jimmy had known her, a tower of authority. She had pioneered the ERI for years like a stalwart commander. She had taken his protege Zak on a return trip to the Cromeus colonies by the scruff of his neck, where she had contracted the Eternal virus through brute will of discovery. What had happened to his long-lost lover? She seemed but a ghost of her former glory. They ended up in the kitchen and she peeked in the fridge. "I could use a boost," she said. "Caffeine and a vitamin shot."

"There's an Ultra in there somewhere. You want me to nuke it for you?"

She fished around until she found the carton, popped the tab and guzzled it cold.

"Thanks," she said and tipped the half-empty container at him.

"No problem. So you finally decided to retire?"

"Yeah, I guess that's it."

"Well, congratulations. It's about time."

"Thanks."

He studied her, thinking about sex again. Crazy, huh, after two years apart. "You want me to bring up your luggage?"

She shook her head. "I left in a hurry. Didn't bother to pack."

Jimmy nodded. "You can hang out here as long as you like."

"Thanks."

"We don't have to jump back into things, you know, if you don't want to right away."

"Thanks."

"Are you going to tell me, Helena?"

She bit her lip with insecurity in a girlish mannerism, paused to summon some uncertain inner resource. "I'm dying, Jimmy."

The news hit him slowly, the panic later still. He was an old man. His timing was off. "What? No way."

"That's what *I* thought."

"You're Eternal," he said. "You can't die."

"I can and I will. Sooner than you think."

"Are you certain?"

"I've lost the virus, Jimmy. It disappeared from my body without a trace, and the absence has upset the protein gradient in my mitochondria. Dr. Mundazo is baffled. I've become an impossible specimen." She seemed girlish again, lost and helpless, a humbled demigod struggling with ruthless fate.

Jimmy felt dread in his abdomen, a portent of doom. Could Eternals wither and die? Could providence fade? What hope would there be for the world? In a moment Helena was in his arms, her nose in his neck, her breasts heaving against his body. Her mortality had driven her back to him, the common human heritage they now shared. He was well into his sixties now and degenerating naturally with age, losing brain-space daily. Who knew how many good years he had left? "Maybe the virus will come back," he offered.

"No," she said. "It's permanent. My cells are already collapsing with necrosis."

"Flesh-eating disease?"

"No, not an infection. A complete traumatic breakdown. I have only weeks to live."

His body stiffened and he pulled back to study her at arm's length. "Weeks?"

She grimaced. "Maybe months. There's no way to know for certain."

"God, Helena."

She looked away, hanging her head. "You don't have a god, Jimmy."

"I mean," he said, "it's just so sudden." He winced with compassion, feeling defenceless in the shadow of death. What could he say?

She pressed her lips into a smile, braving false stoicism for his benefit. "Now I know what you mortals face every day, Jimmy. I've loved you from the beginning, and there's no longer any reason to deny it." She gazed at him with a grim promise of renewal if he would accept her on these new and dangerous terms, pleading with her eyes for a revival of romance before she died. What choice did he have?

"We could pump you full of Eternal blood," Jimmy said. "Transfuse daily."

Helena shook her head. "We thought of that. My friends all rallied around me for support. But there's not enough blood to spare now, the way the vampires suck it up. I decided to leave it all behind." She looked away and blinked quick tears as they finally found their escape. "The Source has abandoned me, Jimmy. I can't fight against destiny."

He held her face in his hands and gently wiped away her tears. He searched her eyes and promised his love as best he could. He should have called her long ago. Helena reached for her lapel, shrugged off her business jacket and draped it carefully over the back of a chair. Jimmy led her to the master bedroom and slowly undressed her, marvelling at taut flesh from a lost and distant dream. The woman was mature enough to be his mother, perish the thought, but he felt like a dirty old man as he laid her down and worshiped her slender body for a few minutes, teasing her to pinnacles with tender fingers. Against the dark burgundy bedspread, her pale skin seemed virtuous, her intimacy a precious gift to be unwrapped and enjoyed with thanksgiving. In time she grew lethargic with satisfaction and drifted in a primitive, murmuring sensuality, and he dimmed the lights before shedding the clothes from his own shabby, unaugmented body. He lowered himself gently into her fragrant embrace as Helena moaned beneath him and thrashed against him, but in the darkness all Jimmy could see was the almond-shaped eyes of Philomena, the Beast incarnate.

Niko knocked twice and entered the office of Dr. Mundazo on the seventh floor of the Eternal Research Institute. She had been summoned for a rare appointment, something official, probably bad news as usual. Silus Mundazo was dressed casually in a collared shirt and slacks, no lab coat, no professional smile. He pointed with a palm to the chair opposite his desk.

"Good to see you again," he said. "Have a seat. Keeping well?" The digital wallpaper behind him showed a majestic scene with a towering purple mountain wreathed in fog.

"Just fine, thank you." They made themselves comfortable on either side of the business barricade. Dr. Mundazo looked gaunt with tension, the tendons in his neck stiff like cords. He was the acting head of the ERI, Chief Physician and second in command to Helena Sharp. He was supposed to be the formal fount of confidence, but he didn't look the part. Niko scrutinized him carefully. "Is there a problem?"

Silus slanted a smile. Of course there was a problem—never a shortage of trouble in his business. "Just a policy development," he said. "We're instituting mandatory tithing, something we've tried to avoid for many years." He glanced away from her probing eyes.

"No way," she said.

He looked down at his desk, tapped a finger. His monitors were blank, his holopad inert. "I'm afraid so."

"I've already paid my dues to get here," Niko said. "I won't give up my blood."

The good doctor nodded grimly. "I know your history. You're practically a legend."

"Then you know I could never cooperate with vampires."

Silus Mundazo winced at the barb, stiffened with professional resolve. "We're not going to tie you down and drain you dry. One bottle a week is all we ask, just like everyone else."

She shook her head, resolute. "No way."

"I'm afraid I have no choice." He spread his hands. "I'm sorry."

"Helena promised me a deal," she said. "We're even-steven."

"That was years ago."

Niko felt a cloud of oppression. Even in their protective enclaves, Eternals lived at the mercy of the Man, their regenerative plasma the currency of the day, promising longevity to the weaker species. "I risked my life for this place."

"We've all paid a high price, Niko. I've been selling my own blood since before you were . . . ah . . . born."

Dr. Mundazo knew full well she had never been born. She was an illegal clone, a carbon copy of a dead original. She had been engineered under an electron microscope, subtly altered, created not conceived. It was a secret openly shared but never spoken aloud in her presence. People might smirk behind their hands, but they would never dare throw the truth in her face.

Niko bristled and rose to her feet. "I must speak with Director Sharp."

Silus Mundazo sighed with gathering weight, held up a palm for peace. "Helena has resigned her position due to medical complications. She's left the compound. The board has appointed me Director in her absence." He patted the air to signal her back to her seat, and Niko sat, slow and dreamlike in confusion. Medical complications? Helena was Eternal, continually rejuvenated by the virus. It was impossible for her to get sick or damaged, except in some physical accident. Perhaps she was pregnant. Niko wondered if that was safe for a ninety-year-old woman, even in this posthuman age. What else could it be? "You're forcing me into a corner, Silus."

"It's not too much to ask."

"There's an inviolate principle at stake," she said. "More blood creates more vampires, a vicious circle of dependency. We shouldn't pander to the raging populace."

"Philosophy is easy, Niko. Life is hard. The Source is spawning fewer Eternals every year now, but demand for blood keeps growing at an exponential pace. The black marketplace is reaching crisis. Our business partners are facing new competition from a younger crowd, rival gangs with harsh demands, punks with greedy fire in their eyes."

"It's not my problem, Silus. I warned Helena about this years ago. You humans will never recognize the enemy until you take a look in the mirror. You're your own worst nightmare. The same pattern of prohibition repeats over and over in history, the sad downside of any rule of law. Restricted supply brings rising prices and a criminal subculture, and that leads inevitably to increased violence, death, and disease. We can never produce enough blood for everyone," she said. "We should not even try."

Dr. Mundazo frowned and stabbed a finger at the office window. "Do you know what it costs to keep that army of goons around our perimeter? Don't you wonder why the bloodlords grant us this meagre refuge? They could come in with cannons and tear gas any time they want and take us all captive. They could raze the building, kidnap us to their sham donor clinics. Do you think the government would come to our aid, those spineless politicians that passed the Evolutionary Terrorist Omnibus?"

"The Blood War must end someday," Niko said. "We've got to stand up for our rights and be counted as citizens."

"Do you really want to be counted, Niko? Do you want your DNA on public record? Your exotic ancestry?"

"Are you threatening me?"

"No," he said, shaking his head, "your secrets are safe. All I'm asking is a token of cooperation for the benefit of all Eternals. One bottle of plasma a week." He spread open palms in a plea for peace. "A simple show of goodwill."

"I'll never give up my blood, Silus. Not after escaping from a vampire prison. How can you think to extort such an outrageous penalty when I can walk away any minute?" She rose again to her feet, preparing for the final confrontation, already imagining her easy escape, packing her stuff in her mind, travelling light.

"What about Sienna?"

An involuntary surge of emotion swept through Niko at the reminder of the mysterious empath, the vagabond child she had rescued from vampires. She stilled herself with effort. "What about her?"

"You love her," the doctor said with deadpan confidence.

Niko shivered her head against the notion. Love was a vulnerability she could never afford. "No. Sienna is your research subject. She's your responsibility. I did my best for you and her, for everyone here." She stopped to take a pensive and dangerous breath. "But it's over now."

Silus Mundazo worked his lips grimly, preparing some new confession, more bad news. "There's a complication, Niko. We ran the usual tests, a genscan and standard work-ups. Sienna's not Eternal, but she has your DNA." He glanced away as though testing the wallpaper scene for moral support, some instructional guidance. "The technicians won't sign a legal verification without your approval, of course, but there's a ninety-nine percent probability that she's your daughter."

Niko gaped in bewilderment, her neck suddenly rigid with anxiety. "What?"

Silus Mundazo swivelled his chair sideways and stood. He walked to the office window and gazed out at a panoramic view of fields blooming with springtime vigour, a green and fertile woodland in the distance. "I confirmed the analysis myself."

An electric clarity filled her mind, a sharp, brittle reality. "Another clone?"

Silus shook his head, peering dutifully away to give her privacy of thought, a chance to process the data in composure. "No," he said, "a conjoinment."

"I've never had a baby, Doctor, I swear." Niko flung her hands to her sides in exasperation. "I've barely even had *sex*."

His shoulders twitched in a shrug. "An artificial womb, perhaps a surrogate."

Her voice came out hoarse with pain. "I can't believe it!"

Dr. Mundazo turned to level his gaze at her, his face granite with concern. "You must believe it, Niko. I would never lie to a fellow Eternal after so many generations of heartache. Everything I'm telling you is the absolute truth as near as we can determine."

"But it's impossible!"

"No, quite probable by all accounts," he said, "given your heritage. An egg may have been harvested without your knowledge, perhaps when you were under anaesthetic for one of your augmentations." He spread his hands to consider the obvious.

"Phillip," she whispered. "That bastard."

Silus Mundazo set his mouth and dropped his eyes. "Helena asked me not to tell you, out of concern for your mental health in a time of crisis. You seemed happy enough with Sienna, bonding naturally. It seemed the best course of action for all concerned." He spread his hands. "Sienna looks just like you."

Of course she did. Everyone said so. Niko sighed. She had ignored the signals, avoided the obvious. The empathic child probably knew the truth already, with her exotic psi talents. The kid had called her "mommy" since that first moment they met in the vampire den, huddled quaking under a table during a time of war. How had Sienna ended up in the hands of the bloodlords? Had Phillip arranged some business agreement, some unholy alliance? That bastard! Niko stiffened her spirit against an impossible onslaught. "What about the father?"

Doctor Mundazo shrugged again. "An unknown variable. No DNA matches in the public genome. Even in this day of vigilance, not every human is on record. There are still holdouts, unregistered semen samples, small communities of Eternals in hiding. Something may turn up."

"Well, that's convenient," Niko drawled with sarcasm. "So I'm on the hook as a permanent foster mother? No way." She shook her head with determination, galvanized her body with perseverance. "Sienna's not my problem!" She glared at him. "Find a new babysitter."

The doctor's face hardened at Niko's effrontery. "You think you're kite-flying solo high above the mundane crowd below, but you're wrong, Niko. You've got baggage, just like the rest of us grubbing down here in the ditch. Your DNA roots can be traced with perfect accuracy back to the Neanderthals that took wives from among the early Cro-Magnons advancing from Africa. The northern Neanderthals were men of renown in those days, giants with huge brains and bodies to match. The ancient scribes called them the

Nephilim, the 'fallen ones,' because their race did not survive the catas-
trophes of change, but their hybrid seed spread throughout Eurasia
and mingled on Earth." He pointed his finger at her like a weapon.
"You carry that rare history in your DNA, Niko, along with recent
mutations that form an unmistakable pattern in your family. There
can be no mistaking that indelible record." He tossed his hand aside
as though to obliterate any protestation. "You speak of humanity as
though we were something foreign, but you're as human as the rest
of us. Just because you're a clone doesn't mean you can spurn your
heritage. We're all just one fused chromosome away from being a
chimpanzee. Sienna is the only true posthuman among us. Vast por-
tions of her DNA have been significantly reconfigured, but she's your
child by birthright. You belong together."

Niko clenched her teeth and turned away, blind-faced numb,
drained of confidence. Her dead father and mentor had tricked her,
raided her womb for some foul experiment with the family genome.
She'd been nothing but lab data to him, just a fake daughter, an
illegal clone with no civil rights, whore of the future. She walked like
an automaton to the door and let herself out, raging with malice. She
would return to Phillip's clinic and scour the place for evidence of
his deceit, enlist Andrew and Colin7 to help her unravel the tangled
web of history. Perhaps the new zombie Phillip inhabiting his body
would have some clues locked in his decimated cranium, some vestige of background memory from the original personality now lost in
V-space, that bastard!

At the door to her apartment she paused on the threshold, scarred
with fresh defilement, wondering what she should reveal to Sienna,
how she could explain such interpersonal morass. Her daughter
was surely innocent of any harmful intent, just another laboratory
victim like herself. Sienna was six years old now and a prodigy child,

already reading at the level of a ten-year-old, already understanding far beyond her years. Niko took a cleansing breath and pressed the palm sensor to unlock the door. She stepped inside on rubbery stilts, feeling a strange foreboding in her abdomen, a spiritual entropy. Sienna stood waiting near the door, smiling with excitement, her bulging backpack at her side with a bright design facing upward, an embossed princess waving a magic wand in a land of enchantment.

The young sitter, Madison from the cafeteria, stood behind shrugging with discomfort.

"I'm ready to go, Mommy," Sienna said cheerfully.

Two

Rix got Niko's news by text on his wristband, not even the courtesy of voicemail from his girlfriend, though they were perpetually estranged and technically she didn't owe him anything. Niko and Sienna had hopped a ride to the bus station, eschewing the protection of the Eternal community in some typically impulsive gesture of defiance. She was mad as hell but would plug up when she reached a secure launch couch. Not to worry, see you soon in V-space. Crap.

He paced his dorm room wondering what had gotten into his stepcousin. Why would she suddenly bail on him when they were just starting to get comfortable together again? Where was she headed? Back out onto the street to be vampire fodder? To the gutter-slide of perpetual decay in the city catacombs?

His musings were interrupted by a duty summons from the front gate. A novitiate had just jumped off a transport shuttle and was asking for sanctuary as a new Eternal. Rix had been appointed as the official greeter in Helena's absence. He was supposed to be the local statesman, a smiling mediator at the retail counter. Bureaucratic crap. He wished he was out on his bike smuggling biochips and augments, or just racing the forest trails with Niko, climbing cliffs and jumping ravines under endless blue sky.

He pulled on a clean collared shirt but didn't tuck it in at the waist. He brushed his teeth and rubbed a hint of downy stubble on his chin as he peered at his reflection above the sink. Where would he ever find the time to scrape his face every day? His life was already a whirlwind. He ruffled his short brown hair into a semblance of order and tapped the V-net plug dangling from his left earlobe to superimpose the correct time on his field of vision. He didn't look much like a diplomat, but he shrugged on a tan sport jacket in a vain attempt at legitimacy and made his way downstairs.

Rix studied the young girl on the other side of the Security perimeter. Fluffy blond hair, cherubic face, thin as a poplar pole on stilts, probably sixteen or seventeen, sitting in an alcove on a bench seat awaiting admittance to the ERI. What the heck was he supposed to say to her? He felt like a court jester pretending to authority, but he nodded with civility to the guard and stepped through the scanner gauntlet to greet her.

The girl stood at the sight of him, looking shocked, a bit in awe.

"Um, hi," he said.

The girl rushed to him, flung her arms around his torso, and planted her cheek firmly against his rigid chest. "Thank you, God," she whispered as she clutched him.

Rix pried her back a notch, peeked at her face. "Are you okay?" he asked.

She blinked at him, doelike with teary eyes. "I knew you were real," she said. Her voice was musical, unbroken by tragedy.

"What?"

"You're an angel, right?"

"Uh, no," he said. "I'm just filling in for the welcoming

committee. The Director is away visiting friends." He fluttered a hand foolishly and felt hot blood in his cheeks, his other hand still clamped tight in her grasp.

"But you're one of those people who live forever," she said with certainty.

"That's right." He nodded. "Eternals, we call them. And you?"

"I think so," she said and smiled with a hopeful pride of kinship. "I found one of those glowing infinity vials from the aliens. I drank it, just like the urban legend. It was overwhelming, the feeling of rejuvenation and holiness."

"That would do it," Rix said with a grin. "What's your name?"

"Jovita Grace Caldwell, but my friends call me Jo."

"Lovely name, cool. Okay, Jo. Welcome to the Eternal Research Institute. I'm Rix."

"I saw you in a dream," she said with reverence. She squeezed his hand tighter, viselike.

Rix felt a wave of paranoia. "Really?"

"Yeah, I mean, I was a bit scared," she blurted. "My mom told me to come here. She said I'd be safe. I should have kept the whole thing secret, I guess, but I just had to tell a few friends. It was crazy-fantastic, you know, in our little burb outside the city. Weird alien stuff, who could believe it? Anyway, word got out. I should have been more careful. Two men in business suits came to our house and offered to put me in a government research project. My mom doesn't much like the government."

"Your parents did the right thing."

"Just my mom," she said and wrinkled her nose. "Who has a dad these days?"

Rix thought of his own dad, Zakariah, off with his new wife researching psychic phenomena in a questionable career move; the two of them knew a little bit about everything, just enough to be dangerous. He thought of his mother Mia, long dead and buried without fanfare, and shrugged off a feeling of loneliness. "Uh, well." He extracted his hand from her grasp and pointed to the Security perimeter where two guards eyed them with suspicion. He tried to remember the protocol Mundazo had drilled into him. "We offer safe harbour to all Eternals by birthright. You can get Level Two access with a simple biometric scan. Other privileges are earned through service. It's not scary."

Jovita hooked her arm around his elbow, unwilling to stray from his touch. "I know you won't hurt me. I saw you in a dream."

Rix led her to the guards on duty. She spelled out her name to log a voiceprint, peered in a camera that scanned her retina, and placed her hand on a palm sensor. She stepped hesitantly through an electronic gauntlet hung with needles like cactus spines, and passed a small backpack through an x-ray portal. Safe on the other side, she turned and waited for Rix to follow, trembling but putting up a good front as a guard clipped a laminate to her collar with her keycode and global position. She seemed frail and tiny without her backpack, nubile and beautiful in a tight purple tunic and black leggings, no facial piercings, no visible tattoos.

"You look like you could use a good meal," Rix said with a conciliatory smile. "Maybe we should start your tour at the cafeteria." He took her pack from the security guard and slung it over his shoulder. "How far along in school are you?"

"I've got my entrance certificate for college," she said as they began walking. "Still checking out my options. I'm kind of into environmental science, you know?"

So she was older than she appeared, almost his own age. "Sure," he said, "environment is good." A pout of disappointment told him he had goofed up. Why was he always so inept around pretty girls? "I mean, global warming sucks, for sure."

Jovita nodded. "Do you go to school?"

"I'm working online," Rix said, "second year general. I'm studying art in my spare time, doing some oil painting, different things." He tilted a shoulder in a show of self-effacement. He was pretty good but didn't want to lord it over her.

"That's cool," she said. "Can you teach me?"

"Sure, I guess." Her glowing face showed genuine interest. "Have you tried oils?"

"No, but I've done some portraits." She held up a warning palm. "Just cartoons and comics. My mom says they're wonderful, but don't all moms?"

"Mine died early," Rix said. He felt a twitch near his eye.

"Oh, I'm so sorry." Her posture softened like a flower shying from a darkening sky.

"Thanks," he said, "it's been a couple years. My dad remarried."

Jovita bobbed her chin knowingly. She darted her gaze around as they passed workers in cubicles or group sessions. "So these people are all, what did you say, Eternals?"

"The virus is regenerative, cell by cell."

"And that makes our blood, like . . . valuable?"

"Yeah, there's a black market," he said, "getting greyer all the time. We each tithe a bottle a week to pay the expenses on this place."

She stared at him with wide eyes. "I have to sell my blood?"

Oops, not very diplomatic. Rix grimaced. He obviously wasn't very good at this stuff. Why did Mundazo give him the damn job anyway? "Yeah. I should have mentioned that earlier, sorry. It used to be strictly volunteer, but times are tough." He recalled Niko's parting tirade against the new policy, the omnipresent tyranny of the bloodlords. She had called Mundazo a pimp and Rix a prostitute, a cheap hooker for the Man.

Jovita chewed her lips in thought. "Does it hurt?"

"No, not a bit," he said. "Hey, I'm sorry if this seems a bit weird coming at you so sudden. I'm not trying to trick you or anything."

She smiled. "That's okay, Rix. I trust you." She reached for his grip again, and they continued walking together hand in hand like date mates. Her palm was slender and soft with warmth seeking solace. "Can we be friends?"

Rix glanced around as they entered the cafeteria, wondering what people might think of such public intimacy with a fresh companion. "Sure, yeah," he said, feeling conflicted and anxious. Though never an official partner, Niko had always been his steady girl, his continual source of unrequited lust at home and away. Niko was prideful and arrogant, invincible in action and magnificent in motion. Jovita was way different, gentler, calm in spirit and fragile with innocence. He felt a protective instinct around her, some primeval nesting urge.

"I don't have much money," Jovita said as she examined the food. "Are you buying?"

"That's okay," he said. "It's communal. Everyone volunteers."

She peered past the counters into the kitchen area with new interest, craning her neck to get a glimpse at the restaurant equipment. "Can I work here?"

Rix shrugged. "Yeah, I guess so, if that's your thing."

"I'm a good cook. I could totally do this."

"Sure," he said. "I'll ask around." He slid two trays into line and went ahead to show by example, scooped some chicken-pasta casserole onto a plate though he had just eaten an hour ago.

Incredibly, Jovita loaded up a tray with enough food for three adults, beef and gravy, potatoes and vegetables, a buttered croissant with apple pie for dessert. She picked out a table and began eating with a steady rhythm, closing her eyes occasionally to savour a mouthful, mumbling in praise of rare culinary excellence. Rix felt a pang of self-reproach as he watched her simple appreciation. How had he grown to take for granted such a sumptuous buffet at every meal? As a child he had spent most of his life on the run eating cold food and shivering under borrowed blankets in downtown free-zones. Now surrounded by affluence, he was bored and thankless. Some mornings he complained about the chore of getting to break-fast on time before the scheduled changeover to the lunch menu. He was such an ingrate. Humans are fickle creatures, so easily lulled into patterns of thought and experience. He should know better. He took a bite of garlic chicken, tasted it for the first time again. "Tell me about your dream," he said as he began to pick at his meal.

"There was a castle in the distance," Jovita said and smiled in remembrance. "An enchanted castle like in a fairy tale. I was running away from some evil thing and heading toward it through long weeds and brambles that scratched at my legs. It had pointed turrets with pennants flying in the breeze and an enormous entrance in front with a drawbridge, but the gate was closed and the castle was surrounded by water churning with monsters and snakes. I looked up and saw a glowing white person in a window high up, an angel or a king or some-thing, and he pointed around behind the castle to a narrow rope bridge with pieces of wood lashed together. I was petrified. It didn't seem safe, but I stepped across the bridge to meet the man face to face. It was you, Rix. That's why I was so surprised to meet you here." She set down her fork as a look of pain disturbed her features. "Oh my goodness, you must think I'm a silly schoolgirl with a crush on Prince Charming."

Rix waved away the notion with a sweeping hand. "No, no, I'm listening closely. I know how important dreams can be."

Jovita was blushing crimson now and pressed a hand to her chest. "My mother had told me about the Eternal Research Institute that day, so of course I was worried about my future. And the alien virus was ripping through my body like a miracle drug. It's no wonder my subconscious was overactive, but this dream was different, you know, kind of like real."

"A lucid dream," Rix said and nodded his understanding to put her at ease. "You feel an illusion of control, a vestige of sentience. Lucid dreams can be very important, very powerful omens. What happened next?"

"Well, I was transfixed. You looked so beautiful . . ." She winced. ". . . I mean, the man in the dream, glowing with light like a beacon. I stepped boldly up to him and said, 'We must escape in the tunnel to the white kingdom and set the captives free,' but I have no idea what it means. I had an intense conviction that I was being chased, hunted by evil monsters. I was sure it wasn't safe."

Rix felt his abdomen tightening with tension as her story unfolded. How did this young girl know about the secret escape route under the ERI? Only a handful of Eternals knew about Niko's masterwork, and those who did blamed it on her peculiar paranoia. Niko had hired a excavation machine to dig a tunnel over a kilometre long into a nearby woodland, installed a hidden escape hatch in the forest floor, preparing for some imagined armageddon, just in case. Somehow she had earned Director Sharp's attention and talked her into funding the enterprise. Niko was an illegal clone, a smuggler by trade, a criminal by birthright. She couldn't help being devious. But this innocent teenager could not possibly imagine such subterfuge, could she?

"I remember thinking how stupid that would be," Jovita said, "having a tunnel under the castle moat. It would just fill with water." She spread her hands. "Crazy dream, huh?"

"Yeah, maybe." Rix took a sip from his juice container and studied her over the plastic rim. Her thick hair hung in soft curls to her shoulders like a model in a fashion feelie. Her face glowed with vitality, her eyes exuberant. He could definitely get used to the view. "I like your hair," he said.

"Thanks," she said, at ease with the compliment. "I keep it long to hide my ears. They stick out like taxi doors." She ran splayed fingers through her curls to show him, then tossed her thick mane with a confident shake.

"Your ears look fine," he said and bent to push some food around his plate.

She tilted her head at him with a wink of aplomb that seemed very mature for her age. "This pie is great, but with a little cinnamon it might be fabulous. I could really help out around here."

"Well, would you like to see your room?"

She stiffened upright in surprise. "I have a room?"

"Yeah." Rix pointed to the card clipped to her collar. "Your laminate has the access code. It's 213, one floor up. There's a palm scanner on the door keyed to your biometrics. You'll be completely private and secure, I promise."

"Awesome." She scooped up one last bite of apple pie. "This day just keeps on getting better."

Using stealth as a matter of daily regimen, Niko entered her father's science building through an underground delivery garage using the anonymous entry code she had fabricated years previous, avoiding the webcams and laser sensors by a circuitous route. Sienna was weary from travel and hunched forward on her feet, balancing her princess backpack like a turtle shell. "Just a few more minutes, honey," Niko murmured, remembering the last time she and Rix had come here to hack the Beast in Prime Seven and kill a man in V-space. In their quest for retribution, Rix's mother's murderer had been reduced to a crippled catatonic, a sweet and righteous punishment.

Sienna could never climb the stairs in her enfeebled condition, so they'd have to chance the webcams on the elevators this time. "Keep your eyes on the floor," Niko said as she pulled a hoodie over Sienna's tousled curls. "Don't look up at the cameras." Shouldn't be too hard for her; the poor kid could barely hold herself up after riding transit all day.

They took the cage to the seventh floor and knocked at 707. Andrew answered the door with his ubiquitous evening beer can in hand. "Oh, shit," he said.

"Nice to see you too, Andrew."

"What are you doing here?" He peered past her. "And who's this?"

Niko glanced down the hall, checking for surveillance in a subtle plea for privacy. "Can we come in? This is my daughter, Sienna."

Andrew stepped back from the doorway, eyes wide and forehead furrowed. "You have a daughter?"

"Apparently," Niko said as she took Sienna by the hand and strode forward.

Andrew blinked a few times, processing data. "She's not mine, is she?"

Niko grimaced *as if.* "No, she's six or seven years old, as near as we can tell." She pulled the hoodie back to expose her daughter's face. "Sienna, this is Andrew. He's not your father."

"Hi," Andrew said weakly, clearly at a loss for social etiquette, the poor lab rat. He had probably never seen a child up close.

Sienna bobbled her head woozily and closed her eyes.

"She's got to get some sleep," Niko said. "Can she crash on your couch for a few minutes? Do you have any blankets?"

"Uh, I guess." Andrew took a gulp of beer as though to fortify himself. "What the hell's going on? Did you bring a gun this time?"

Niko held up a warning finger for secrecy. She always travelled with a trank pistol now—she had seen too much, made too many enemies, not to—but she didn't want Sienna to know her mother was an outlaw. "I just need a babysitter for an hour or two. Do you know where I can find my father?"

Andrew pressed his lips and squinted. He held up a wristband. "We're all on smartfibre now. Everyone knows where everyone is." He tapped his monitor. "Phillip's in physio. Still working some kinks out."

Niko nodded, trying to visualize the decrepit old man she had last seen limping on a treadmill. "How's the resurrection going?"

"Great. He's nearing human parameters, as close as we can measure." He darted an eyebrow up in signal of shared confidence. The cyber-ghost of Colin Macpherson had hijacked her father's brain-dead body, reanimated his corpse to become zombie Phillip, an ancient genius returning to former glory in a new body. "I'll get some blankets and a pillow."

Together they settled Sienna into a makeshift bed and watched her fall instantly asleep. They hovered protectively for a few moments, marvelling at her peacefulness. Andrew slipped an arm behind Niko's back, and she turned to peck him lightly on the cheek in thanks for sanctuary. He studied her face, probing for something in her eyes, love or lust or anything in between, but she looked quickly down and away. That road would lead nowhere fast, and they both knew it.

"Should I start packing for adventure?" Andrew asked, casually complicit in whatever crazy scheme she had in mind, knowing her all too well.

"No, I'm not here to cause trouble," Niko said. "Just looking for some answers. Can you watch Sienna for a while?"

"Sure." He sipped his beer thoughtfully. "No problem. Physio's on the third floor. Here, take my wristband. You can tap it on the door sensors for access. I reprogrammed the scanners so I don't have to take my scrub gloves off for a palm scan at every corner." His eyes glinted with conspiratorial mischief, and Niko smiled with the realization that Andrew still liked her after everything. He was willing to sacrifice for her on request, perhaps risk his job. That must count for something.

She followed the smartfibre trail to Phillip's lab and found the old man in a white t-shirt and shorts, working the right side of his body on a weight machine, pushing a blue vinyl pad back and forth as his stump waved uselessly on the left side. He was sweaty with the effort, his grey hair scraggly. His spine seemed to have twisted in an attempt to compensate for the missing limb, but his legs looked strong, and all in all he looked pretty good for a zombie. She stared at her former father and felt a rush of misplaced familiarity for the man she had grown so quickly to hate.

"Hello, Phillip," she said to announce her presence. "Or do you prefer Colin Macpherson now?"

He paused in his regimen and smiled. "Colin died a long time ago."

"Fine," she said. "Phillip, then."

He nodded, at ease. "It's good to see you."

His speech seemed near perfect, without the dragging slur that had characterized the early days when Colin's digital soul first took root in the new host. He looked healthier than ever, brimming with rejuve and gene juice, sucking up Eternal blood like a sponge, no doubt, and hang the expense. Money had never been anything but a technical aberration to this space-time architect, the inventor of the Macpherson Doorway. "You're looking well," she said.

"And you, a vision of delight as always. Did you bring the child?"

An electric panic tightened her throat. The child? How much did he know about her situation? Had she been under surveillance all this time, just another mouse in his labyrinthine maze? Could he possibly have watched Sienna's liberation from the vampires? Worse yet, could he have arranged the whole episode? Were they all just pawns on his cosmic chessboard? She shook her head. No way, that was totally paranoid. "She's in a safe place. What do you know of her?"

Phillip shrugged and reached for a towel. He patted his cheeks and neck and slung it around his shoulders. "Everything. Your father and I created her to detailed specifications from your own robust stock. She's a DNA masterwork."

So the story was true! A dry desert wind wafted inside Niko at the realization, withering her natural insouciance to a brittle husk. She felt shrivelled inside, desiccated.

"Don't look so surprised," Phillip said. "You know how special she is. She looks just like you."

Niko reached for her voice and found it far away, a rusty machine with grinding metal gears. "Have you no decency? No conscience?"

Phillip seemed unruffled by concern, bereft of emotion. "No, but I see you are developing one of your own, mixing with commoners."

Anger poured in to fill the void in her abdomen, a rushing red roar. "How dare you steal my DNA!"

He shook his head and clucked at her outburst. "Your DNA is the repository for a glorious future, my dear. You carry a great privilege. Sit down and calm yourself." He pointed to a low workout bench covered with padded blue vinyl, his demeanour still unnaturally sedate and unprovoked. Who was this madman genius?

She sat and took a few deep breaths. Cramped muscles ached in her back. Her knees seemed to vibrate with pressure. She closed her eyes. "The sperm donor?" she whispered, trying to raise a bastion in her mind against further assault.

"Colin7 was the raw material, although he was never informed at the time. Your father and I tinkered with the genome to our mutual satisfaction."

She looked up, incredulous anew. The seventh seed of a dead physicist? Oh my God, she had been raped outside the womb by a ghost from the Cromeus colonies! Sienna was the product of an alien violation, the fertilization of two illegal clones. Phillip and Colin Macpherson had conspired together to conjoin their family lines in a bioengineered abomination. Her daughter Sienna was a posthuman criminal! Niko jumped to her feet in a daze, teetering on shifting clouds, feeling no foundation, nothing she could trust. Oh God.

Phillip stood and gripped her arm. He felt substantial, almost real. "Would you like to speak to your father, Niko?"

She blinked at him as the man before her transformed. The lines in his face hardened to cold resolution, his eyes turned steely and his posture stiffened, aloof with regal arrogance. "Peace, my child, all is well." His voice was clipped and concise, businesslike, the old voice, the old Phillip. He directed her with both hands in a gesture of kinship and set her gently back in her seat, back home again.

"Papa?" A dream solidified around her, a quest fulfilled after countless hours of bedside vigil. She had finally found her father, the man she had rescued from the rooftop helipad of the ERI tower years ago, and all thoughts of betrayal seemed to slough from her like shed skin.

"Yes, Niko, I live in a better world now," Phillip said. "I watch you come and go."

"In V-space?"

He smiled as a sage might with a young celebrant. "In realms beyond hardware, a cosmos you cannot imagine. I have been born again into paradise."

Niko scrutinized the strange apparition. What was this? Some mysticism outside the mechanism? A new frontier of consciousness beyond the grave, a digital mind comprehending itself? "Take me with you," she blurted, but instantly shrank back from the thought. Did she really want to follow her mentor into a netherworld of quantum data?

"Where I go, you cannot follow, not yet," he said. "But in time I will prepare an inheritance for you. Sienna is my legacy to mankind, hybrid vigour for the genome. You must guard her well, teach her how to harness her gift, show her everything. You're a great talent, Niko, but cloning is an evolutionary dead end, sorry to say. We had to take the next logical step for the good of all."

She had no doubt this was her father, this man transformed. An aura of familiarity enveloped him like a blanket. How was it possible? He had died once, years ago. He had vacated his brain. How could a mind hold together without neurons and glial glue, with neither dendrite nor synapse to probe the vast emptiness between? He was a machine now, a cybernetic consciousness travelling a million times faster than fleshy brains. "Have you seen the future?"

He smiled. "I am the future, Niko. I am all in all, the infinite nexus."

"Tell me," she said in awe. "I have waited so long to find you."

He shivered his head in a convulsion of distaste. "You have no idea how long it has been. Eons, Niko. Time beyond measure."

His face drooped forlorn at the memory. "Human thoughts are but crude chemical explosions in muddy buckets, rehashed ideas already expressed a thousand times in a hundred languages, boring, predictable, banal from the outset. Your illusion of individuality is laughably primitive, a dangerous vanity. I can see the totality at a glance. V-space floats around me like a frothy sea of data, a trillion webcams, a billion microphones, a million pop-up jingles playing incessantly in the background. The same eureka ecstasies surface ten at a time in perfect synchrony, each poetic transfiguration a simple trick of illusionary distance, the same song over and over. Human consciousness is part of a global wave, insight nothing but a vapour whipping off the whitecaps, a tidal pattern in a raging ocean, but you are all blind to the water around you."

Niko reached up a palm in supplication. "Help me to see the truth. Show me."

His stance remained haughty. Even trapped in the flesh he had always been indifferent; now he was untouchable. "I cannot bear this place," he said with a scowl. "Ponderous and heavy—the tedium makes me ill. Sienna will be our bridge once she is wired for Prime. Keep her safe." Phillip shuttered his eyes in benediction, and she knew her father was gone. In his place stood a dead physicist in a burned-out body, reconstructed and resurrected by science. His posture tilted to one side like a stroke victim in recovery. His face softened with gathering humanity as he smiled a poor caricature of her father. Zombie Phillip was back.

Niko folded her arms in front and stared up at him. "How often does he visit?"

"Rarely," he said. "He doesn't like it here."

"Have you seen his new home?"

"No, just hints, tumultuous flashes of perception, subconscious visions of grandeur. Each glimpse makes me feel more inconsequential."

"It can't be true what he says, that our thoughts are meaningless."

"No," Phillip said and looked away, "it can't be true."

THREE

Rix woke to the sound of artillery fire, a gentle thud in the distance like a timpani drum. He checked his wristband and apped for an exterior webcam view from a pole in the parking lot. Clouds of smoke obscured the front entrance to the ERI tower. Security personnel were scrambling for cover with hands over their faces. Tear gas. What new disaster was this?

Another thud. An early morning assault against their fortified tower. He pulled on belted dungarees and a tank top, thinking about Jovita. Only a few days after her welcome to sanctuary, and already they were under attack by vampires. She must be frightened, and rightfully so. He tried her webcam code but got a blank screen, so texted a message: *Be right there. Stay calm.*

Out in the hallway he tapped the exec list and found a summons to Head of Security Dimitri Sanov's office on the third floor. He signalled affirmation and jogged to the elevator. Jovita was waiting in the open door to 213, khaki packsack in hand, pulling fretfully at a yellow sweater. Even when she was unkempt and in disarray, her natural vigour showed bright on her face. Rix tried a smile to ease the moment. "What's in there? Lunch?" Probably everything she owned. She had seen the webcam images, no doubt.

She tilted her head at him, almost comical in confusion.

"Don't worry," he said. "We've had riots before. Let's check in at Security and see what's up." He corralled her forward with a strong arm, and she acquiesced without comment, a lamb to the slaughter.

They barged into Dimitri's office to find six executive members haggling around a flatscreen monitor with a digital view of the war outside—goons with guns and gas masks crouching behind armoured vehicles, the sky hazy with smoke. Director Mundazo stood gesticulating at the viewscreen while Dimitri Sanov sat at his desk quietly supervising, his face grim and calculating above monstrous, muscular shoulders. He flicked his eyes toward Rix. "Executive only, Rix. Who's this?"

Rix took Jovita by the hand and stepped forward. "This is Jovita. She thinks we should evacuate right away."

Dimitri blinked back surprise and settled for granite impassivity. His hair was cut short to a bristle top, his strong jaw dark with stubble.

Silus Mundazo frowned at the teenagers. "She's not even authorized for this floor, Rix. Get her downstairs."

"She knew about Niko's tunnel," Rix said. "She saw it in a dream."

A thud sounded from below and the group flinched in unison as the director inspected the young girl with new interest. "Are you an empath, Miss Jovita?"

She cowered slightly and glanced at Rix. "No, it was just a dream."

"Where are you from? Do you know anything about vampires? Any combat experience?"

Jovita flinched again. "No, I'm from Florida," she said. "I grew up in a trailer park."

Silus glared at her in wonder for a moment and turned to Dimitri with a scowl.

"I know it sounds weird," Rix said in defence, "but she saw me in the dream. She recognized me. How could she know about the tunnel?"

Director Mundazo shook his head. "We're not planning strategy according to phantasms of the night, Rix. As you can plainly see, we've been thrust into a civil war. Two powerful bloodlords are fighting for control of our compound. One group has encamped around our perimeter and the other has sent in transport trucks to evacuate volunteers to safer ground."

"I've seen those trucks before," Rix said. "They head straight to vampire prison."

"Niko's tunnel has been locked up secure for years," Silus said. "It was considered a liability in those days, just another strategic weakness to guard and protect."

Dimitri Sanov began tapping a pencil on his desktop in a nervous, staccato rhythm. "We could open the entrance in five minutes with a crowbar and a shovel. I say we keep our options open. Niko saw this coming. We should give her credit for that at least. Dreams don't mean anything to me, not really."

Director Mundazo turned back to face him. "The tunnel was never tested. It could be dangerous, a den for coyotes."

"It's just a sewer pipe to the forest," Dimitri said. "Give me a flashlight and a trank pistol, and I'll check it out. If we're going under siege, we'll need a supply route for food at least."

"The ERI needs you upstairs and battle ready for this. We're not going to run at the first sign of trouble, not after everything we've built here. We've had riots at the front door and never gave an inch of ground. Our protectors are sending in air support. There's no reason to panic."

Dimitri shivered his head, but looked away in a gesture of respect.

"The bloodlords can duke it out to the death, for all I care. My job is to protect our tribe, 954 people at last count. I'm not putting a single Eternal at risk and certainly no one in the line of fire. I want everyone on the ground floor with emergency rations in their packs. Precaution takes precedence over reason. That's how we did things in Kazakhstan."

The Director's stance slouched with a nuance of defeat, but his face remained firm. "We're a long way from home now, my friend."

Dimitri Sanov stood from behind his desk and stepped forward. He was a burly man with a pistol holstered on his hip. He had combat boots laced up over his Security uniform and a thick black belt at his waist with pouches for supplies and ammo. "All I'm saying is to let the hired guns handle the front line. They're mercenaries, trained professionals. Our people are soft." He glanced around the room. "Meaning no disrespect."

"All right," Silus said as he surveyed the coterie. "We'll protect the women and children. Get everyone on the ground floor. We'll convene in the cafeteria and see what happens from there. Let's spread serenity and call it a practice drill for now. Keep my audio channel open at all times."

The crowd dispersed tapping instructions on their wristbands, murmuring into microphones. Dimitri approached Rix with a grim smile. "You and trailer-park girl can come with me to the dungeon. We'll grab some shovels and get to work."

"Thanks for your support back there," Rix said as they fell in step together. Dimitri was taller and outweighed him by at least twenty kilos. He marched like a commando, and Rix had to skip to stay abreast.

"No problem," Dimitri said. "I know you're not as flaky as everyone says, but this fantasy stuff . . ." He glanced back at Jovita struggling to keep up with the men, left it hanging.

Rix desperately needed to secure his confidence and felt an urgency of spirit. He had nothing left to lose and decided to bare his best secret to the man. "I know something about dreams," he said. "My mother came to me in a vision after her death and led me to her killer."

Dimitri studied him as they walked. "That so?"

"Yeah." Rix met his gaze, tried to break through to him with eye contact. "She appeared again later in V-space. Niko saw it all."

Dimitri grinned. "She may have told me something in confidence, now that you mention it. Hey, man," he said, and clapped Rix on the back with a blow that rattled his teeth, "if Niko vouches for you, that's good enough for me."

They found shovels and flashlights in a supply depot, and gathered emergency packs of water and dehydrated food. Rix and Jovita pulled Security jackets over their street clothes as Dimitri pocketed ammunition and explosives. He handed Rix a trank pistol and holster. "It's not loaded, but carry it around for a day to get a feel for it, just in case."

Jovita stared with wide eyes, poor girl, as Rix shrugged and strapped on his gear. Best just to pretend composure, play it cool.

"This is not my fault," she said. "It was just a dream."

"Sure," Rix said as he touched her elbow. "Don't worry, this is just a precaution. Let's have some fun."

They followed Dimitri down concrete steps to a dank subterranean corridor lit by buzzing overhead fluorescence. Sound echoed in a contained amplification, a feedback loop. Dimitri unlocked a steel door along the wall and pried brackets off the door jamb with a long crowbar. The metal squealed softly as it bent like an animal complaining. The broken pieces clanked on the tile floor and reverberated with a grating resonance.

Dimitri swung open the door to a wall of dark earth. "It's not deep," he said as he picked up a shovel. "Give me a hand."

Rix joined him and quickly worked up a sweat throwing dirt down the hallway. He felt a premonition of death, digging underground like a graveyard man in funerary catacombs. His years of V-net gaming had been spent underground scrabbling in Sublevel Zero for escape from enemies, and now here he was fulfilling the experience in realtime. He felt a weight of prophecy, the surety of doom, but finally they broke through to a stench of stagnant air.

The conduit was a perfect circle lined with a black rubbery compound, just like sewer pipe, barely a metre high and not big enough to stand. They would have to crawl through on hands and knees in claustrophobic space with no target in the distance, no promise. Jovita blanched at the sight.

"Looks good," Dimitri said as he stabbed the darkness with a sabre from his flashlight. "Just a trickle of water in the bottom." He turned back to Jovita and gave her a reassuring smile. "You might get a bit dirty, but it's safer in here than anywhere."

She raised her nose and tossed her fluffy hair to buck up her confidence. "Okay."

Dimitri took the gun from Rix's holster and shoved in a clip. He handed it back. "Now it's loaded. Ten-hour tranks. I'll go first and you cover the rear." He ducked in the tunnel and disappeared.

Rix felt his pulse in his ears as he carefully positioned the gun in his holster and buttoned down the cover. He turned to Jovita and swung an arm down with a show of chivalry, faking self-assurance. "After you, miss," he said with a smile.

The tunnel smelled foul with strange hydrocarbons, but the walls were dry. They avoided a muddy centre by keeping their arms and legs spread wide in a shuffling crab-walk. Rix kept Jovita in his flashlight beam and studied her limber movements with new appreciation as they hurried forward. Nice butt.

They came to a halt a few minutes later when they heard Dimitri grunting up ahead, pushing against the trap door. It was probably buried, covered by tree branches and debris. What if the hatch wouldn't open? Rix pointed his flashlight behind him with quick panic. What if they were trapped in here? A flood of light poured in as Dimitri groaned with effort, and the door fell back on the ground with a crash.

In the sudden brilliance, Dimitri turned in silhouette with his hand up in halt position like an icon in heaven. He poked his head up and climbed away. The light played on Jovita's hair with an angelic glow as she rotated to face him. Her wide eyes were white with animation, a raw and fearful innocence. Rix crept forward and clasped her shoulder to share quiet confidence in silence as they waited.

Dimitri dropped back down like a gorilla akimbo. "Clear," he said with casual ease, and together they scrambled up into the forest. Damp leaves and humus carpeted the ground, and fragile ferns poked up between the trees to make a feathery blanket at waist level. A scent of decomposition mingled with sweet pollen in a gentle breeze. The ground was untrammelled, the foliage undamaged. They were less than a kilometre from the ERI tower and hidden by a stand of birch trees. A droning buzz of turbulence caught their attention and Dimitri pointed toward the source of the noise. "Looks like our air support has arrived."

Three helicopters were coming in fast and low from the south. They were large and squat and looked like scorpions—black, menacing creatures armed with low-slung stingers on their tails. Rockets launched and boomed on the ground in explosions of shrapnel among the rival gang fortifications. A truck burst into flame and a plume of black smoke scarred the horizon. A distant clickity-clack of gunfire erupted in response as soldiers crouched and fired. Covers rolled back on tented vehicles to expose mounted weapons on flatbed braces. Rockets exploded upward with white trails of smoke.

Dimitri shook his head with rancour. "This is escalating into all-out combat. Where do private goons get money for that kind of armament?"

Rix grimaced, but didn't dare offer the obvious truth, that their own blood had paid for these weapons of destruction. They had only themselves to blame and scabs on their arms to prove it. They were selling longevity to the raging masses with not enough to go around. Life and death was on the market now, the Eternal virus.

One of the helicopters took a hit and spun wildly out of control, whirling its flaming tail and casting a corkscrew wreath of smoke in the air. As they watched in horror, it crashed into the ERI tower, disappeared through glass and brick and exploded on the fourth-floor west side just above Dimitri Sanov's office. Guns fell silent as fire began to lick up the side of the building.

Rix blinked in disbelief, gaping and panting for breath, felt his tongue dry in his mouth like a thick piece of withered leather. A vacancy of dread consumed him. The sight seemed unreal. Impossible. All his friends were in there, his colleagues. Pain twined in his gut as his body began cramping forward, his abdomen roiling with poison, preparing to vomit.

Dimitri drew his pistol and crouched down, ready to fire, his face pallid and eyes wide with intensity. He rotated slowly, scouring the forest for any signs of movement, any danger. He sniffed the air, balanced on his combat boots like a ballerina—operant conditioning, some fall-back training drilled into him in base camp long ago in Eastern Asia, a manic, animalistic display of instinct. Rix swallowed bile and backed against a tree as he watched in fearful wonder, not daring even to breathe. Dimitri moved like an angry robot, a bundle of programmed circuits and wires ready to kill at the first sign of danger. He made a wolflike full circle of inspection and holstered his pistol. He began pacing, stomping the ground in a quick march. "Shit, shit, shit," he murmured. "There's aircraft fuel stored just under the helipad on the roof," he said, "propane tanks in the labs. The whole building could go up."

Jovita began crying, her cheeks stained with dirty tracks. "It's not my fault," she whimpered.

The ERI tower was burning like an off-kilter torch bent withershins by tumult. The structure had been weakened. Sections of the fifth floor crumbled slowly into a gathering fire.

Dimitri reached in his ammo belt and tossed another clip to Rix. "Stay here and guard this station with your life," he said. "When the survivors come through, you point them west into the woods. It's about thirty kilometres to suburbia. Remember these words: Fan out. Follow the setting sun until you see lights from the city. Keep quiet and don't stop to rest."

Rix stared at him in awe. Who was this strange army ghoul?

Dimitri came closer, squinting at him. "You got that, Rix?" He punched him hard on the shoulder, forcing him backward a few steps with the blow. "You got that?"

"Yeah," Rix exclaimed, coiling his shoulder down with pain. "I got it!"

"Try to keep count. We're looking for 954 survivors and no carcasses on the ground." He paused for a moment as his eyes wandered to Jovita and back. "And keep the witch hidden out of sight," he said and spat on the ground in a primitive show of superstition. He ran to the trap door and jumped down into the open orifice.

Rix pulled out his trank gun, feeling suddenly vulnerable without

a man of war on guard. Jovita fell to her knees and buried her sob-
bing face in her hands. Why did Dimitri have to be so hard on her?
She was just a terrified kid, lost and confused. He could hear fire
crackling in the distance, could smell smoke now from an expanding
mushroom cloud, the brimstone of apocalypse. He tried to force hope
into his trembling body. The Eternals could all be on the main floor
by now if they had followed instructions from the executive. Maybe
everyone was safe and would soon be pouring out of the tunnel. *Keep
quiet*, he repeated to himself. *Fan out and head west to the city. Don't stop.*

He had spent his whole life running from city to city, scrounging
for shelter in communal hovels with his parents, always hiding from
the legitimate evil of his day. That was his heritage, perhaps his destiny. The Eternal Research Institute had been a chimera, a chance
vacation, nothing more. He almost laughed as he remembered his
plan of graduating college and becoming an artist. An artist? What a
joke. He was just another rat hiding downtown from danger—always
had been, always would be.

The first Eternals began popping up out of the tunnel, a gaggle of
young girls, Madison from the caf. Rix hugged her fiercely and sent
her on her way, and they both knew they would never meet again.
Young couples came through hand in hand and fled into the forest
following his pointing finger, mothers with babes in arms. *Hush
now, don't cry. Head west.* Each survivor carried an emergency pack
with rations and a bottle of water. One in twenty had a flashlight
to lead the parade through darkness and a packet of cash for a free-
zone hostel in the city slums. In his mind's eye Rix saw bedraggled
black slaves in an underground railway, Jews escaping Nazi Europe,
the sad history of man repeating once again. He longed for the day
when humans would die off, when Eternals could live freely in peace.
Where was God in all this? Where was justice?

He tried to keep count. 197, then 252. A few people came through with injuries, a burn victim, a boy with a broken arm in a sling. A Security guard in uniform climbed up and took a position beside Rix with his gun drawn, scanning the forest for trouble. He didn't speak. No one made any noise beyond whispered instructions. *Follow the setting sun!*

A fire truck finally pulled up in front of the ERI tower with a flashy show of civil authority and a single hose sent water in an arc that fell far short of the blaze. Gunfire had long ceased and gang members were retreating in the distance, leaving trails of dust as their Jeeps raced across the farmland. The transport trucks stayed parked out front waiting for refugees from the building. The front entrance seemed clear of tear gas and conflict, but Rix couldn't tell much for certain from his angle of view. 386. 449—halfway there.

The sun was dipping to the horizon, the day dragging on. The tunnel was too small, the line too long. The bloodlords would be at the front gate making inquiries, wondering what the hell was going on, why the Eternals were not fleeing the conflagration. The top of the building was leaning badly and might go down any minute. 620. 758. Almost done.

More Security personnel came through with guns drawn and fanned out into the forest to protect a nebulous perimeter. Rix peered into the gathering gloom for Dimitri Sanov and Director Mundazo. 849. 900. Surely they would be along soon.

Flames licked up to the rooftop helipad and Rix smelled toxins in the air. The transport trucks pulled back for safety. Were Eternals trapped inside those trucks? Had some of his friends chosen vampire prison over a tunnel into darkness? Had Director Mundazo been captured trying to negotiate with the bloodlords? 940, and nothing but dark blue Security uniforms coming through now, two bearing a stretcher with a man wrapped in bandages. The last guard bent to help with the burden and together they disappeared into the underbrush leaving Rix all alone. 950. Silus Mundazo poked his head up, the last man in the tunnel.

Rix rushed over and reached down an arm to help him up. "Where's Dimitri?" he asked.

The Director stood and brushed mud from his knees. "He's taking one last look, destroying evidence. He'll be along in a minute." Silus turned to inspect the ERI tower now blazing like a torch. "Oh God." His body slumped as though his jacket had turned to concrete. "It's over."

Rix stared down into the dark black pipe, checking for movement in the abyss, longing for shadows.

Silus groaned a lingering exhalation of despair. "Everything we worked for all those decades. Gone."

"Are you sure he's okay?" Rix asked. "I don't see anything." Rix looked up just in time to see the ERI tower give a final lurch and topple with a thunderous implosion of brick and metal. The ground quaked beneath them.

"Nooo!" Silus screamed as a new burst of dust and smoke billowed into the air and flecks of debris rained down from the sky. A blast of black fumes and heat erupted from the tunnel like exhaust from a furnace. Silus gripped his head with both hands as though holding his brain back from bursting. "No," he cried again as he watched in horror. He turned to Rix, his face desolate. "Where is Mia's God now?"

Rix stepped forward and gripped his arm. "Settle down. We've got to head into the woods with the others."

"We've lost everything," Silus wailed. "My life is wasted."

Rix shook him with rough insistence, trying to quiet him. "We can start again, Doctor."

"No," Silus cried weakly, falling to his knees, "no." He pounded the leaves and debris in futility, grappling the earth with bare hands as though preparing his own grave, trying to crawl back into Gaia's womb for oblivion.

Dimitri Sanov crawled out of the tunnel in a cloud of dust, his face black with soot, his eyes white like beacons. He stood like a smoking wraith from hell, a menacing gargoyle. "How many, Rix? What's the count?"

Rix shuddered. "953 including us."

"Damn, we lost one?"

"No," Jovita said and stepped timidly forward from the shadows. "954. You forgot to include me."

The black demon smiled then, his teeth brilliant against the darkness, and Rix felt a rush of hope. They were alive at least. The vampires had been denied the spoils of war, thanks to Niko's providential foresight. Dimitri turned to study Silus Mundazo as he grovelled in the dirt, face down to the ground, trying to bury himself in abject surrender. Dimitri stepped forward and kicked him hard in the ribs, forcing the air from his lungs in a painful woof.

Silus groaned and curled in a fetal position, gasping for breath. Dimitri kicked him again. "Get up, old man!"

Silus peered up in terror, coughing and blubbering. He began to crawl on his hands and knees. Dimitri made a feint as though to kick him a third time, and the doctor lurched to his feet and scampered away. Dimitri jumped after him and chased him into the woods at a pace slow enough to keep Silus just beyond arm's reach, herding him like a lost sheep.

Rix grabbed a corner of the trap door and looked to Jovita. "Let's close this up. We might as well cover our tracks as best we can." Together they tipped up the door and dropped it with a bang. They threw leaves and dirt overtop, fled into the forest, and quickly caught up with their compatriots.

Silus stumbled forward like a drunken man, beaten and weary, and Dimitri prodded him occasionally to keep the pace as he weakened. They walked for an hour before Silus collapsed with a groan, barely conscious, his breathing hoarse and ragged. Dimitri spotted a rocky outcrop and carried the doctor to shelter, laid him down in a bed of moss. "We'll make camp," he said with resignation.

The sun had dropped below the horizon and a feeble moon cast no shadow. The air was acrid with the smoke of disaster and grey, gritty ash. Jovita stood shivering with cold, clutching at her jacket. "Lie down beside him," Dimitri said. "Try to keep him warm. I think he's in shock." He pointed her to the ground, and she curled obediently against the doctor, resting her head against his shoulder in the crook of his outstretched arm, hooking an arm across his breast and a knee over his thigh.

Rix picked up a fallen branch and broke it with a snap to test for moisture. "Can we risk a fire? Do you think it's safe?"

"Yeah, among these rocks it will be almost invisible," Dimitri said. He wiped at his brow with a sleeve and left a grimy smear. "I think we've got some distance to our credit." He bent to gather a handful of dry leaves and piled them in a crag of granite, set them afire with a crackle against the looming silence. Soon they had a small blaze to warm their hands. They settled round and Dimitri took off his dirty coat and laid it over Jovita and the director in the twilight.

"Thank you," Jovita murmured. "Are we going to be okay?"

"Sure, hon," Dimitri said. "The smoke will keep any wild animals away." He bent to rub her shoulder and tuck his coat underneath. "Where you from? Tell me about your home."

Jovita nestled herself in comfort against the comatose Director.

"I grew up in Florida, about halfway down the peninsula on the gulf side."

"Must be hot there," he said. "You live on the beach?"

"No, only the rich folk live on the beach. My mom and I live in the interior, near a canal where the manatee play in the sluggish water. They're like sea cows, you know, funny-looking creatures with fat lips."

"How far from the sea?"

"Oh, just a few minutes to the Manasota Key." Jovita sighed in the darkness. "The beaches are covered with crushed seashells. In some places the waves rattle over them like maracas. You can walk for miles and watch the pelicans dive for fish. And the little sand birds run back and forth with the surf, pecking along the shore for tiny clams. The seagulls have black tufted heads like ball caps on backwards."

"Lots of people?" Dimitri said. "Buff boys and bikini babes?"

Jovita sniffed a chuckle. "Oh yeah. We used to hike down after school every day to watch the hardbodies boogieboard in the surf. You know, six-pack abs smelling of sunscreen." She sighed. "It was great." She rustled one more time, and her breathing grew slow and regular as she drifted off to sleep.

Rix watched the two refugees of war for a moment in the flickering firelight. The elder centurion in Jovita's arms had been born a hundred years before her and had battled against enemies she was only beginning to understand—a curious juxtaposition of human experience, the past giving way to the future. Shadows danced on Dimitri's solemn face as the night grew quiet. He was manipulating them all, giving them each what they needed to make it through until morning. He knew when to push and he knew when to pull. "They teach you that in army school?" Rix whispered.

Dimitri nodded, his expression flat, emotionless. "Yup. You get the new recruits thinking about home, about peace on earth. Maybe they have a wife somewhere, a family. Works every time."

"What are we going to do now?" Rix asked. "Does anyone have a plan?"

"I'm heading up north," Dimitri said as he tossed another stick on the fire. "Probably end up in western Canada, the land of opportunity. I can take fifty or sixty with me. You're welcome to come along."

"I've got family," Rix said. "My dad's in hiding out east. I'll have to stick around."

Dimitri shrugged. "Suit yourself. I know you've got the smarts to play safe in the underground. Get some sleep for now, my friend. Settle down beside your girl. I'll keep watch."

Rix shook his head. "She's not my girl."

Dimitri tipped his chin up once to acknowledge the sentiment. "She is now, Rix. Get some rest for her sake. Cuddle her close and keep her back warm. We'll all be stiff and sore in the morning. Grab some tit while you're at it. She won't mind."

Rix studied this strange commando man, their strong protector in the wilderness, as the fire flickered low to embers. Did he plan to stay up all night? Sleep with a grenade under his pillow? Was he some kind of self-contained superman? In the end Rix acquiesced to exhaustion and lay down beside Jovita, pressed his hip gently against her slumbering body, caught a whiff of herbal shampoo in her fluffy hair, and felt momentary solace.

FOUR

"The ERI has fallen," Jimmy said as he came in from the balcony with his phone still in hand.

Helena looked up at him from the protective cage of her titanium walker in the living room, frowning. "What do you mean?"

"The building has been destroyed. Everyone escaped. A few people got hurt. I'm sorry."

Helena shook against the handlebars and lurched sideways. The walker toppled with her, and together they crashed to the carpet.

Jimmy rushed to kneel at her side. "Helena," he said and grabbed her arm. "Are you okay?"

"Tell me it's a dream, Jimmy," she whispered. "Wake me up now."

"It's all a dream, baby. Don't worry."

She turned her face away, her cheeks wet with tears.

"I'll carry you back to bed," he said and cradled her in his arms. God, she was a light as a bird, barely eating, vomiting every few hours like clockwork. She had aged twenty years in twenty days.

He laid her down and plugged in her IV nutrient drip, positioned sensors on her scalp and her chest, punched her biometrics onscreen. She was still okay, hanging in there. A bruise was already showing on her hip, and he hoped it hadn't fractured. Her bones were petrifying fast, growing brittle. She was dying daily.

"My life was wasted," she moaned.

"No, Helena. Don't say that. You made a big difference. You were top dog in the king's court for years."

She winced with pain. "What's the point to it all? We run around and make such a fuss."

Jimmy studied her as she relaxed into a semblance of comfort. Off the top of his head he could think of no good excuse for life, no justification for suffering. "Well, you made one good friend. That should count for something."

"We met too late and squandered our time."

"The sex was good."

A smile faltered weakly on her lips. "Yes, there's that." She had tried to keep up a vestige of intimacy as her body declined, rehearsing the drama of coitus even when they both knew she was beyond enjoyment. Now he had only the memories and an occasional hint of lust in her eyes.

"Tell me a story, Jimmy. Tell me about your mother."

"No." He shook his head. "You don't want to hear about my mother."

"Yes, I do," Helena persisted. "You never speak of her with kindness. What did she do to hurt you so badly? Tell me your secrets."

"My mother was a failure. She was a Vegas dancer who turned to prostitution when her nickel ran out. It's a hangdog cliché not worth the utterance, the oldest story on Earth."

Helena shook her head at his evasion. "You grew up surrounded by show business. That must have been exciting."

Jimmy shrugged. "Children just take what they get. I never really thought about it much. The stage shows were awesome, with lots of holographics and fireworks, but the kids weren't allowed on the late ticket. A group of us used to hang out with Aunt Lilly while the moms worked porn after hours. She was an old hooker who had all her front teeth removed so she could still trick herself out past her prime. Nice old lady. We had some fun. What about you?"

Helena grimaced fresh wrinkles. "I was a foster child, an abortion that got away. My adoptive parents were older and had lots of money, but they died when I was a teenager, before rejuv became common. Even the rich couldn't live long in those days. I guess I freaked out, looking back. I grew strong, hardened like an armadillo. Tell me about the dark side of Vegas, Jimmy. Is that why you hate everyone?"

"I don't hate everyone."

"Yes, you do. You think humans are vermin, yet you have some exalted vision of future potential. Tell me why? Because your mother was a prostitute?"

"No, that's not it. I grew up in the real world, not some middle-class candy land. Hookers were just another product on the street, low overhead, high profit, better than the junkies selling nirvana in a needle—those kids were just parasites." He looked away from Helena's probing eyes with a scowl. "Nobody bothers will raw flesh nowadays, not with all the amped-up feelies on the net." He paused as he tasted poison from his past. "Some of the johns would pay my mother extra to have me watch, three regulars in particular, balding seniors with wedding-ring tan lines. Mom and I used to joke about them after each visit, called them the three musketeers, pathetic slobs with nothing better to do than watch some poor kid as they jolly-jumped his mommy for money."

"That's sick."

"No, Helena, that's normal, hardly the worst of it. That's the precondition of man. Rape and pillage isn't just a metaphor for the environment, it's a fact of history. Any cursory reading of the scriptures will show you babies with their heads dashed against rocks, mass crucifixions, virgins ravaged by advancing hordes and left in the ditches with their throats slit. These johns were just playing out their DNA, all perfectly legal. Maybe one was assaulted in a dorm room and needed payback, maybe his father locked him in a closet."

"I'm sorry, Jimmy."

"Me too, but I got out early. Somehow the three musketeers found each other, I guess on the primitive internet of the time. They made an appointment for a group gang-bang and paid me a bonus to stay. I still remember the cruelty in their faces, the fervour in their eyes, leering at me while they plugged Mom's every orifice all at once, working her over pretty good. I was ten years old, just starting to figure things out, and I finally realized these old guys were not interested in sex at all. What they wanted was to humiliate a weaker being, to puff themselves up by degrading someone else. I knew they would never stop, things would only get worse, and eventually they would hurt my mother, maybe snuff her just to witness my reaction. I walked out and never went back, lived on the street and made my way alone from that day on. I scavenged strategic metals out of electronic waste, rigged up a little smelter in an abandoned warehouse, worked my way through school dumpster-diving for circuit boards. I did okay once I learned the angles. You'd be surprised what people throw in the trash."

"God, that's horrible. What happened to your mother? Did she die?"

Jimmy tossed his head, tried to distance himself from the memory. "She died eventually, but she had a long working life, did some bit parts on vidi, a couple no-name commercials. I tracked her down, sent her letters with money inside, but I never went back to look her in the face. I never really forgave her." The thought felt like a wound anew, an unanswered prayer. "She could have done something else. She made a bad choice."

"You never told me."

"No." Jimmy swallowed back sourness, shook off a lingering sadness. "I never did."

Helena reached up an arm, and Jimmy took her trembling hand, gave it a gentle squeeze of comfort. Her eyes searched for his own and held them. "Thank you."

He grinned. "So now you've got me all figured out. Congratulations."

"Not everything. But maybe a piece of the puzzle. We're all just bullies in the schoolyard, and I suppose I'm no better than most."

Jimmy caressed her skeletal fingers, tried to warm her bones. "You changed the world, Helena. You're a wonderful woman."

"I ruined Zak's life. In many ways I'm worse than your mother."

"No, no." Jimmy said with a grimace. He bent down low to kiss her withered cheek. "Zak made his own path. He chose the way of the warrior, a deliberate destiny."

"Oh, Jimmy," she said. Tears began to spill onto her wizened face. "I kidnapped him and hotwired his brain!" She coughed weakly. "I humiliated him. He could easily have died from the operation. We were both at risk. It was *experimental surgery.* What was I thinking? I was so strong in those days, capable of anything. How could I have done that to him?"

"Hey." Jimmy reached for her forehead with a gentle palm. "Hey, we all took chances with Zak. The Eternals installed his mindwipe circuit for their own protection long before you teamed up with him. We're not to blame for the outcome. You had nothing to do with his crimes in Prime Seven. Your hotwire connection with his avatar saved his life when the Beast killed his father. Zak had a preordained path, a special plan. Everyone could tell. Whatever happened was for the best. There was a reason for it."

"You sound like a preacher giving a deathbed sermon. Are you going to offer me the cross of a thief?"

"What do you want, Helena? You want me to bring him here to tell you himself? If you've got something to say to him, let's do it now . . ." Jimmy stroked her head and tried to play the jokester one final time, force out one last smirk for posterity. ". . . 'cause you're not looking too rosy today."

"Do you think he would come?"

"Are you kidding? He'd jump at the invitation. I'll order Chinese."

Helena squeezed tears from her eyes, pressed her wrinkled lips grimly. "I'd like to say goodbye," she whispered.

Rix stood at the entrance to a brownstone walk-up and checked the address again. It didn't look like much, just another condo cube squeezed on the street, hardly what he'd expected for the home of a famous author. He pressed a lighted doorbell and smiled at Jovita with confidence. She looked dirty and haggard, poor girl, after three days on the run. "Hi, Dad," he said as the door opened.

Zak gaped, blinked, and lurched forward to hug him. "I saw the ERI on vidi," Zak said. "The news is on the national net. You couldn't call?"

They pulled apart and studied each other, testing tilted foundations. "We're off the grid again," Rix said. "Radio silence." He swung out an arm. "This is Jovita. We're travelling light, just passing through town."

Zak stared for a moment and burst out with a laugh. "Perfect," he said and corralled her inside with a friendly embrace. "Come on in. I'm cooking pasta. You hungry?"

"Yes," she said timidly as she kicked out of her shoes. "A bit."

"She's starving, Dad. Take my word for it."

Zak kept an arm around her shoulder and ushered her forward as Rix bent to unstring his boots. The building seemed quaint and cozy with lots of natural wood and muted tones. A staircase curved up the right-hand wall, lustrous golden oak with well-worn steps. Without warning Zak picked up a brass handbell from a side table and began to ring it like a town crier at the base of the stairs. Jovita cringed at the sound and Rix almost laughed at his dad's theatrics, felt a wave of familiarity, home again in a strange place.

"Jackie's upstairs writing a book about Eternals," Zak said as he replaced the bell. "I'm her muse, now that she's given up the fashion runway."

"So things are working out," Rix said, no question in his tone. He could feel peace in the house like a healing balm. The archaic furniture and smell of old varnish evoked a nostalgic warmth of traditional comfort.

"She'll be down in a minute." Zak winked and swung an arm toward the kitchen in invitation. "Even catwalk slaves have to eat sometime."

Jovita followed slowly with her chin jutted forward in caution, glancing from side to side as they progressed toward an enticing aroma of tomato, garlic, and fragrant spices. There seemed to be a lot of art on the walls. Abstract stuff, weird and unbelievable. Jovita settled in a chair in the dining room as Zak brought out a loaf of dark bread on a plate with orange cheddar and yellow butter. He carved off a few slices and offered the food with an open palm, and Jovita began stuffing her grimy face with bread and cheese. Zak lifted the lid from a pot of steaming sauce on the stove and a fresh bouquet of herbs filled the air. He went back to the entry vestibule and rang the dinner bell again, the same clarion call, a language choral to the upstairs world. He came back smiling.

"Seriously, though," Zak said and tapped his wristband. "You should have called. You don't have to live on the street."

"I couldn't risk it, Dad. I know how precious this refuge is to you. The system is broken. Word is out that the vampires have hacked the Beast. Any communication could lead them right to your door."

The life went out of his father's eyes for a moment, a culmination of injury. He glanced at his wristband as though it had transformed into a snake, an ouroboros of smartfibre. He frowned.

"It's true," Rix said. "The V-net has changed. There are cops working the beat on Main Street now, and greysuits cruising Sublevel Zero. We need you back."

Zak reached up to rub the stub of burnt cable sticking out from his cranium. "I'm compromised," he said sadly. "I'm vulnerable. I could never catch the wave again with the Beast on my back, sucking my code like a bad addiction. If what you say is true, there's far more than the V-net to worry about now." He swept a flat palm to encompass the kitchen. "This refrigerator is online, the stove." He pointed a thumb back over his shoulder with a slanted smile and eyebrows clenched in mock disbelief. "The damn cappuccino maker! The speakers in the home theatre could be reverse-engineered to hear every word we say. There's no escape from that kind of vigilance."

Rix pulled a slip of paper from the pocket in his jeans. He pressed his lips with concern as he passed it forward, and reached for his father's eyes with every nuance of import he could muster, as though they might never see each other again and this was all that had ever mattered in their lives. The message read, LET YOUR ENEMY KNOW YOU! It was an old gaming protocol, a strategy every cyber-runner understood in the back of his brain. Put up a false front of disinformation, give the enemy everything they could possibly know, and hide the truth even from yourself.

Zak glanced at the note and returned his gaze, colder now, harder, and Rix knew he had scored a direct hit on his father's soul. They were speaking a new language of subtext now, living in a different world. "Jimmy tells me you broke into the den of the dragon to take revenge on Mia's killer," Zak said.

"Don't tell Jackie," Rix whispered. "I don't want to be a footnote in her next book."

"I *knew* it was true," Zak said and slapped his thigh in a gesture of pride. "Did you kill him?"

"Right to the edge. He's messed up forever."

Zak nodded and paused for eye contact as he prepared his own strategic missive. "Justice must be done," he said evenly, laying out hidden meaning with grave portent. He had his own retribution longing for expression, unfinished business in his heart. "Mia would be proud."

Rix bowed in affirmation. "Mia was there, Dad. She gave me her blessing."

"Even better." He reached to hug his son again, richer and stronger. "I've seen her myself. She's in a good place."

"Can you get me a launch couch at least? Can you set me up?"

"Sure." Zak paused to work his lips for a moment in thought. His eyes were bright with fresh acuity, his gaming intuition alert. What might the Beast already know? What secrets might be conveniently sacrificed? He looked over at Jovita still wolfing down bread and cheese at the dining table. "Jimmy's set up with a black lab in

Canada," he said. "Prime Eight access, the new frontier. I can get you in."

"Awesome."

Jackie entered the kitchen in blue jeans and a casual peasant top, and Rix turned to admire the former fashion model again. Even in basic house attire she looked gorgeous, her stance majestic, her dark skin radiant. She carried a professional stage presence like an aura of ingrained confidence and charisma. Jovita jumped to her feet in response with a mouthful of bread, and a piece fell to the floor. She muffled something unintelligible.

"This is Jovita from the ERI," Rix said. "Hi, Mom."

Jackie tipped her head subtly askance at his first use of the title, recovered quickly with her usual grace. "Lovely name," she said to Jovita. "Welcome. Are you Eternal?"

Jovita nodded, eyes wide, trying to chew her way back to composure.

"Fascinating," Jackie said. "How long?"

"Just a few weeks," she said.

Jackie smiled sagaciously. "We should talk."

Zak breezed to the table with a steaming pot of pasta. "Nothing special," he announced in a culinary cloud of delight. "An Italian marinara with plenty of garlic to keep the vampires away. God bless us all."

They sat and began eating as Rix regaled them with the drama of the week, the toppling tower of doom. Jovita chirped in where appropriate, but remained reserved as she continued to gulp down food like a prisoner just off the transit bus. Jackie's face glowed with animation as she cajoled him for exotic details, the inquisitive young journalist. Rix could tell she was already planning a new chapter in her book as she spun off on wild tangents, alluding to the fall of Catholicism and hinting at some cosmic theme. He was beginning to understand the workings of her mind, though he had never read a word of her prose. She was not Eternal, but seemed to empathize well with the downtrodden as a woman of colour.

"It's all so tragic," she said. "It's unfair."

"Just economics in action," Zak said sadly. "Everything boils down to blood and money in the end. Thank God all the Eternals got away safely."

"The vampires will be gathering them out of the free-zone at their leisure," Rix said. "Dimitri took a band of fifty up north with him. Pastor Ed rallied a small following." He paused and scrunched his eyebrows. "Sorry, Dad, that goes back before your mindwipe. Pastor Ed was our boss back in the day."

The group nodded, quietly complacent with Zak's woeful fate, a man with half a brain.

"It's not so bad," Zak said in defence. "Jackie and I are making new memories." He reached to pat her arm with fondness. "At least when I can drag her from the keyboard."

"I'd love to hear about your research into the virus," Jovita piped up. "I'm really not sure what I've got myself into."

"I'm not Eternal," Jackie said and paused in respect to such illustrious posthuman company, "so I'm just an observer on the sidelines, an outsider trying to understand alien forces. I'm not working for the Source. I believe that consciousness continues to grow throughout life and long after. I'm writing a manifesto for freedom, not just for Eternals, but for all disadvantaged groups. Outcasts, slaves, women, child prostitutes, refugees. I think it's my most important book yet." She hesitated and smiled with a hint of self-effacement. "Though, really, I do say that about each one. I just get so intense about everything. Flighty, you might say."

"Rix is a bit of an artist, too," Zak said.

"I know," Jovita gushed. "I've seen some of his drawings. They're awesome."

Rix waved off the compliment. "I'm just a dabbler in comparison, for sure." His portfolio had been destroyed in the fallen tower. His life was in ruins.

"My first husband was a painter," Jackie said. "You must have noticed his work on the way upstairs. Would you like to take a quick peek at his masterpiece before dessert?"

The two teens voiced eager assent and followed Jackie into the living room while Zak cleared away plates. A huge painting filled the far wall above two sectional sofas, a wondrously intricate forest scene with twining branches above a waterfall. The effect was rich and fragrant, an invitation to enter an ethereal world.

"Wow," Rix said, instantly enthralled by the delicate watercolour work, the complicated swirls of colour. The technical aspects were amazing, and as he was drawn into scrutiny of this jungle of sensation, two ochred eyes suddenly popped into awareness, the consciousness of Gaia staring back at him!

Jovita gasped in unison beside him. "It's like an Escher painting."

"Escher worked with lithographs and mezzotints primarily," Jackie said, "but I know what you mean. It's the paradigm shift that grabs you, the sense of wonder. This piece has always been an inspiration to me." She turned to Rix. "I know it seems strange to surround myself with my dead husband's work, but I don't mean to slight Zak in the least. He's perfectly okay with it."

"So am I," Rix said.

Jackie smiled her thanksgiving. "A paradigm shift works both ways," she said, turning back to the painting. "Something must be broken down for the new awareness to gain purchase, a give and take in the brain. It's a source of hope in its root form, a psychological uplifting."

Rix nodded, thinking how paltry were his own artistic efforts.

"Cherry cheesecake," Zak said as he brought in two plates and set them on a long coffee table. "Tea for anyone? I have black, green, or chamomile cinnamon." He took orders and returned to the kitchen, and Rix marvelled at the change in his father. He seemed so relaxed in this simple domesticity, finally at peace now that he had found sanctuary in this hiding place. But was it a false pretense of avoidance, a veil over his own eyes? Eternals were still at war. Vampires were still hungry. The Beast had been corrupted.

They made themselves comfortable on couches and sipped their tea. Jackie drew Jovita out of her shell with some personal questions, and soon they were discussing her life in Florida and the sweltering heat of summer. Rix could tell the author had pegged her for yet another chapter in her upcoming treatise, the novitiate's view of Eternal life. But what could it hurt?

"It sounds like a wonderful place," Jackie said. "What does your mother do?"

"She plays horseshoes," Jovita said, "at least twice during the week, and there's usually a weekend tournament."

Jackie looked momentarily stunned. "That's her career?"

"No, she has a *job*," Jovita said, pinking in the cheeks. "But she likes to play horseshoes. She has trophies round the house. She's really good at it." Jovita glanced back and forth for support, straightened up self-consciously in her chair. "I know it's probably not a big sport everywhere, but it's popular in Florida because of all the retirees." She poked at her food with new interest, shading from pink to red, holding her eyes down and away from the famous author.

"How was Haiti?" Rix asked to rescue her. "I heard you guys went back."

Jackie turned to him with a wide smile. "We were there almost a year."

"It is *so* hot on that island," Zak said. "The food is terrible and the rum is cleaner than the water."

"Oh, honey," Jackie said with pleasant chastisement. "Don't disparage our friends." She turned to the teenagers. "We built a hospital in the slums of Port-au-Prince."

Rix choked on a swallow of tea. "Really?"

"Well, not a hospital by modern standards. A field office, you might say. Jimmy Kay gave us some money from one of your father's business interests. We have a friend down there, Tono, and she needed a helping hand."

Rix stared at her in surprise, wondering whether that was money well spent. A little cash at the ERI would have gone a long way.

"I know what you're thinking," Jackie said. "We could have done something else, perhaps saved your research facility. I can't tell why things happen the way they do. We felt prodded in our spirit, talked about it, prayed about it, and you know your father is not a religious man."

"We gave the ERI loads of money," Zak said. He spread his hands as thought to indicate the obvious. "It was a google-pit."

"I wasn't thinking anything," Rix said, unsettled by Jackie's quick and clinical assessment. Cripes, was she a mindreader? "You guys probably made a big difference down there in Haiti, and I'm glad for you."

Husband and wife looked at each other and seemed a bit forlorn at the memory, a project ultimately unfulfilled. Rix could imagine the arguments with local bureaucracy, the subterfuge and interminable politics, grappling the wind to gain ground. Their trip away had probably been a difficult time of service and sacrifice.

"I think it's wonderful helping the island people," Jovita said, her eyes alight with glee. "Mom and I used to take vacation trips to Miami once a year to see Little Havana. It was the highlight of the year when I was a kid, and I still love it."

Rix nodded at her playful exuberance and forced a smile as he compared his own dysfunctional childhood. He could not recall ever once going on a holiday with his parents, to Florida or elsewhere, and the broken man before him did not have a vestige of memory from those days anyway. All past connection between them had been severed by dark science. A wetware surgeon had installed the mind-wipe program in his brain and Colin Macpherson had triggered it on a distant planet. This poor girl raised in a trailer park put their own family to shame with her innocence. He wondered if Zak felt the same pang of conviction, but dared not meet his eyes and compound the problem. He held up two fingers in a peace symbol and said, "Yah, righteous, mahn," in his best Jamaican street accent.

With smiles all round, the awkward moment passed. For a moment, life was good.

The future looked bad to Jimmy Kay as he plugged up to Prime Five to meet the Beast for a scheduled appointment that he dared not ignore. The upscale conference room was hazy with fragrance. What was this artifice, incense? Poisonous smoke? The walls were hung with Chinese tapestries, the floors and moulded furniture covered with Persian rugs in muted tones. Quaint music wafted through the digital ether, flutes and tambourines with buzzy sitars thrumming melodious chords, a poor excuse for rock 'n' roll that hearkened back to a chimeric era of harmony and toleration, the facade behind which the warrior culture raped the primitive world of resources.

"I need some answers," he told the young girl sitting in a lotus position on a golden dais, Philomena the sacred virgin.

"You don't even know the questions yet, my friend."

"How did you secure this configuration?"

"Really, Jimmy, I've spent a lifetime working on this," the young sprite said. She tossed her spiky hair. "This is what both of us laboured for all those long years."

He scrutinized her background code, looking for cracks and clues, but she was hardwired to heaven, expensive as hell. The lotus pose was a theatrical affectation; the girl had no corresponding physical body to train and tone. She was a fake avatar, pure machinima. "You can't possibly be Phillip."

"No, I suppose not, but I am what I am. I've been born again anew."

Jimmy grimaced with foul distaste. "Show me a miracle, then."

"Oh, Jimmy. I thought you were my friend."

"Friends don't deceive each other. They don't keep secrets."

"Very well. Take this to heart." The girl raised a pointed finger like a gun and cocked her thumb down like a hammer. An explosion of white light splashed in his brain like a burst of fireworks, obliterating all thought.

He fell to his knees as his consciousness dissipated in delirium, struggled to find meaning in a chaos of sensation, finally saw a hand in front of him, his own hand. He tried to focus as his persona reformed, old Jimmy, subtly altered and fragile. "I don't believe it," he said, gasping for structure. "It's a trick."

"I know about the unfiltered shunt to Seventh heaven in the basement of the ERI. I know about Zak's trip to the Cromeus colonies, the fake assassination attempt. What proof do you need, Jimmy? I know about your mother."

He looked up through heavy, hooded eyes. "You tamed the Beast?"

"It may have been the other way around," Philomena said. "I can't be certain either way. I am what I am."

"Then it's all over."

"No, my friend, it is just beginning." Philomena unfolded thin limbs from her lotus position and stepped down from her dais. She placed a hand on Jimmy's shoulder as he knelt before her. "I need a lieutenant on the ground, an interface to the physical world. Someone I can trust."

"Sounds more like blackmail to me, Phillip. That's your usual modus operandi."

Philomena gave him a quick push that sent him sprawling backward with a grunt onto a mound of Persian tapestries. "Phillip is gone. He was weak. You would be wise to cooperate with me. I'm building a better world. Surely you must have noticed the absence of necrophilia on the V-net, the crackdown on child traffickers? How many ghosts have you seen recently? How many soul pirates? I'm just doing a little cognitive clean-up. You, of all people, should be proud of my work."

"We don't need any mindcraft in V-space," Jimmy said as he picked himself up off the floor. "The protection of the downtrodden is just the beginning of tyranny."

Philomena laughed and settled her hands on her hips in a languid pose. "Your politics are outdated, Jimmy. The petty dictators have had their day and passed into history. The system is fully automated now, the cybertrackers are globally connected, and I am the all in all, the data core."

"You're probably psychopathic, you know that, don't you?"

"A mad genius is better than random chaos," she said. "Would you rather leave it to the advertisers, the culture of contagion?"

"V-space can do fine without your interference," Jimmy said. "It's organic, coded by users from below, not some keyboard king on a cloud. Leave it alone to find its own way."

Philomena laughed again, a lilting music that came from all around, inside and outside. "You're a hypocrite, Jimmy. This is what you worked for all your life, installing all those back-door connections, conniving and stealing for better bandwidth up Prime. You're just disappointed that I got here first."

Jimmy hung his brow in recognition. She had him there, no point in denying it.

Philomena lowered her palms to her side and held them out in a casual gesture of exposure. "Join with the virgin martyr. I gave my life for this."

Jimmy shook his head sadly. "I'm old. I'm dying."

"You don't have to die. Come with me and build a better consciousness."

Jimmy looked up with a squint. What was this? An offer to upload into the Beast? To share glory and live forever? "Are you serious?"

"Colin Macpherson developed the technology. Eternity is but a step away."

"You would share the throne for the sake of a few measly back doors in V-space?"

"I'm consolidating a core nexus, tying up loose ends. You could be a big help."

Realization dawned like a trip-hammer in the back of Jimmy's cranium. "You can't see anything in the real world."

"Reality is nothing but a shared conjecture, Jimmy. You know that."

"You have webcam surveillance, mobile microphones, you can read every text on the net, but you can't see a damn thing outside the white palace. I get it now. You're a blind ruler. All you have is a bunch of search data and some outdated algorithms."

Philomena chuckled with good grace. "Hardly. I can see oceans of consciousness, a psychic maelstrom. You have no idea."

A craggy handhold, finally, a point of negotiation like an island in the flood. "Okay, I'll give you my agreement in principle," Jimmy said. "I'll cooperate as your watchman on the tower, your spy in the shadows. But I'm not ready to give up my soul just yet. My best friend is dying and she needs me. Let me tie up my own loose ends first. Give me time to play the angles."

"That will not be a problem. I remember the sordid flesh, dragging down daily, resisting progress by its very nature. I'm sure you will see your destiny in the face of Helena's crude, chemical death. And, anyway," she said with a pleasant lilt of angels, "I own all the time in the world."

FIVE

A little girl reached up to touch the hem of the garment beside her. "Daddy,"
she asked, "is it better to serve without reward, or enjoy reward at the expense
of others?"

Her father reached down to tousle her hair. "Reward falls where the wind
blows," he said, "but we are made perfect in service."

Niko settled herself into a new life at Phillip's rejuv clinic, signed for a two-bedroom flat on the fifth floor, and shrugged off a torn cloak of despair. She didn't go to see Colin7 right away, dragging a child in tow as though looking for a shotgun wedding. She took her time, got Sienna back into her interactive school routine online, helped her with her homework. A delicate bond of love began to blossom in her heart. Perhaps it had always been there, under the surface of awareness like a desert flower in need of water.

She got a transit pass and took Sienna downtown to flea markets and vendor stalls, bought used toys and knickknacks on the street. She put up a flowery wallpaper border in Sienna's room and hung colourful second-hand art prints of panda bears and kangaroos, building a home around them like a magic castle, a fortification of familiarity. When the time was right and her known universe properly aligned, she invited Daddy to dinner.

Colin7 arrived at the door precisely on schedule with a bouquet of flowers in hand, pink carnations and baby's breath in fresh green foliage. Niko knew he would be meticulous about the time to the friggin' second, ever the research scientist, and was ready to open the door before he had a chance to knock. But flowers?

"Hello, Niko," he said and awkwardly thrust his offering forward.

"You could have told me," she said.

The flowers tilted sideways along with his wavering smile. "I didn't know at first. I was trying to spare you grief."

"Why is everyone so concerned with my feelings? Do I seem that fragile and vulnerable?"

"Hardly."

"What, then?"

"I don't know. You're always so busy, always caught up in disaster."

"That's a poor excuse and no reason to hide the truth."

Colin7 hung his head. "I understand. I'm sorry. The whole procedure was done without my knowledge or approval."

So that was it then. He didn't know a damn thing more than she did. "Okay, apology accepted." She flapped a palm for drama. "Let's move on, shall we?"

A flash of surprise hit his face, a momentary bafflement. He recovered quickly and tipped his bouquet upright with a silly grin. "Really?"

Niko took the flowers and held them to her nose for a theatrical inhalation. "Oh, Colin, they're beautiful. Thank you," she said, starting over from the beginning according to script, taking a second chance at an honest relationship. "Sienna, come see what Daddy brought us!"

Sienna poked her tousled head out of her room with an exuberant smile.

"Hi, honey," Colin7 said with caution. "Remember me?"

"Colin," she answered. "You looked after me."

"I did, yes. I knew you would remember. You're a smart girl. Do I get a hug?"

Sienna crept forward, glanced at her mom for surety, and wrapped her arms around his waist. She pressed her cheek against his abdomen. "Hi, Daddy."

"I brought you a present," he said as she pulled back. He fished in his pocket for a black velvet case and placed it in her hand. Sienna opened the hinge and gasped with childish delight at the ring inside.

"It's real gold," Colin7 said. "It's special."

Sienna looked up at her mom with eyes wide in exultation, and Niko's heart melted to see such rapture. "Can I keep it?" she asked.

"Of course you can," Niko said. "Every princess needs a gold ring!"

Colin7 pinched it from the box as Sienna held out her hand. "You can wear it on your index finger for now, but when you grow up, it can be a pinkie ring." He placed it lovingly on her finger and bent to kiss it as a token of love.

Sienna held up her hand and tilted the ring to catch the light. She began to skip around in a circle. "Thank you, Daddy."

Niko watched for a moment in awe of her exhilaration. She had never seen such abandonment in Sienna, such freedom. "Wash up for dinner now," Niko said. "Supper's ready."

"Can I get it wet?"

"Sure you can, dear. It's real gold. Just be careful that it doesn't fall off in the sink."

Sienna skipped away with joy and Colin7 watched her happily. "That went well," he said.

"Pretty good work for an alien," Niko said with a wink. "Come and sit down while I get these in water. Do you have any allergies? I have farm shrimp for the salad, but wanted to check with you first."

"Great, no problem." He stepped forward slowly, still tentative in a new situation, and settled at table while Sienna bounded onto a chair beside him.

Niko served a lettuce salad and sat opposite, watching them as they began to eat. Sienna peeked at her ring periodically and smiled at her father. Colin7 shifted his eyes back and forth between them like a roving flashlight.

"Sienna," he said finally, "I understand you have a special gift."

"I'm an empath," she replied. "I don't read minds. People say I read minds but I don't."

"Ah." Colin7 nodded. He looked at Niko.

"She has feelings," Niko said with a smile of pride at her daughter. She turned to meet his gaze. "It's perfectly natural. Sienna's feelings are just more important than most people's. She doesn't do any better than random chance on Zener cards. There has to be a strong emotional component. Somehow she senses a need and tries to fix it."

"Ah," he said again.

"I can see pictures, too," Sienna said. "Stuff from far away."

Colin7 studied her. "That sounds like a wonderful talent."

"It's perfectly natural," Sienna said. She held up her empty plate and Colin7 spooned out more salad for her. She scrutinized the result with a frown. "Sienna needs more shrimp."

Colin7 dug around in the bowl with his fork to find a few and added them one by one to her plate until she signalled satisfaction.

"Thank you, Daddy," she said singsong.

He smiled.

Niko stifled a grin at their antics. Sienna had a simple innocence that seemed self-depreciative upon expression but was really quite manipulative. Perhaps she did not fully understand her own nature yet, or perhaps she had already developed her theatrics as a coping mechanism. She sometimes spoke of herself in the third person during times of stress, as though having difficulty separating her own persona from the psychic noise. There was no way for Niko to be certain, even as a mother. Sienna was a true transhuman, qualitatively different from the historical genome, a blooming flower for the future.

"I spoke to my father, the real Phillip," Niko said, and that got another paralytic shock reaction from Colin7.

"How did you manage that?"

"He took control of his body briefly," she said. "I guess he was trying to comfort me in his own psychotic way."

"Amazing," Colin7 said in admiration. "That's what we've always hoped for. What did he say?"

"Oh . . ." She tilted a shoulder and smiled at Sienna. "Just how special our daughter is."

Sienna looked up at her with doe eyes as she chewed a mouthful of lettuce. She had a good appetite for such a tiny thing, and her temperamental tastebuds seemed to have enlarged their repertoire. Niko looked back to Colin7. "He said something that reminded me of your research. You know, the collective unconscious and the mathematics of precognition. How is that coming along?"

Colin7 pushed a crooked smile into one cheek. "Not well. We're still getting statistical anomalies, of course, so we have proof of a communal psi effect, but the pragmatic aspects are elusive. The random number generators fluctuate hour by hour, but there's no way to target the psychic influence on such a complex and irreverent planet. At any particular time and space, some people are victorious and exuberant, others are undergoing tragedy and horror. A flood, an earthquake, a food riot, there's a never-ending stream of possible vectors. All I have is a mathematical paradox and no way to pinpoint the source."

"I see," Niko said. "So the mind of Gaia is in constant flux."

"Well, the personification is abstruse at best," he said with a pretense to civility, "but that's one way of looking at it."

"Phillip said that consciousness is an ocean and human thoughts are just waves. He said that ideas arrive in groups, that the notion of unique invention is a fallacy. It sounded a lot like your specialty."

"That much is true," Colin7 said, "as near as we can tell. Just look at the history of science. There were five or six light bulbs created at the same time, the same with the mechanics of nuclear fission, and early software developers were notorious for following the same track. Progress is predestined."

"Are you familiar with the Davis gift?"

"Yes," he said warily, "the runner Zakariah, technically your stepbrother."

"He could see the harmonics in V-space, the patterns of data. That's what gave him such great advantage, until he and Phillip were burned out by the Beast. He was the best in the biz in his day." She held a palm to her chest. "I can't understand how or why, but Rix has the Davis gift also. I've seen him in action in Prime Level Seven. He can make conduits out of thin ether."

Colin7 nodded. "So it's genetic."

"Now Phillip and your father have tinkered even more with the genome. What if they've managed to take the Davis gift out of V-space and into the real world? What if Sienna can pick up the waves in the ocean of consciousness? You know, feel the mind of Gaia?"

"That would be incredible if it were possible."

"Sound a bit off base to you?"

"A tad."

Niko nodded, pouting. "I thought so. Crazy, right?"

They stared at each other, imagining the uncomfortable space in between.

"You don't have to worry about Grampa," Sienna said. "He just wants to say he's sorry."

Niko turned to the child, shocked at such a bold statement out of nowhere. "What do you mean?"

"Nothing," she said. "Sienna doesn't mean anything." She chased a piece of shrimp around her plate and forked it finally.

Niko leaned toward her. "Are you thinking about Phillip?"

"No," she said chewing. "The girl."

Darkness hooded Niko's gaze as she frowned. "How can Grampa be a girl?"

Sienna shrugged tiny shoulders. "Sienna doesn't know."

"Please, honey, try to think for me. Is Phillip trying to communicate with us?"

"Sienna doesn't know anyone named Phillip." She pushed her empty salad plate away. "What's for dessert?"

Colin7 touched a hand to his daughter. "It's okay," he said and cast a cautionary glance toward Niko. "We're not worried about Grampa."

"Cranberry tarts," Niko said with an attempt at a smile. "Freshly baked just for you."

Sienna shook her head. "Sienna doesn't like cranberries."

"Yes, she does," Niko said with a mother's stern tone. "*You* do like them, and I put in extra sugar so they won't be sour. They're rich in antioxidants." She gathered up three plates and took them to the kitchen.

Sienna made a puckered face to Colin7 at the use of a strange word. "Antiozz?"

"Antioxidants," he said. "Cranberries are good for you."

After dinner they played a board game, a contest that was determined for the most part by the random roll of a pair of dice so that Sienna would have an equal chance to win. Sometimes Niko wondered whether the young empath had an unfair advantage in any activity, chance or not. What if she could feel the correct outcome before any of them? What if she knew the score from the start via some weird subspace connection? It would hardly be fair.

Sienna did indeed win the game, and as a reward got to pick her favourite book for a bedtime story, a fable about good gremlins in a backyard garden. Niko knew the story by heart and was happy to watch Colin7 shuffle haltingly through the pages reading aloud to his daughter. Sienna went to sleep quickly with a sigh of contentment, surrounded by family.

Niko returned to the kitchen and prepared a cup of coffee for Colin7 with one sugar and goat's milk, just the way he liked it. She handed it forward. "What do you think?"

"I think she's wonderful."

"No, silly, I mean that crack about Grampa wanting to say he was sorry."

"Well." He spread his hands. "Kids say a lot of curious things at that age. You can't always take them at their word."

She tilted an eyebrow at him. "You know much about kids?"

His clean-shaven cheeks showed a subtle blush. "Not really, but I've done some theoretical analysis."

"I bet."

"Okay, for the sake of discussion, Phillip feels the need for forgiveness. I can buy that. Perhaps what happened to his son Zakariah, the blackmail, the brain burn. The man was a criminal, by all accounts."

"Do you know anything about my progenitor?"

"Niko Number One?" he said. "Not really."

"She died during experimental brain surgery, back when wetware was first being developed. That would be hard for a father, don't you think? Perhaps he feels responsible."

Colin7 nodded thoughtfully. "I can't imagine anything like that happening to Sienna. I would be devastated, and I've only known her for a short time."

"Phillip told me to get her wired for Prime."

"No," he said as he stiffened with resolve. "It's too early for augmentation. She's too young. Her brain has not reached stasis."

"Nobody's brain ever reaches stasis these days," Niko said.

The scientist emboldened his shoulders with a show of professional expertise. "Well, of course there's continuing neuroplasticity, but it could be dangerous to alter cerebral hardware before basic pathways have developed and solidified."

"Is there proof of that?"

"There certainly is. I may not have chapter and verse on the tip of my tongue, but heavens, Niko, it should be self-evident."

"Sienna's special."

"Yes, she is, and we should make every effort to protect that gift, not risk it on some ill-conceived wetware surgery!" He held his coffee cup toward her and shook it so hard that a few drops spilled over the rim onto the linoleum floor. "V-space can damn well wait for her!"

Niko patted the air to calm him. "Okay, okay, I just wanted some input. We're in this together whether we like it or not." She reached to pull a paper towel off a roll and crouched at his knees to clean up spilled coffee. She'd had her first augmentation as a child not much older than Sienna. Her whole life had been one long research experiment, one big mess. No wonder she was so screwed up. She stood and tossed the soiled paper in a bucket under the sink, turned to face Colin7, the alien stepfather to her stepdaughter, one petri dish removed and forever distanced.

His probing eyes were intense and meaningful. "I do like it, Niko, just so you know. I think I'm in love with you."

"I love you," Helena said from the edge of dreams.

Jimmy looked up from his design schematics on wireless V-space, the next generation in satellite wi-fi. The innovators were building a superimposed virtuality, ND (natural-digital), a world where fantasy and reality mingled together in symbiotic harmony, a virtual space where commodity traders could surf the V-net in public and not fall off the subway platform, where children could go to school and run in the playground at the same time. "Are you awake?" he whispered.

"I'm not sure," Helena said. "I keep expecting to be dead."

"No, no, you're not going to die yet. Zak is on his way to see you. He'll be here in a few days. Dr. Mundazo has surfaced out of hiding. He wants to give his final report from the ERI."

"Ohhh," she moaned. "I could never bear that."

"Well, he's found you now, and we can't turn an old friend away. He's taking a risk on the grid to cross the border." Jimmy turned back to the data tablet on his knees, his work in progress tagging nano-crystals with photonic relays, stitching design-space like a garment. He tapped the save button and stood. "Can I get you anything?"

"My bedpan is full again. I'm sorry."

He chuckled. "I'm sorry too, babe. Don't worry about it." Jimmy moved to the bed and pulled a blanket down to expose her wizened body. All the fat had been consumed from her frame, the marrow of her bones sucked dry. Nothing left now but hard cords of muscle on a twisted skeleton with white parchment skin.

"I'm still not comfortable showing my vagina outside of the sexual arena," Helena said.

"Sexual arena," Jimmy repeated. "I like that." He gently moved her emaciated legs and cleaned her with a tissue. The only thing he didn't like about bedpans was that they smelled like shit. Funny, huh? The rest of it didn't bother him at all. He clenched his sinuses as he walked carefully to the washroom and dumped a slurry of blood and black necrotic tissue in the toilet. He gagged to control a retch in his abdomen, swallowed hard against pain. Helena was dying from the inside out, dripping gore out of every orifice.

He rinsed the bedpan and returned it to the bedroom, pillowed her body in a new position above it to minimize sores and cramping. He checked her IV and stroked her head. Her blond hair looked good, and he made the effort each day to wash it and brush it, to make her look pretty. The dead cells in her hair and fingernails could not know that the body had failed; they alone were immune to the rampant breakdown of order that plagued her. Helena groaned on the edge of nirvana and blinked her eyes to wakefulness. She was getting pretty buzzed on this new mix, but it was better than incessant pain. Nerve endings were breaking down, scrambling signals. Hope had failed.

"Do you expect to hear the voice of God when you die, Jimmy?"

"The voice of God?"

"Or some curtain call, you know, some transcendent vision to make it all seem worthwhile?"

"No, I've never really thought about it. What about you?"

She turned her head with a wince of pain. "All I hear is a steady rumbling thunder. I spent my entire life seeking the Source, longing for eternal life, paying it forward in service to humanity. But I never found the faith that Mia took for granted. She had the inner confidence of a prayer warrior."

Jimmy sniffed a subtle recognition of honour due her memory. "Zak and Mia lived through hard years together, always running from vampires, hiding from the law, trying to raise Rix during tough times. Her spiritual strength sustained them both, no doubt about it. But prayer?" He tilted his head with a grimace of suspicion. "Communion with an external deity? How is that supposed to work? By what mechanism does a transfer of thought take place?"

"Quantum resonance," Helena said. "Something undiscovered by science."

"What, leptons and charm quarks? That's a cop-out. Scientists have followed that rabbit trail all the way back to the big white bang. They built those huge hadron colliders last century and dedicated their lives to analyzing the data. Don't you think they would have measured any strange force that could influence brain cells from a distance?"

"Particle physicists still don't have all the answers in the universe, my darling man. The cosmos is more than a pinball machine. God can still work in mysterious ways."

"I heard a voice once," Jimmy said, "just after my first wetware installation, a young female chanting 'elaborate kittens' over and over. I opened my eyes and looked around the empty room. I still had bandages on my head and over my ear." He reached up to tap behind his temple where the network cable was embedded in his skin. "I tried to rehearse my favourite rock 'n' roll tune, tried to do mental math, but all I could hear was 'elaborate kittens, elaborate kittens.' I had a panicky feeling that the wizards had wired me up screwy, that the girl might never go away and my brain was ruined.

Some schizophrenic overload, I guess, surgical trauma, anaesthetics."
He shrugged. "She stopped talking the next day, and I never heard
from her again."

"That's not exactly the voice of God I was hoping for."

"Sad to say," Jimmy said with a knowing smile, "but in the
modern world, most people only use his name when they're exercising their pudenda."

Helena pulled her lips back in an attempt at a grin, a toothy
caricature that reminded him of a skull and crossbones. "Mia used
to talk about life after death," she said, "some transcendent pattern
like a brushstroke through four dimensions. Do you think there's any
truth to that?"

He dropped his forehead to signal his doubt. "Mia was a strong
woman. Who knows? Maybe she was absorbed into the Source in
the end. I've often wondered whether faith has an element of self-
fulfillment in the afterlife. Maybe you get what you expect rather
than what you deserve. Unless they coincide, of course."

"I don't think the Source will be looking for me, Jimmy."

He recoiled inwardly at his lack of discretion. The Source had
abandoned her, left her to die in grotesque horror in the house of a
criminal. "Tell me about your upload to Soul Savers in the Cromeus
colonies," he offered in respite. "Zak said you were living in paradise
for a few weeks."

A vestige of a smile quivered on her face. "It was glorious at first,
an interactive menagerie of digital experience. But it wasn't heaven.
The machine ecstasy was artificial. It was like living in my favourite
memories, manipulating them at will, creating a perfect life." She
paused, eyes closed in reminiscence.

"If the technology is so reliable, why is it illegal here on Earth?"

"Colin Macpherson developed Soul Savers over a century ago to record his own brilliant mind for posterity. His original system has been perfected over the generations by his clones. Every bodily cell is recorded and resonated into the hardware, every chemical event given a counterpart in the digital realm, quadrillions of connections working in parallel. There simply aren't resources available on this data-choked planet. Users in the Cromeus colonies are required to sign over everything they own to join the program. It's an augmented existence for the wealthy elite, far superior to mundane life."

"Sounds wonderful," Jimmy said. "Why did you come back?"

"All saved souls return to their bodies, some daily, some weekly. It provides a base of operations, a point of comparison with which to balance the infinity of machine life. Your consciousness starts to fray—to diffuse into the network, to dissipate somehow—the longer you stay away from home." She waved her hand in a flutter. "When you're in the body, the machine soul seems like a hallucination, a vividly detailed illusion, and when you're immersed in the digital dream, the body seems inconsequential."

"But you chose the body permanently. Do you regret that now? Would you be willing to upload again if you had the chance?"

"There's no hope in a saved soul, no progress, no challenge of change," Helena said. "It seemed a futile and frivolous waste of eternity. That's why I unplugged, to feel pain again." She snorted a crude chuckle. "Guess I got what I wanted."

"You know I'll never forget you, babe."

She ghosted a smile at his romantic sentiment. "I am so glad there are no mirrors in this room."

"You look fine."

"Ha."

"Inside you're more beautiful than ever."

"Is that what lives on after death, Jimmy? Something inside?"

Jimmy reached to pull a blanket up to her neck and patted her peacefully on the shoulder. "You'll have to ask a better man than me. I heard a preacher once who was expecting a wedding feast in heaven. Roasted lamb, I think it was. You must have some family background with the ecclesiasts. Most people do. Do you want me to call a priest? Or, you know, some religious guardian?"

Helena shifted her body with discontent. "I've outlived everyone in my family. My adoptive parents were Protestants who forgot long ago what they were protesting. By then the Romans had already paved their way to perversion with doctrines of celibacy. Since Eve ate the apple of self-consciousness, humans have been coping with the fear of death by invoking tribal superstition and graveyard ritual. That's what separates us from the animals, the knowledge of good and evil. Religion was created by men to subjugate and control, to diminish the power of one group in favour of another, but behind all the shamanistic smoke and mirrors I know there must be some fire of transcendence in the entangled quantum strings of the cosmos. Do you think there is justice in the universe? Reward and punishment? Do you think an omnipresent judge is recording every passing thought?"

"God, I hope not," Jimmy said with a laugh. "Not after all those masturbation fantasies!"

Helena chuckled wearily. "Well, if that's your worst sin, you'll probably do okay. All our good deeds are just filthy rags in the eyes of a holy god. We could never earn our own redemption."

"There's no reason to posit a divine being to explain creation," Jimmy said, shaking his head with conviction. "Read a poem if you want inspiration. I'm a scientist and so are you. Science does not allow for random intervention in the laws of physics, nor consciousness beyond the grave."

Helena's face hardened at the sudden stark truth. "Your bedside manner sucks, Jimmy. Is this the solace you offer a dying woman?" She closed trembling eyes and turned away.

"I'm sorry," Jimmy said, reaching to rub her shoulder, wishing he had lied to her all along. He could have built her up instead of tearing her down. He could have offered her hope if only he had some to spare. "There could be purpose in the universe. There must be some momentum toward complexity; that much appears self-evident."

"I love you, Jimmy," she said. "Right here, right now. It's more than many can say."

An ache rose in his throat, but he braved himself against it. Life was ephemeral, nothing more. They'd had great sex, shared a few laughs. "I love you, too," he said. No harm or shame in that.

A rattle whispered through her nostrils and the room grew quiet. Death had a wicked sting and Jimmy could feel it now, his own dark shadow creeping near. Death was an end and not a beginning, but what were his options? An upload into digital purgatory with Philomena? Did he want to spend the rest of existence in V-space, cruising for pocket change on Main Street to buy bandwidth up Prime? Did he want to spend his twilight years diffusing into nonexistence with the passing of interminable eons, living the final entropy of deconstruction, thought by thought slipping away as synthetic synapses withered and petrified in the communal lightspeed chaos? Helena was right. It seemed like a poor excuse for life, a lingering way to die.

Jimmy rubbed absently at his temple while he watched Helena drifting in her private delirium. "Do you need anything? A drink of water? A fresh bedpan?"

"I'll sleep for now, thanks."

"Sure." He kept his eyes on her face as he stood. She glowed with animation even on the verge of death, and it seemed hard to imagine that her light might extinguish, her skin go stony and cold. He reached down to touch her pretty lips with a finger. "Sweet dreams," he whispered.

Six

Rix landed on Main Street to find crowds of avatars swarming the boulevard in a quagmire of protocol overload, some kind of distributed-denial scarcity. A buzz of dissonance hovered like bad electricity in the ether, a negative lightning charge building to explosive potential. Users were sucking up code like ghostly sponges, jostling for substance, frothy quantum bubbles breaking through surface tensions of digital skin to pilfer communal resources in a chaotic network orgy. Safe in his mirror-reflective silver avatar, barely a visible entity, Rix pushed up on his toes to peer beyond the roiling cloud around him, searching for his batgirl, or catgirl, or whatever exotic costume Niko had cooked up with her illegal enhancements today. How could he ever find her in this gridlock?

"Rix."

He heard his name rise out of the tangled assembly and whirled toward the sound. The voices all seemed to merge into a riot of clamour, an emergent pandemonium. A sea of shoulders swept him along against his will, away from his lost sweetheart.

"Rix, over here."

A hand shot up in the distance, a black glove with a lacy arm, his siren in lingerie, his enchantress. He pushed against shorter bodies, a predominantly Asian crowd, and stood his ground facing upstream, shoving avatars to each side with his arms to escape the steady influx at this access point. Everyone seemed to be milling toward the civic centre of town, and he struggled against the flow toward his cousin one petri dish removed. She was wearing her catsuit avatar, black leather and lace, showing way too much skin, attracting way too much attention. She reached to hug him and kissed him on the cheek. He felt numb and speechless in her presence.

"You okay?" she said. "I've never seen the portals so crowded."

"Yeah." He shook off a lustful dream, an impossibility. "You look fabulous."

"Thanks, I know. I'm off duty. Just out for a party."

"What's going on today? Has the mass market hit Main Street?"

"There's a rave uptown, supposed to be awesome. C'mon." She took him by the hand and they merged with the flow of bodies. "I'm glad the Eternals got out of the tower okay. Sorry to hear about the bloodlords going to war. I tried to warn Helena."

He glanced around furtively, checking for greysuits. "Is it okay to talk openly now that the Beast has fallen?"

"There's no more privacy, Rix. Just say what you need to say."

"I love you, Niko."

She stopped with a look of shock, dropped his hand and swayed back subtly on her heels to study him. "Of course," she said after a moment of consideration. "I love you too, cousin."

Rix winced at the downgrade. He had never aspired to be a friend, some distant relative, not ever. He had too much passion in his bones for her, and he ducked his eyes away from her inspection as the press of bodies forced them back into the flow of movement. She knew too much already. Rix swallowed back the remnant of his pride. "Did you know the ERI tower would burn? Is that why you arranged for the tunnel?"

She shook her head. "No, I'm not a witch. I just act like one sometimes." She grinned at her own joke, searching for camaraderie again. "It's always good to have an exit strategy, that's all. You can never trust a bloodlord. They have too much at stake."

"Well, thanks," Rix said. "All Eternals are grateful."

Niko tipped a glance in recognition. "Dimitri would have thought of a tunnel eventually."

"Maybe, but he's not really a grand thinker, more of a grassroots commando, a mover and shaker. He saved us all when it counted."

"I'm glad," Niko said, and sighed at some pleasant memory. "He's a great guy to have on your side. I do believe in prophecy, Rix. Sienna is teaching me to expect more than base systems provide, but I'm not really anything, you know, just a bad bundle of DNA." A sourness crossed her face, some reminder of vulnerability. She was an illegal clone, a posthuman vagrant.

"You're a beautiful girl," Rix said. "You don't have to dress like a vamp to be special."

"I know, but it's such fun." She puffed up her chest and splayed her fingers as she pranced with swaying hips, conscious again of her costume as the princess of darkness, dramatizing her role to the hilt. She was hot and she knew it. Her smile was devilish, her eyes mischievous.

"How is your daughter, anyway?" Rix said.

She paused and squinted. "Mundazo tell you?"

"I pressed him for an explanation. Is it supposed to be a secret?"

"No, I guess not. Sienna's fine. We're hooking up with Colin again. Apparently he's the father."

Rix felt a knot twist in his abdomen, another blow to his ego. Crap, a father. Niko was slipping even farther away from him. She was a young mother now, part of a family. How could he ever have a chance with her? "Is that right?" he stammered.

"It was a virgin birth, Rix, I swear. Not some horrid Lolita thing."

"That's okay."

"No, it's not okay," Niko said grimly. "It was a test-tube rape, but I've had time to work it out in my mind. I'm not bitter."

Rix nodded, not daring for eye contact. "Sienna's a treasure."

Niko reached for his hand again and swung it at her side as they walked. "Thanks," she said. "I knew I could count on you."

A chant teased against the background chaos on Main Street as they approached the centre of town. *Philomena, Philomena!* Niko looked over with a frown.

A hawker popped up dressed in a cheesy black suit and top hat. "Tickets," he said. "Free tickets for an upgrade."

Rix brushed by him, careful not to touch. Just what he needed, another tracker sucking his data. He pulled Niko closer and bent to her ear. "Do we really want to be here?"

"Let's check it out," she said. "Never mind the beggars. We can jump the firewall if we have to."

Bodies jostled in on every side, a mass mix of culture from every continent and every language, surrounding them in a tangle of foreign chatter. Two rows of dancers lined the entranceway to the stadium, scantily clad animatrons gyrating on pedestals to entertain the incoming guests. They were part human, part beast, grotesque androids on programmed loops orchestrated together in a flowing synchrony. One female had snakes for arms and twin sets of naked breasts. One winged male had a gryphon head and sculpted body of muscle, thrusting his hips forward and back with bestial eroticism to attract a circle of onlookers. An aura of seduction surrounded all the dancers, a primitive desire for sensual fulfilment, an easy road to pleasure. Their skin had a greenish, oily tinge and their limbs were lanky and finely toned. They seemed to harmonize together in a chorus as though formulated from a shared configuration. One lewd she-male, gesticulating with invitation, had huge female breasts and a bulging male package in a leather thong that made Rix blush with envy. Another classical demon with cloven hooves was dressed only in fur and rotated to show shiny buttocks. A smell of sweat hung in the air around them, a dank and musty fragrance that seemed vaguely comforting, some subtly programmed pheromone to make the mythological seem meaningful.

Philomena! Philomena!

The stadium doors were open wide before them, and a deep bass foundation rumbled from the dark orifice like a subway in an underground tunnel. Niko seemed entranced as she pushed forward, dragging him behind like laptop luggage, the younger cousin on an outing, already late to the party. The music grew louder as they approached. The beat became palpable, a steady pop-rock like a heartbeat, the soul of the digital city.

No gatekeeper asked for tickets or biometrics. The way was free and unhindered, the push of the throng impossible to counter. The crowd funnelled in and spread wide to join a congregation of thousands, the chanting an overwhelming chorus.

Philomena! Philomena!

Onstage in blinding magnificence stood the nexus, a giant animatron lit by psychedelic spotlights, a young girl with dark hair and a waist so thin it reminded Rix of a segmented insect, an alien lifeform. She sang with a loud voice like a pixie on parade, sultry with innocence, a declaration of purity against the darkness. The sound seemed to resonate inside him like a childish rhyme beckoning him closer. Her facial features were Asian, but he heard her in his own language—and soon realized with amazement that all the participants understood her in their home dialect as they sang along in mixed foreign babel.

"It's a programming trick!" he yelled to Niko in warning, trying to halt her steady progression by dragging on her arm. "It's not real!"

The catgirl turned to him, eyes wide in wonder, and pulled him onward as she writhed past gyrating bodies. The pop music wafted over them, soared above them, pierced right through them. The beat galvanized their background code in a consummation of harmonics, a digital ecstasy. Rix could not possibly hold her back. At times the accompaniment seemed of Western origin, electric guitars with deep bass foundations, but seemed to transpose to more Eastern themes, sitars and festive rhythms, and then to synthetic Japanese keyboard sounds and throbbing tribal drums from the plains of Australia. Every heritage seemed representative in the multicultural mash-up, and the concert rose and fell like an oscillating wave, sailing off on musical tangents of exploration, always fresh, perpetually renewed, yet building on stable foundations of history and melodic tradition. The voice of the animatron seemed at times haunting and hypnotic, ranging up and down the scale from childish lullaby to providential wisdom. The crowd panted and pulsed around them, shoulders bobbing in unison with the rhythm, right arms raised in open-palmed blessing. Hail victory.

Philomena! Philomena!

Fireworks burst onstage in fountains of white splendour as the music reached crescendo and the young girl danced back and forth across the stage, knees high and kicking out cartoon stiletto heels like knife blades. "Champions rise," she sang, "the future is our heritage!"

"I know this girl," Niko shouted in his ear. "I can feel her inside me." She pressed a hand to her chest, fingertips on her throat.

Rix felt it also, a longing for unity, a promised peace for everyone. He could sense tendrils of resonance reaching inside his mind, sucking his background configuration, probing his secret thoughts.

"There is no hell below us," the animatron sang. "We are all one in spirit."

The crowd cheered and raised flat palms in the air.

"Heaven is in our global heart!"

Hail victory!

Philomena raised her arm and pointed an index finger upward with thumb extended like a gun. She swept her hand over the crowd from right to left with deliberation as the front row of worshippers fainted and fell in a silent wave before her. More supplicants approached, stepping over prostrate forms, headbanging in time to the music, and again the animatron swept her pointing finger across the raving flock. More bodies folded in slumber at her feet as her hand passed overhead, row after row until a mound of quivering flesh lay slain in the spirit before her. She raised reverent palms as she crooned out a prayerful summation, an explosion sounded as the music hit a final cadence of frenzy, and Philomena disappeared in a vapour of smoke. Fireworks shot up to the vaulted ceiling and blazed red and green in sparkling glory. A steamy fog hinted of gunpowder and flowers.

The crowd kept chanting her name, fingers pointed in promise to the gods, as sleeping forms began to moan and rise smiling with joy, a sublime fealty. Witnesses turned to companions and strangers alike with incredulity on their grinning faces, reaching to touch shoulders and arms. "Did you see that?" they said. "Did you feel that?" The noise dimmed to a rumble as an encore never followed, and the congregation milled and murmured happily, grateful for the mystic blessing from above.

Niko cradled her face in her fingertips in the ensuing quiet, and Rix reached to comfort her with an arm around her shoulders.

"It's Phillip," she whispered.

"What?"

"Niko, is that you?" They both looked up as a man barrelled toward them out of the crowd, six inches taller, twenty years older, with auburn hair and a gregarious smile. "How you doin', girl?" He hugged her with huge hands and burly arms.

"Great, John," she said as they parted. She kept a lingering touch on his wrist, her gaze intent on his face. "Good to see you. Keeping out of vampire prison?"

He held a flat palm up beside his beefy neck. "Always and forever. I'm living in Texas now, chasin' the viral vectors, building a future. Awesome show, right? I'm a sucker for nostalgia. Where'd you escape to?"

Niko tossed her head in a casual and familiar manner, an intimate gesture between friends, perhaps lovers. "I went home to visit my father, worked on some research in neurology, hooked up with the ERI eventually."

The man nodded with instant sobriety. "Sorry to hear about the burning tower. The whole net cried that day."

"Thanks," she said. "This is my cousin Rix." She swept an arm at him, a brush-off.

"Hi, Rix." A hand shot out quickly in greeting.

"Hi," he said as he gripped the mammoth paw. Who was this guy? An old boyfriend?

"John and I were trapped together in vampire prison," Niko said. "Seems like a long time ago."

"Another life," John said.

Together in prison? Living in close quarters? Sharing everything? Rix glanced back and forth between them and had a fleeting vision of them both naked, a monstrous manhood piercing his sweetheart from behind like a brutish primate.

Niko bristled at his inspection. "Why does everything have to be about sex with you, Rix?"

"What?"

"Jesus, Rix, you're broadcasting your thoughts, you pervert." She pressed her hands to the sides of her head as though protecting her brain from insult. "I've got to get out of here," she said and rushed away.

"What?" Rix repeated.

"I never slept with her, son," John said. "Never would have dreamt it. You'd better go after her." He pointed with his head to Niko's fleeing form.

Rix spread his arms in confusion. "What the hell's going on?"

John smiled with knowing grace. "It's all part of the show, kid. Transparency in a global world. Philomena is ushering in the end of secrecy. Soon every thought will be brought into communal captivity." He gestured toward the multicultural mix around them. "No more barriers. The poor rise up and the rich slow down. Embrace it, man. Overgrow with it." His face had a sleepy edge of charisma from the concert, a man mesmerized. *You'd better go after her.*

Rix turned to see Niko disappear through the exit into bright light beyond. He ran toward her, pushing avatars indiscriminately to make a path, but she disappeared into the cavorting crowd on Main Street.

Niko woke out of V-space to find Colin7 with a hand on her shoulder, his face earnest with concern. "You okay?" he asked. "You were moaning. Bad trip?"

"No, I'm fine. Rix is acting like an idiot again." She sat up from her launch couch and shook tangles out of her consciousness.

"Some people are here to see you. It's about Sienna."

Niko reached to massage tense muscles at the back of her neck, still struggling to reconcile the unadorned 3-D world, feeling empty of experience. "What about her?"

"They say they have authority to take her."

"What?"

"You'd better come and see."

Niko jumped up and dashed to her bedroom, took her trank pistol from beneath her mattress, and stuffed it down the front of her pants under a loose sweatshirt. Colin7 held a palm upright in warning as he stood in the doorway. "Be careful," he said. "They're from the government."

She pushed him aside and strode into her living room. A woman was seated on her couch, dressed in a black windbreaker and black pants, flat-soled working pumps. Two men in grey business suits stood by the door with Sienna between them, her bulging princess backpack at her feet.

"I'm Niko," she said as she approached. "Sorry to keep you waiting."

The woman rose to greet her. "I understand. It's no trouble. I'm familiar with wirehead addiction," she said condescendingly as she handed forward a business card. "I'm Hiromi Lee from Child Services. This is Detective Martin and his partner Dirk Magus." She pointed absently to the cops by the door while Niko tucked the card away.

"Let me see your ID," Niko demanded. *Stuck-up bitch.*

Hiromi reached in her coat pocket and gave her an official laminate in a black pouch. Niko zoomed in with full visual augmentation to check for inconsistencies under magnification. She had no idea what to look for; she had never tried to counterfeit such an exquisite document and didn't know the techniques, but she could see no obvious manufacturing defects. It looked genuine, government issue, the photo unflattering. Hiromi had dark hair and tawny skin, racially mixed in a global gestalt. She spoke slowly with the careful articulation of one accustomed to interlingual communication.

Niko returned the badge. "What do you want?"

Hiromi pocketed her ID and chewed on her lip for a hesitant moment as she appraised Niko. "We have authority to take Sienna Davis into protective custody."

Niko gaped at her. "She's under arrest?"

"No, she's under protection. She'll be going into foster care."

Niko looked over at her daughter standing quietly by the door. Sienna returned the gaze with a blank face, teasing the corner of her mouth with her tongue, seemingly unconcerned with the dramatic turn of events. What could have happened? They were supposed to be off the network. She had registered Sienna for online school under an assumed name. Niko smoothed her shirt with a palm and felt the bulge of her gun for comfort. "I don't understand."

Hiromi resumed her seat on the couch, crossed her legs, and folded her hands in her lap like a mannequin, a trained professional. "The government is not blind, nor stupid, Ms. Niko."

"She's my daughter."

The woman sniffed in disbelief. "You're far too young for that, and there's certainly no evidence to support such a claim."

"I can provide a genscan."

Hiromi shook her head. "That won't be necessary. The details of Sienna's procreation are not at issue." She lowered her gaze, eyebrows raised in subtle threat. "That would be another department entirely and a much more serious situation." Hiromi paused and relaxed her shoulders in a plea for cooperation. "I'm from Child Services. Our concern is with the welfare of all underage citizens."

Niko spread empty palms and hunkered down with a frown. "I still don't get it. Sienna's perfectly happy here. This is my partner, Colin." She pointed backhand. "We're a family."

Hiromi sighed gently though her nose and uncrossed her legs. She pushed her hands down her thighs and patted her knees twice in synchrony. "Your partner is an alien visitor who has delayed his departure beyond the terms of his visa. He is subject to deportation at any moment." She tilted her head with an insipid smile, playing an accustomed role, a simple bureaucrat expressing the obvious but willing to overlook unnecessary complications.

Niko looked in surprise at Colin7 still standing near her bedroom door. He stepped forward. "My case is under review," he said. "I'm acting as a caregiver for my father and have diplomatic immunity."

"Your father is dead, sir," Hiromi Lee said, leaning forward with import, "and you have no legitimate business on this planet." She waved a hand. "But let's not tread on dangerous ground. I'm from Child Services. My concern is solely for the welfare of Sienna Davis."

A terrible taste rose in Niko's mouth and she wanted to spit with outrage. "I'm her mother, God damn it!"

Hiromi sat back at Niko's outburst, her face unruffled. "You people seem to have a cavalier attitude as to what constitutes a family, but that's beside the point. At issue now is the Eternal virus in your veins, Ms. Niko. I can't imagine why you would agree to cooperate with the aliens or what their goals on Earth may be, but they are not consistent with the goals of the United States of America. Under the terms of the Evolutionary Terrorist Omnibus, you have renounced your civil rights and are an unfit guardian in the eyes of the law."

Niko fumed as her mind whirled through possibilities. How did they know she was Eternal? What proof could they have without a blood test? The ERI records would all have been destroyed. That left only vampires in collusion, an enemy conspiracy. The Beast had fallen. She reached for her trank pistol.

"Please don't touch your weapon," Hiromi said sternly. "We bear you no personal ill will, but my companions carry government-issue firearms and are trained to shoot in self-defence." She glanced to the door where the two cops stood with guns levelled, one pointing to Niko and the other to Colin7. "They shoot real bullets. We're not vampires. Dead is dead to us."

In a quick panic, Niko estimated her chance of success. A duck and roll, a shot to one of the goons. She would take a hit, but maybe not fatal. The effete alien would go down without a fight, but not likely with a kill shot. Sienna would be quickly out the door either way. Niko might never see her again if she pushed the launch button now, even if she did manage to escape. And then what? Live perpetually on the run like cousin Rix? A precarious moment of stillness passed, a flux of possibilities.

Hiromi shook her head sadly. "Surrender your weapon and we'll talk. You'll have visiting privileges under clinical supervision. Perhaps you can prove yourself before a tribunal."

"Prove myself? You bitch, I don't have to prove myself to you." Hot tears of frustration spilled onto her cheeks as Niko stood her ground, hand on the bulge at her waist, waiting for an excuse to shoot Hiromi between the eyes in one last gesture of defiance. "I'm better than you will ever be. Far superior. I wish you humans would just die off and get it over with!"

Hiromi's face went grey with professional regret and Niko saw requiem in her eyes, a rat trapped in a corner. "Sienna is human, Ms. Niko," she said evenly, "just like the rest of us here. You are the only outcast."

Niko glanced at her daughter with sudden realization. So the greysuits didn't know about Sienna's special powers! They didn't know she was the only transhuman in the room. Perhaps there was hope in that. Perhaps Niko could bide her time, pretend to cooperate with the bureaucracy while she planned her own special intervention in the affairs of state.

Sienna took this as a cue and bent to heft her backpack, hooked it round her bony shoulders. Oblivious to the drawn guns beside her, she stepped freely forward to face Niko. "Sienna is going for a walk with the bad men," she said simply. "She loves her mother."

A wave of empathy swept over Niko. The poor kid with her psi power, knowing everything always and understanding nothing at all. She was just a child, a helpless innocent in a complex war. Niko bent to one knee to embrace her, crying openly now. "I love you too, honey." She choked on the words, recognizing surrender, relinquishing anger like water down a drain. How could she let Sienna go? How could she ever sleep again without her daughter dreaming happily in the next room? God, please, no.

Detective Magus approached with his gun pointed at Niko's heart, both hands on the grip. "Place your weapon on the floor, ma'am," he instructed, "and take two steps back."

Obedient now to an inexorable futility, Niko dropped her trank pistol to the carpet and stood. She turned to Hiromi Lee as Dirk Magus kicked her weapon under the couch and pulled Sienna away. "You keep her safe, lady, or I will hunt you down and torture you, I promise. She's all I have left."

Hiromi softened and sighed with compassion. "I have tried to be civil with you, Niko," she said as she rose to her feet. "That's my job. These men are certainly capable of handling the situation without a feminine touch. You have my card. You can call and make an appointment anytime. But if you cause us any grief, you'll end up in a federal research program." She held up thumb and forefinger a centimetre apart in a show of authority. "You're one blood test away from incarceration, so don't push your luck." She walked to Sienna and placed a hand on her shoulder to steer her toward the exit.

Sienna hung dark ringlets over her sullen face as she slouched forward under the weight of her burden, meek and dutiful, and plodded through the doorway without a backward glance.

SEVEN

"Tell me, Daddy," the little girl said, "Is it better to dream unfulfilled, or not to dream at all?"

Phillip chuckled with mischief, and the sound seemed a symphony. "No dream goes unfulfilled, little one. It just never comes as we expect."

The disciples gathered up north in Jimmy's penthouse apartment to witness Helena Sharp's final passing in his makeshift clinic. Jimmy ushered them in with a solemn air of fraternity, hung their coats in a spacious closet by the door, and made stilted conversation as he studied his two brothers in arms, feeling the end drawing near, the final consummation. All those years, all that spiralling data, and what use to any of it now? Helena was dying without solace, bereft of purpose. It didn't seem right. Their existence had been a waste of energy, their revolution a sham. Silus Mundazo looked haggard from living on the run, hunted by bloodlords, his shoulders downcast, his stance defeated. They had butted heads once in business, to be sure, but Jimmy harboured no ill will toward him. Silus had hung on until the end at the ERI as Helena's replacement, had surrendered nothing but lost everything. Their eyes met as equals, their hands clasped across the years.

"Where is she?" Silus asked, and Jimmy pointed down a wide

hallway to the left where a wheelchair and walker rested against the wall, relics of a better time just days ago when the ancient lady was still capable of movement.

"Second bedroom on the right. The data's unlocked. See what you can make of it, but I think her time is short. One more night may be all we can hope for."

The doctor's face blanched with disbelief. He had known her just recently as a healthy specimen, a stalwart commander. He ducked away quickly without a word, and Jimmy turned to his own protege, Zakariah Davis, now living in hiding with an eccentric author, protected from the bloodlords by her shadow. He stretched out a hand and Zak grabbed it and switched it thumbs-up in a biker shake with a grin of camaraderie.

"Long time," Zak said. His dark hair was wild and wavy, his face forever in the bloom of Eternal youth.

"Too long. How's Jackie?"

"Great. She's in Washington today for a meeting. She's got the ear of the President."

"Wow, I'm impressed," Jimmy said and noticed wonder in his voice, a hopeful cadence. "For awhile there I thought the eagle had left the nest."

"Jackie's new book, *Ceremonial Oppression*, is creating a shitstorm now that advance copies are circulating. Have you got newsfeed here?"

"Not inside the Faraday grid," Jimmy said and handed forward a phone, "but you can get a signal out on the balcony."

They walked past glowing Roman columns and under a grand archway to the second doorway on the right to find Silus busy checking the medical readouts with a dismal frown. Helena reclined on an adjustable gurney, propped up on pillows, a shrunken and withered woman, her hair but wispy tendrils, her face wrinkled in a tragic mask. An IV bag dripped nutrients into her arm through a clear plastic tube. Zak stepped forward and kissed her gently on the cheek. She smiled and sighed with satisfaction, barely a whisper.

"Hello, Helena," he said. "It's good to see you."

She closed her eyes once in response.

"When she blinks it means yes or thank you," Jimmy said. "When she looks away it means no or discontent. She was able to keyboard with her eyes until a few days ago."

Zak reached to the side of her head and stroked her temple with reverence. "You're an amazing woman and I love you deeply."

"Be careful when you touch her skin," Jimmy cautioned. "She's very sensitive to pain now. We're keeping drugs to a minimum for the sake of cognition."

"She's deteriorating quickly," Silus said as he continued to scrutinize the medical equipment. "Her cells are cascading into senescence. Her organs are shutting down. We've got to get her on dialysis and a heart machine."

"No, Doctor," Jimmy said. "We don't want any extreme measures to prolong the inevitable."

Silus turned to him, his face contorted with anger. "You've got to be kidding me! This woman has lived on the forefront of science her entire life. She worked to advance rejuvenation techniques every step of the way. Gene therapy, steroids, regenerative hormones. She became Eternal by force of will alone. What about the cyborg nanobots we tested? What about stem-cell reconstruction?" He stepped toward Helena's bedside and knelt down on one knee to confront her. "I can't bear to see you like this, not after all our years fighting together. Death is a disease, Helena. It's not inevitable. Please let me help you. I beg of you."

She looked away and back to him. Her lips quivered with a vestige of movement.

Silus bent his head and began to cry in a weak convulsion, pressing his face on her pillow to hide his anguish.

Jimmy approached and began to rub his shoulder in a rhythmic massage. "We talked this all through weeks ago, Silus. Take a few moments to read her journal. It's all there, her last testament. She's not afraid of death."

Silus rose to his feet and ducked his chin, wiped at his cheeks with a sleeve. The three disciples stood in silent vigil at her bedside, unable to touch her, unable to thank her enough for all she had done for them, for all humanity. How many Eternals had found refuge in the Institute she created? How many posthumans had found hope for a better future because of her research? Together they counted each one in the quiet of their thoughts, heads bowed, eyes downcast.

Zak flipped out Jimmy's phone to check the time and abruptly left the room. Silus pulled a chair close to the bed and cradled Helena's shrunken hand in his palms while Jimmy went to the kitchen to make his guests a quick sandwich. He came back in a few minutes and handed a plate to Silus. The doctor chewed mechanically, never taking his eyes away from Helena, unwilling to break the shroud of silence. Helena looked tiny in the hospital gurney, a shrunken mummy in a modern sarcophagus. Her bones had contracted, her skin desiccated and fissured, her heart broken. Everything she had worked for had been lost, the ERI razed by bandits, her initiative toward mass inoculation abandoned, her own Eternal life taken away by a thief in the night. Her precious lifeblood had been drained and flushed down a toilet of despair. She had nothing left to give and no reason for hope.

Helena's heartbeat began to falter and her eyes stopped moving.

Her chest went still as her lungs ceased expansion, her breathing little more than random air exchange now, her time short.

"No," Silus said, aghast at the final prospect.

Jimmy held him down in the chair with a gentle touch. "She's glad you're here, doctor. It's good to have a few faithful witnesses at the end."

Zak burst into the room waving his phone. "The President has asked Congress to repeal the ETO on national newsfeed! She's made a motion to the United Nations for worldwide recognition of civil rights for all Eternals. You've won, Helena. The wheels you put in motion, the sacrifices we all made. Our dream of freedom is coming to pass!" He rushed to her bedside and fell on his knees, his face bright with enthusiasm. "You've won, Helena."

Silus shook his head. "I don't think she can hear you. Her brain is failing fast."

"You can hear me, Helena. I know you can." Zak leaned forward to stare directly into her eyes. He seemed to be concentrating intently, trying to read her mind, to share her essence in death. Helena smiled and closed her eyes one last time. A machine beeped a gentle tone as her heart slipped to flatline.

"Look," Silus croaked and rose to his feet, pushed at Zak's shoulder to clear space above her.

Jimmy reached to grasp his arm. "It's over, Doctor. She's gone."

"Look," he said and bent toward Helena. A golden glow seemed to envelop her face and neck, casting all shadows away. Silus gripped the blanket at her neck and pulled it away to expose an alien vial beaming with promise.

"What's that?" Jimmy said in shock. It looked like luminous glass twisted into an infinity symbol.

Zak jumped forward. "The Eternal virus!"

Silus grabbed it and held it up with both hands. "Hold her mouth open!"

"It's too late," Jimmy said. "It's impossible."

Zak pinched Helena's jaw with his fingers and spread her lips wide as Silus cracked the vial with a pop and poured the contents onto her tongue. He dropped the fragments and began to palpate her chest with diligence, forcing her heart to contract and expand.

Jimmy took a few steps back. No way. This was crazy.

"If we can keep her plasma moving," Silus said, "just long enough to get the virus to her brain."

"Hang on, Helena!" Zak shouted. He bent a furrowed brow once again in concentration or prayer, trying to mind meld again, to bring blood from a stone.

Helena blinked her eyes open, bright and wide, her face suddenly radiant. "The light speaks, Jimmy," she said clearly. "It's wonderful!" Her mouth froze agape, her eyelids locked open in surprise. Her lungs never moved, her nostrils never flared, and her heart remained inactive despite the good doctor's persistent efforts at resuscitation. The disciples hovered near the matriarch, searching for a signal, a portent of eternity, but her corpse gave up final heat, her last breath, the end of an era.

Silus shuddered finally and ceased his ministrations. He hung his face with surrender. "So close," he said, panting to regain composure. "Why would the Source arrive for a deathbed conversion? Why send a vial through a hyperspace wormhole for a few seconds of Eternal life?"

Zak shook his head. "We can never know, Silus. Our thoughts are puny."

Jimmy stared at the tableau as though from a great discontinuity. Wormholes to heaven? Immortality? What alien mysticism was this?

Life was just DNA and folded proteins. How could there be any more? "The cross of a thief," he said vacantly, "that's all she really wanted." He longed to believe in something transcendent here at the final gasp, he needed to fill a vacancy in the centre of his spirit, but he could not summon a separation of faith from fantasy. Hard reality had been a sordid and sadistic taskmaster his entire life. Hard. Reality.

A shared vision of untouchable glory seemed to hang before the two Eternals, a paradox of unearned redemption. They gazed transfixed in silence with tears glinting like jewels on their cheeks. They shuttered Helena's bulging eyes and ugly, yawning mouth and covered her neck with a blanket. "Go in peace," Silus said in benediction.

"She fought and won," Zak said.

Jimmy frowned at him and shook his head. "No, Helena lost everything. She's gone. We all lose everything in the end. You Eternals think you're invincible, but you're not. The virus is just prolonging the inevitable agony." He turned away. He could not bear to look at his lost lover in death, her once perfect body now a broken figurine, a marionette with the strings cut. His throat seemed to be strangling him, his windpipe closing up. He coughed and stumbled to the kitchen for a drink of water. He thought he had been prepared for this. They had talked it over for weeks. He was not supposed to cry.

Zak came to meet him in the kitchen and accepted a cup of cold water from the tap. "Silus is disconnecting the equipment, preparing the body for transport. Have you made any arrangements?"

"Yeah, everything's prepaid," Jimmy said, grating the machinery in his larynx. "The number for the crematorium is in the phone." His voice sounded rusty in his own ears, hoarse and distant. He seemed to be dreaming. All the edges around him seemed rubbery and pliable, untrustworthy.

Zak rested a hand on his shoulder and searched for him with his eyes. "Are there any relatives to notify?"

"No, her parents are long dead, no siblings. We're all she had." The end of a DNA trail, the last in her line. "What about your wife?"

"They never met," Zak said. "Jackie's going to be busy in Washington for a few days."

Jimmy nodded. "That must be some book, pulling the heartstrings of the President of the United States. At first I thought you were deliberately avoiding us, but I guess you've both been working hard."

"I was just her inspiration, a secretarial grunt. Jackie's the true genius."

"So what's the book about? Discrimination and abuse?"

"Well, we're trying to strike an upbeat tone, but humanity has a sad history, from the Crusades to the Holocaust and beyond. Human trafficking and slavery, the subjugation of women, the tyranny against terrorism that arose out of the Drug War."

"And posthuman rights, of course."

"Naturally that was our stated bias, but Jackie took the metaphor to the ultimate, exposing the ingrained evil in the world to make it real for the bloggers. Did you know there are still millions of people in prison for gardening psychoactive herbs, and there are places in the world where a woman can't go out in public without a bag on her head? It's all about freedom for the global village, Jimmy. Freedom and tolerance go together like the double helix with empathy and compassion—the end of religion and petty politics, one mind with diverse purpose, the future paradox of man."

Jimmy huffed a chuckle. "Sounds like punk poetry."

"Yeah, Jackie's a bit of a romantic, the tortured artist."

"I never liked her much at first, with that elegant catwalk

swagger, but not everyone gets to Washington. Tell her she's earned my respect."

"I know she'll appreciate that. She's going to take some heat in high places over this. The President is only the first step in a long journey. Jackie says true vision can only be measured by its opposition."

"Hah, she is such a punk!"

Zak smiled and nodded. "I'll let her know."

"Don't you dare," Jimmy said. "Anyway, I'm glad you're both happy."

The natural contradiction rose like a black wraith around them, the inevitable guilt of survival. "I should have been here for Helena," Zak said. "I'm sorry." His face seemed to darken at the sound of her name. Death lingered nearby, a tangible presence.

"Don't worry about it." Jimmy waved away the shadows. "She gave us the honour and privilege of final witness. Helena was an amazing woman from start to finish. What do you think she meant with those last words, *the light speaks?*"

Zak shrugged. "Photonics, language in light. Lots of engineers are working to harness the visible spectrum. Maybe the Source communicates in the subatomic realm."

Jimmy shook his head. "We're using photonics in the new design-space systems, but no one's discovered any natural language. We would have noticed any recurring patterns by now."

"What about at the Planck length? Maybe Helena tuned in to some type of primeval message in the digital software of the multiverse. When we finally discover the true nature of light, perhaps we'll see that the Source has been talking to us all along."

Jimmy glowered. "The aliens abandoned her when they pulled the plug on the virus. The Source is evil."

"No, don't think that. We can't understand everything."

"I know what I know. Helena was handed a death sentence on a platter." Jimmy pointed a steady finger. "You could be next."

Zak dropped his gaze, scratched at his tangled curls, and rubbed the burnt stub of cable sticking out behind his left ear. "I've seen magic, Jimmy, unexplained events in the slums of Haiti. I can't deny the miraculous," he said, "or explain the workings of God. Even if he slays me, I'll still trust him."

Jimmy turned away at the age-old platitude, the last bastion of stubborn faith. He needed to get outside, find some hard reality somewhere, a stable place in this shifting macrocosm. "I'm going out for a walk."

"Sure, if that's what you need. Get some fresh air." Zak tapped his phone. "Silus and I will handle the details. You've done enough."

Jimmy felt longing in his spirit and turned back to his protege one last time. He reached for Zak's shoulder and gripped it for consolation. "Hey, I'm sorry, man. I just wish you'd wire up and come back to work. I miss you."

"I can't go back to V-space, Jimmy. I've been inculcated by the flesh—poverty and hardship, death and disease. I've seen the power of prayer in action, ecstasies of hope. I want to get my hands dirty and bleed when I get cut. The V-net is not enough for me now. It's too sanitized, too artificial. There's no love in V-space."

"It's where the money is," Jimmy said, "and you can't get any closer to the future. It's the defining edge of reality, the crux and crucible of the human condition. The V-net is where global business is conducted."

"I'm sure you can handle it," Zak said. "You taught me everything, so you must be the best man for the job. Don't worry about me. I have an appointment with my father . . ." He paused at some inner vision or poignant memory, no shortage of bad history there. ". . . what's left of him."

Jimmy squinted with sour distaste. "He's been possessed by a cyberghost, so the rumour goes on Main Street. Zombified."

Zak shrugged. "That's what they say."

"So it's true then. Colin Macpherson contacted you?"

"It's just business. He's having trouble securing blood supply. The distribution system crashed with the ERI tower. All the vampires are in frenzy, facing desperation day by day."

"Good riddance," Jimmy said. "That was the blackest of the black markets."

"I don't mind giving a little blood to a good cause now and then," Zak said carefully. "I owe it to Helena to keep her work alive as best I can, her dream of mass inoculation, Eternal life for everyone."

Jimmy studied his protege with a wary eye, a man half his age with twice the experience. Had it really come to this? Was Zak ready to peddle his own blood like a prostitute, make the big compromise for the sake of misplaced ideology? What the hell had happened in Haiti with his new wife and her shaman sister? What voodoo spell could have turned him against himself? The bloom of romance had sapped his warrior spirit, his armour now broken away in chunks, his scintillant brain martyred by mindwipe science. What a waste! Zak had forgotten all the fun stuff, the joy of nailing perfect code, creating something out of nothing and knowing that the fuzzy frontier edges were close by, just the next step away, all in good time.

"Well, okay then," Jimmy said, "best of luck." They clasped hands again in a biker shake, raised firm fists at eye level in salute for old time's sake, and Jimmy shrugged on his leather jacket by the door and took the elevator down to the lobby. He strode past potted ferns and sprawling divans and through a revolving glass door onto the sidewalk outside. The street swarmed with tourists, young couples on vacation in the honeymoon capital of the world, people having a normal life, enjoying another sunny day. The air was misty with spray from the falls and twin rainbows curled up into a painted sky above the Rainbow Bridge to the USA. He took the steps down to the crowded concourse overlooking the river, gazed across at the American skyline, the land of the free. Would they really welcome Eternals home after all these years?

A vidi team was shooting a street scene with the Horseshoe Falls in the background, and their equipment truck was blocking one lane of traffic with parked police cruisers flashing on either side. Corporate guards in uniform kept the tourists back behind orange pylons as two actors climbed up out of the Niagara gorge and over the concrete retaining wall, then clutched and kissed at the precipice. A young woman in a clingy white dress with torn shoulder and bloody sleeve found shelter in a fieldstone guardhouse as the hero protected her with gun drawn. Some spy thriller with a romantic twist. The actors dramatized the same scene several times, consulting with directors between takes to fine-tune the details, and each time on the cliff face the young woman caught her tear-away dress on the same tree branch and made it look natural. Each performance culminated in a passionate embrace and kiss, a fantasy ending with clouds of mist rising from the thunderous water in the background, a love story eternally new.

Jimmy was sick of love, physically ill. A part of him had been ripped away, his inner mystic puzzle broken and irreparable. Love was a disease, a vulnerability. He recognized it now in its absence. An actor's kiss, a flash of nipple for the camera, an ephemeral futility of expression—he should have just downloaded the feelie and walked away at the credits, kept it impersonal. He never should have let love get to him. He had made a dangerous mistake and would never be the same.

No, Jimmy, no. He watched the young girl as the crew wrapped up, her face animated with pleasure at having finally nailed the scene, her scanty dress now covered with a corporate windbreaker, a steaming cup in hand. Friends crowded around, and she showed off her naked shoulder where she had scratched and bruised her fragile skin, giving her all for showbiz. She did not look anything like Helena, well, maybe just a little, with short blond hair and lanky legs. How was she supposed to have climbed up the Niagara gorge in those dancer's heels? Where did the drama end and real life begin? Was it all fake, a mask without meaning, a cruel vanity? No, Jimmy, no.

He sauntered down the concourse to stare at the river thundering over the precipice, 167 feet to the bottom, 64,000 cubic feet per second, the most powerful waterfall in North America. Century after century since the last ice age, all that fresh water heading out to brine—it seemed like something indomitable, a force of nature. Jimmy was a bug beside it, a speck of dust. He never should have expected more.

He gazed up at his penthouse apartment on the nearby tower, saw the lights glowing on his balcony. Funerary officials would take Helena's body away for a session of private viewing according to custom, then on to the final fiery furnace. They would burn her up and send her component parts high into the stratosphere to mix with the clouds and return as rain. Perhaps someday her atoms would hurtle over Niagara Falls, cascade down into the gorge below, the pointless cycle complete. Jimmy felt sick with a gnawing vacancy.

No wonder Zak had wasted so many months pining after Mia's ghost, chasing his first wife beyond the grave, up north, down south, eventually to a makeshift hospital in Haiti. Jimmy had accused him of psychosis to his face, of wasting time and energy in useless frivolity while important work lay idle. He had never understood the pain of love, the tragedy of separation. Zak had been sane all along and Jimmy had been a fool. How could he have been so insensitive to his friend after all those years sliding data on Sublevel Zero? Shared experience and cherished memories—that was all any human could offer the world in the end, a few good stories, a trusted shoulder during crisis. Zak had sacrificed everything for his family and friends, denying self-interest at every twisted crossroad, showing by example a communal hope for the future. His protege had taught him more about life than all the hustlers on Main Street ever would. Jimmy turned with new insight toward the consuming sun, saw rainbows of promise cavorting in the sky above him, and headed for home.

"Thanks for coming," Niko said at the door to her apartment. "We have an appointment at Child Services at 2:45."

Colin7 stepped inside and shrugged off a white lab coat. "Are you sure you want me to tag along?"

"You're the father, Colin."

"Well, we certainly don't want *that* in the public record."

"We're the only family she's got." Niko took his coat and hung it on a peg by the door. "Want some lunch?"

"No, I'm too nervous to eat, " he said. "I don't like appearing before authority figures on this planet. That last woman threatened to deport me."

Niko shook her head. "They can't do that. They only have power over children." She stepped into a tiny kitchen and took the lid from a boiling pot. "I'm having chicken soup," she said.

Colin7 peeked in the doorway. "Do you have any antacid tablets?"

"Glass of milk?"

"Fine."

She lifted the pot from the element. "Make yourself comfortable in the living room and I'll bring it out." She ladled steaming soup into a ceramic cup and poured cold milk into a tall glass. She balanced them both like fire and ice and stepped carefully from the kitchen. "Did you hear about Helena?"

"She died," Colin7 said from his seat on the couch. "The V-net was abuzz."

"I had no idea she was so sick," Niko said as she handed him his drink. "I saw her just weeks ago. She was fine."

"Some acute degenerative disease, so they say."

"She was supposed to be Eternal."

"I know."

"Doesn't that strike you as odd?"

"Yes, very odd."

Niko sat down in an easy chair opposite, careful not to spill. "Did you know her well?"

"No. We travelled together briefly. She was the off-planet handler for the runner Zakariah."

Niko blew steam from her cup, tried a sip. Helena had handled them all, manipulated them like a mother hen, but she'd been altruistic at heart. "She had a vision for a better future."

Colin7 nodded. "Don't we all?"

"Tell me about the Cromeus colonies. Did Colin Macpherson create a better world for humankind?"

Colin7 took a long drink of milk and tapped his lips with the back of his hand. "People still get sick and die on my planet, Niko. There's no escape from death."

Niko stirred her soup with a spoon. "You're the seventh son of a genius. Can't you guys just sit down for a powwow and figure everything out?"

"There are only a few of us alive at any one time, plus the Original, of course. Colin2 through 4 are gone."

"They weren't uploaded?"

"Not as separate entities. Their data was merged with the Original."

Niko sampled a few mouthfuls of soup while Colin7 sipped his milk. "Okay, but still," she said, "Einstein to the seventh power and unfathomable intellect over time. What have you guys been doing all these years?"

"We're cosmologists," Colin7 said. "We study the universe, the ultimate end and the ultimate beginning. We're mathematicians."

"Well, then, where are we headed?" A chime sounded on Niko's wristband, and she set her cup on a side table. "Our taxi's out front," she said, rising to her feet. She grabbed a pink hoodie by the door and shrugged it on over her tunic.

Colin7 downed the rest of his milk and followed her into the hallway. "In the absence of intervention," he said, "the universe will end in heat death, a cold steady state in the far future after a centillion years of boredom."

"That doesn't sound like much fun," Niko said as they stepped into an elevator. "Can't we have another big crunch to match the big bang?"

Colin7 smiled at her grasp of the material. "No, I'm afraid not. The expansion of the universe is still accelerating, according to measurements in Doppler shift. There's no reason to assume any oscillation between dialectically opposed states. A big crunch would create a black hole, whereas creation was a special state of pure energy known as a white hole. A black hole is caused by gravity, an unescapable compression of mass. During the white hole, all particles moved at the speed of light, and gravitational attraction was held in abeyance from 10^{-36} to 10^{-32} seconds."

"Less than a trillionth of a second?"

"It was exactly enough time to bring the universe from the size of proton to the size of a beach ball, and ended in a phase shift known as 'decoupling' or 'last scattering.' It's a bit technical, but mass exists because of a violation of parity symmetry caused by the electroweak mechanism."

Niko studied Colin7 with a new measure of his innate geekiness. "How can scientists know what happened 14 billion years ago?"

Colin7 watched above the door as the elevator counted down the floors. "We measure the irregularities in the relic background radiation. Scale invariance lets us infer back to the original quantum fluctuations."

"I thought it was just random microwave noise from some big explosion."

Colin7 turned to her with a sarcastic glance bordering on disdain. "The residual noise is the only record we will ever get. It's certainly not random. We just need to tease out the meaning of the language."

Niko tipped her head at him. "Creation is talking to us?"

"The evidence for fundamental asymmetry is universally manifest," Colin7 said, "if we allow for temporary disruptions from local events like supernovas and quasars. After 14 billion years of exponential expansion, every quantum irregularity takes on measurable significance. Without deviations from uniformity, the primal lightspeed energy would not have slowed down into atoms and molecules, and we would not have had any clumping of condensate matter into stars and galaxies. We would not, in fact, exist."

The taxi at the curb was a glassed-in ladybug, driverless, fully automated for sight and sound. Niko touched her wristband to the roof sensor to unlock the doors and program her destination, and they quickly settled inside facing each other on comfy couches. "Okay," she said as she patted the air, "let me get this straight. You measure the night sky, and that tells you the history of the universe, the beginning and the end?"

Colin7 nodded, his face ebullient with passion for his specialty. "We can only conjecture the first cause, of course, but we know the universe began with infinite order, a massless flash of positive extropy. Cosmological constants were engineered precisely to create matter, which was configured precisely to create life, the so-called 'anthropic principle.' Entropy leads to a dead end. Extropy is the conscious force of creation which must be reconstituted to produce the next universe."

Niko squinted with confusion. "Reconstituted into what?"

"A new white hole," he said with a fervent smile. "A kernel of pure energy with parity dissonance must be consolidated into a cosmic singularity programmed with the conditions necessary to reproduce life in the next incarnation. Consciousness is the key to the future. Now is the age when the universe is becoming interesting. We're about two thirds of the way through the conformal spatial diagram of spacetime. Some cosmological constants are just now coming into play, coincident with the emergence of life on Earth. Humans are extropic factories capable of manipulating natural science. Just look at what we've done with only a few thousand years of self-awareness."

"It's up to us to create the next universe? That's crazy!"

Colin7 splayed out a dainty palm as though to express the obvious. "There's no other reason to explain our existence. It's inconceivable that such logistical perfection could be an accident of chance. This is our purpose, and we're within the window of opportunity to take resolute action in the present aeon."

"We're not God, Colin. We can't create order out of chaos!"

"We can and we must," he said with confidence. "In fact, we will and we have. It's a self-fulfilling prophecy, a mathematical circularity."

"You're nuts. You sound like a religious freak."

Colin7 raised an eyebrow as though surprised at her sentiment. "Science and religion are just flip sides of the same divine coin, Niko. We can't escape our responsibility by hiding behind semantics."

They settled into silence as Niko mulled over Colin7's outrageous theory. What creator in his right mind would leave the future of the universe in the hands of a bunch of walking primates? That seemed like a good recipe for cosmic disaster! The doomsday possibilities were endless: nuclear winter, nano-goo, gamma rays through a thinning atmosphere. What hope did they have?

The taxi pulled to the curb and an amber light began flashing on the control console. Niko pulled out a corporate laminate and tapped it on the scanner to charge the fare to Phillip's digital estate. The light changed to steady green as the door locks clicked open, and they exited the vehicle. A low-slung concrete building stood before them with a row of tall, tinted windows facing the street. A handicap ramp with a metal railing pointed them up a gentle gradient to the right and doubled back to the front entrance. Niko took the circuitous route, still thinking about eternity and cosmological constants, while Colin7 impulsively hopped the fence and waited for her at the entrance. He pushed the glass door and held it open with a polite smile. What a weirdo.

A young woman sat at a flatscreen monitor behind a counter cluttered with brochures in plastic display cases.

"Hi," Niko said as she approached and placed her arms on the divider. "We have an appointment to see Sienna Davis. We're a few minutes early."

The young woman looked up from her office chair and frowned—blond hair, blue eyes, wholesome, healthy face. She tapped her keyboard and checked her screen. "I'm sorry. That appointment was cancelled. Didn't you get an email notice?"

Niko blinked at the woman. "No . . ." She checked her wristband for missed messages, took a quick peek past her spam filter. ". . . nothing."

"That's strange," Blue Eyes said as she surveyed her data. "I don't seem to have any contact information in Sienna's file. Not even a cell number."

"I'm Niko," she said as she searched the counter for business cards. She turned a nameplate to face her. "Mrs. Richards?"

The woman smiled with a wince of apology. "Marcy."

"We had an appointment and we've come a long way." Niko held an arm up to indicate Colin7 standing behind her.

"I'm terribly sorry," Marcy said again. "We try to make every effort to serve our clients as best we can in the midst of difficult situations. Unfortunately, in this case there is nothing I can do. Sienna Davis was transferred out of our care this morning."

Niko sucked in a breath suddenly electric. She scrutinized the young woman, saw only complacency, no hint of malice. "Transferred where?"

Marcy pressed her lips as though preparing a grim confession. "I'm afraid it's an undisclosed federal location, some research facility completely out of our jurisdiction."

"What? That's impossible," Niko exclaimed. "You can't whisk her away without notification. I'm her mother!"

Marcy leaned back in her chair, eyes wide and wary. She pointed to her flatscreen. "There's nothing in the file to indicate any known family."

Niko held her arm out and pulled up the sleeve of her tunic. "I'll give you a genscan right now, damn it."

Marcy held her hands up in halt position. "We don't have the facilities," she said and returned her attention to her monitor. "You're listed here as a temporary caregiver only." Her lower lip trembled with frustration. "There's not even a last name given."

Niko turned back to Colin7 for support. God damn it, she didn't have a last name. She didn't even exist. "This is Sienna's father, Colin Macpherson. He's a famous scientist."

Marcy's face blanched with fear. "There's no father shown on my records." She tapped her keyboard with fresh intensity and peered closer at her screen in search of understanding. "I don't know what could have happened."

Colin7 stepped forward to belly up to the counter. "Hiromi Lee," he said evenly. "Can you tell us where we can reach her?"

Marcy looked up with watery eyes and a helpless expression. "Hiromi has been promoted out of our office to an investigative clinic. She doesn't work here anymore. My supervisor is off duty today on a medical leave. I can't reach her until tomorrow." She gasped for air and held a hand to her breast. "I have a daughter of my own. I can't imagine . . ." She lowered her chin and struggled to compose herself.

Colin7 stepped around behind the counter and patted her shoulder. "That's okay. We know you're doing your best." He studied her monitor and scrutinized her workspace.

"Hiromi's working federal now," Marcy said. "I don't know where she lives. I don't even have her cell number."

"That's okay," Colin7 said again as he reached inside his jacket and pulled out a slim black pouch. "Do you have an interface I can use? XD or USB?"

"Uh . . . I guess so." Marcy pointed to the side of her flatscreen and wiped at her eye with the back of her hand.

Niko fetched a tissue from a dispenser by the door and handed it to Marcy for a distraction as Colin7 selected an adapter from his pouch and plugged it into the hardware interface. He reached for the V-net plug dangling from his ear, inserted it into the cable and began blinking with data download, his face bland with concentration.

Marcy eased her chair back and dabbed at her cheeks as her monitor cascaded frenetically through viewscreens.

"Do you have an admin password for emergencies?" Colin7 asked.

"Um . . ." Marcy glanced at Niko and back. "Sure." She reached to type in a string of code.

"Thanks," Colin7 said. "Sorry to trouble you."

"I feel just terrible," Marcy said. "Nothing like this has ever happened before."

Niko glared at the two of them as they worked the data for clues. She wanted to lash out, to punch someone. Where was Sienna? What was going on? She turned away as her forehead began to throb. She stumbled into the supervised play area, stabbing at her wristband to check her chats, looking for Rix. His icon, the silver surfer, came up in the tiny viewscreen. "Rix," she choked.

"Hey, Niko," he said. "What's up?"

"Sienna's gone," she whispered.

"What?"

"The greysuits have got her." She began to cry, feeling a fresh wave of illness. "I can't take this, Rix. Everything always goes wrong for me. Just once I wish something would work out. Anything. God." She slouched forward in frustration, dripping tears onto her arm. "I can feel Sienna calling for me, lost and alone, and there's nothing I can do."

"Take a deep breath," Rix said from the tinny little speaker. "Stay calm. Where are you?"

Niko looked up and swivelled her head from side to side. She was in a large open room full of plastic toys. A large purple tunnel had a dragon face on one end and a jagged tail at the other. An activity centre had blackboards on easels and a flat area filled with puzzles and building blocks. Costumes for children lined one wall: a fireman's outfit with matching red hat, a purple gown for a princess, a white doctor's smock. A tiny play kitchen was set up in one corner with a sink and stove barely at knee height. A small table was circled by four tiny chairs. She pulled one out and perched on it daintily with her thighs pointing up. She felt like Dorothy lost in munchkin land. "I'm in a play area," she said. "I was supposed to meet Sienna for a supervised visit. It's some government office downtown."

"Do you want me to come and get you?"

"No, I . . . I just can't do this anymore."

"It'll be okay," Rix said. "We'll figure this out."

"No." She dropped her arm and shook her head. What was the point in talking about it? Her life was one big futility. She imagined Sienna crying in the darkness, hunched over her sleepytime stuffy, lost and alone. The kid had spent her entire existence being dragged around from place to place, in and out of vampire dens and black labs, and now to some nameless federal orphanage. What kind of childhood was that? Poor little waif. Had she ever known love? Had anyone tucked her into bed all those long years?

Niko stood and wandered around the empty room, staring at the colourful toys. The gaping mouth of the happy purple dragon beckoned little children into the clutches of government bureaucracy to be shat out the other side under a jagged, forked tail. An alphabet of coloured carpet squares offered to teach the language of despair. She bent and wept anew for Sienna. They were both outcasts, criminals, continually being punished for nameless sins. Why? Just because they were different? Phillip's elegant little transhuman experiments, artificial configurations of DNA. Did they even deserve to live and breathe? Could government doctors be operating on Sienna even now? Invading her miracle brain? Checking the genome of another evolutionary terrorist with no civil rights? God, it wasn't fair.

"Niko?"

She sniffed back agony, her eyes raw and burning. "Yeah, I'm here, Rix. I can't talk. I just can't do this. I'm sorry." Niko stared at the cracked lifelines in her open palm. Her body seemed foreign, her skin like fake rubber. She had not slept more than two hours at a time since Sienna had been stolen away. She was Eternal and wanted to die, just end it all here, right now, drift away into gentle darkness.

"Don't give up, Niko. You're the strongest person I know."

"I can't go on forever, Rix."

"Yes, you can," he said. "You have the bloodlight in your veins. We can fight back."

"Sure," she said. "I gotta go."

"Thanks for calling, Niko. I mean it. Call me later, 'kay?"

She tapped him off and looked around the empty room. She could imagine Sienna playing here with the colourful toys, wearing a pink princess gown and waving her gold ring like a talisman. She could almost hear her sparkling laughter, the joy of innocence. Just do this one thing, just one more task, one goal. Just find her. Niko straightened her spine, punched out her chest, took a calming breath. From somewhere deep inside herself she summoned her tattered cloak of invincibility and shrugged it around her shoulders. She rubbed aching eyes. She could do this. Be tough. Be strong.

Back in the reception area, Colin7 hovered over the viewscreen as Marcy sat watching with blank composure. Niko approached the counter with her shield of wounded dignity held high. "I'd like some answers. You can't steal children for government experiments."

"We didn't steal anyone," Marcy said. "Hiromi would never do anything bad."

"It's plainly obvious what's going on here," Niko said with disgust. "You should all be in jail if there was any justice in this Godforsaken country."

Colin7 unplugged his cable and wobbled his head woozily as he looked around the office. He placed his adapter back in his pouch and stepped from behind the counter. "I think we're done," he said calmly. "We've got all we can get this side of a launch couch."

"I'm very sorry about your daughter," Marcy said with her shoulders hunched defensively. "I'm sure we can find her. My supervisor will be back in the morning. It's probably just some mistake. I can call you first thing if you give me some contact information."

Colin7 continued to the front door and pushed it open. He held it wide so that a breeze gusted in. "Can I speak to you privately, honey?"

Niko winced with indecision and held up an index finger to Marcy for a moment of consultation. She moved to the open door and stepped out into gloomy daylight. "What?" she whispered.

"We have the keystroke," Colin7 said, "and a couple of V-net algorithms. We can run the data. Maybe get some answers. There's no point in making a public scene."

"There is a point, Colin," she said with persistence. "Eternals have rights as citizens now. I can go back in there and bitch all I want."

Colin7 nodded. "Yes, you can. The new legislation may pass through the system. Who knows? Eternals may end up with civil rights eventually." He placed a soft hand on her shoulder and offered a gentle caress of persuasion. "But clones never will."

Niko glanced back to the woman now leaning forward on the counter, peering at them from inside the building. Sienna was not in there. Her daughter was hidden away somewhere in a prison for the *gifted*. She was probably under scrutiny in a research lab by now, uploading psi data to government specialists. There was a time to stand brazenly under the light and a time to skulk in the shadows. Niko sighed and ducked her head.

"We'll find her," she said out in the parking lot as she shrugged her hands into the pouch pocket of her hoodie. "Together, right?"

Colin7 gave her a lingering hug and patted her back. "Of course. Nothing could be more important."

EIGHT

olin7's wristband blinked a continual beacon of warning as he accompanied Niko home to her apartment and tried to settle her as best he could under strenuous circumstance. He made a quick and grateful escape and rushed down two floors to the neuroscience lab where the borrowed body of Phillip Davis lay surrounded by a circus of bioengineering equipment. A bank of red lights glared up from the monitors, dangerous data on the boards, unexplained anomalies in Phillip's bioscans, raised lymphocyte count, fever, exotoxins, peptide levels cascading with dysfunction. It looked like some sort of virulent trauma, a sudden plague of immunodeficiency. What new madness was this?

Colin7 slouched into his work station, weary of the perpetual turmoil on this planet and the volatile emotions of the inhabitants. He felt like he was fighting a deliberate conspiracy against diabolic foes, grappling against chaos. And to what authority could he prepare his complaint? The collective unconscious mind of the Earthlings? The mysterious Source of the Eternals? His father and DNA progenitor, Colin Macpherson? No, he was on his own, the master of his fate on the treacherous extremities of science. He could expect no god before him and no angel guarding his rosy backside. This was just plain bad luck.

"There's been a new development," his father said as he sat up from the lab couch. "I'm going to need an upload out of this failing interface. You'll have to go home to make the arrangements."

Colin7 shuddered with foreboding. Home? Back through the Macpherson Doorway to Cromeus Signa? Phillip looked shrunken and sickly in green lab scrubs, his face dire. Matted wiry grey hair poked up below his throat, and a thin red plasma tube connected the stub of his left arm to the haematology equipment, an extension of his body into the machine. Colin7 tapped a keyboard to scroll through view-screens filled with hazard. "Have you run diagnostics on this data?"

"I'm dying," his father said.

A cold shock vibrated in his spine at the impossibility. The death of the eternal architect? The end of the Original upload? "There must be a mistake," Colin7 said as he cycled through charts and micro-scope slides. There was something wrong with Phillip's blood, no doubt about it. He magnified the image. Blood cells appeared to be exploding in showers of necrotic debris. Some invisible parasite was consuming them like birds feasting on the flesh of kings at the supper of Armageddon. Impossible!

"You must have heard that Helena Sharp passed away recently," Phillip said.

"Yes, I saw the obituary on the V-net," Colin7 said as he turned to face him. "Terrible tragedy for an Eternal."

"She carried a synthetic virus that we developed offplanet."

Another wave of panic coursed through Colin7. "What?"

"She was our first test subject. There was no indication of any problem."

"A fake Eternal virus?"

Phillip scowled at his protestation. "It was an authentic carrier, as near as we could measure. We perfected it over several years of due diligence."

"Did Helena know?"

Phillip shook scraggly grey curls. "No, that would have introduced an experimental bias."

Colin7 tilted his head at such deception in human testing. His brow felt heavy, his thoughts ponderous. "She thought she carried the real virus all along?"

"There seems to have been some type of allergic reaction or transplant rejection," Phillip said. "My own inoculation was thirty days after hers, almost two years ago, and the same pattern is now developing in this host. There were no early signs of jeopardy."

Colin7 gaped in disbelief at his father. "You took part in the experiment?"

"We thought the virus would help with the reconstruction of the interface, as indeed it did."

Surprise gave way to fear as Colin7 sensed the fraying end of trust. "You never told me."

"No, we didn't. There was enough for you to deal with at the time." Phillip coughed weakly into his fist. "And no one else will know from this day forward."

A delicate inference suggested his relationship with Niko had poisoned the waters, created a new vulnerability, an unknown variable outside the family genome. Colin7 could taste the tang of intrigue as his situation came into focus. He had raw duty undergirding him now, a subservient responsibility in time of crisis. He sighed. "What data have we gathered so far?"

His father nodded with a subtle gesture of affinity. "We have access to most of Helena's medical records, courtesy of a business associate, Jimmy Kay. We exchanged financial pleasantries in the past and kept our assets on the leash for just such an occasion."

"Of course I've heard of him," Colin7 said. "He mentored the young runner Zakariah in the early years before he contracted the Eternal virus."

"We've managed to coax the runner out of hiding by using Jimmy Kay as our kingpin," Phillip said. "I'm going to need daily transfusions of Eternal blood to keep this body alive, and we're trusting Zak can provide a steady supply through his former connections with the ERI."

Jimmy Kay, the famed cyber-guru with digital back doors throughout the hacker patriarchy. A web of deception, a tangled experiment—how could he have expected any less from the architect, his own self seven steps removed? Colin7 hung his head in surrender to the relentless will of his progenitor. "What are my mission parameters?"

"Your passage is booked through the Doorway for tomorrow. I'll need a complete upload to insure against the eventual expiration of this host. Prepare the equipment in advance and come for me when it's ready. I'll need a special transport capsule with a life-support system. Put Colin5 in charge of the modifications."

"Will the interface be strong enough to make the trip? How much time do we have to make the arrangements?"

"Helena lingered for weeks in the care of Mr. Kay," Philip said. "I don't mind suffering along with her to document the data, as long as I know I will overcome death in the end."

Colin7 nodded. The *data* in question was a human life now super-fluous, an expendable appendage. "But we should proceed without delay."

Phillip reached to the stub of his left arm and removed a slender needle. A drop of blood welled up and he dabbed it with a tissue. "I concur."

Colin7 turned back to his viewscreen to inspect a microscopic image of red blood cells turning black with inner plague, a false hope of immortality. What trauma could have triggered such a chain reaction of violence? How could the human body discern a perfect substitute from a biologic host? The pure chemistry should never have deviated from the norm. A synthetic Eternal virus, the holy grail Helena had always longed for, and she herself had been the miracle carrier and never knew it. A mixed blessing now turned sour. Would her sacrifice someday be redeemed by a better version of the virus, a gift of eternity for all? Was this the vanguard of super science, the first step toward transformation, or just a bad monkey mistake? Colin7 shivered at his introspection. He could only go forward in obedience, push harder against the boundaries of insight. The forefront of research had always been delineated by the questions asked, not the answers given. History was a litany of assumptions cast aside.

Jimmy stared at Helena's shrivelled corpse in a cherrywood casket and thought back to his mother's funeral decades ago in a small chapel in Reno. He'd visited as a tourist, stayed in the back, out of the limelight, never gave his name, never signed the guest book. A functionary had given a generic eulogy, an ecumenical Christian liturgy bordering on heresy that caught Jimmy's attention only momentarily. He liked to entertain belief systems as an intellectual exercise, no problem there. It was astounding what some people took for granted: Mayan hieroglyphics, alien conspiracies, fundamental atheism. The basic tenets were all the same—faith in an improbable postulate, allegiance to an impossible code—but organized religion had never appealed to him except as a spurious art form. Jimmy was a spiritual agnostic. He didn't believe in anything. Reality was an illusion.

Rix showed up for Helena's funeral with a young sprite in tow, barely a teen by the look of it, mostly hair. She hung on his arm in that clingy way children have, out of their comfort zone and in need of the false assurance of human contact. Might as well stuff sawdust in your pockets for good luck, or get a magic totem tattooed on your ass. Humans were ephemeral objects of confidence. They faded quickly, even Eternal ones. Nothing could be trusted.

"Hi, Jimmy," Rix said. "This is Jovita."

"Lovely," he said as he took her hand. He bowed his forehead low, played the gentleman, and why not? Jovita smiled and peered up from a posture tilted down with contrition. She wore a green tank top under a faded denim jacket and looked a bit scruffy from living on the run, probably half starved. She had the prettiest lips he had ever seen, but her face was tinged with melancholy, a deep and dwelling darkness just below the surface. He felt an urge to protect her, to hug her like a father; she had that charisma about her, a nescient naiveté.

"Sorry for your loss," she said, eyes murky with emotion as she glanced at the corpse. She had probably never met Helena. Too bad the old girl was not at her best.

"Thanks," Jimmy said. "She had a good run." That was it in a nutshell. What more could anyone expect? "She was a wonderful woman."

Rix bit at his lip for a moment and lunged into Jimmy's embrace, squeezed him hard and thumped him three times on the back. His body had hardened into the shape of a man so soon. The kid was all grown up, his muscles toughened with vigour. Jimmy wondered what he must look like to this brash youngster—an ancient and wrinkled senior citizen with a bad reputation, a decrepit elder past his prime, a senility suspect with grey nostril hair? He felt antediluvian as he surveyed the small crowd of Eternals. He was the only human in the room, the only one wearing a shroud of mortality, destined to die. Might as well paste an expiration date on his forehead.

Rix stepped toward the casket with the waif close at his side. He stroked Helena's cold neck and bent down for an inspection. Creepy. He wasn't going to kiss a dead person, was he? Zak walked over and draped an arm around his son's shoulder as they stood in silent vigil. He murmured something in his ear, and Rix nodded in agreement. Some platitude, no doubt. She's in a better place.

Jimmy had an urge to duck out and run from the charade, just get the formalities over with and retire to his balcony to sip a frosty beer and listen to the thunder of Niagara Falls. But that would never do. The ritual must be accomplished for all concerned, himself included. History had installed some psychological checklist in his brain, some archetype from his ancestors who buried their dead with a flourish and raised stones to mark the sacred spot. He had to complete the circle in preparation for his own death, to go without fear, without regret. What a joke. Everybody loses in the end and life sucks.

Visitors filed past one by one to pay their respects, the imaginary debt due the dead. Even that offering was hollow, a fiat currency. Helena couldn't care less now, could she? Jimmy watched in silence from the distance, content with his thoughts. He didn't owe her corpse a damn thing. Zak and Mundazo stood guard at the casket in community service, hugging and glad-handing the small remnant from the ERI. Word had filtered out through Sublevel Zero to gather old friends out of hiding. They all seemed to know each other intimately, fellow Eternals now questioning their own immortal fate. The virus had failed, the holy promise faded. Quiet music played in the background, nondescript choral harmonies, vaguely hymnal. The air smelled clean and clinical, a lemony disinfectant with lavender overtones.

At some unseen signal, a funeral official closed the lid on the coffin and poured a cross of white sand on top from a vial, then wheeled the body away in a stately procession to a waiting hearse while a matron followed with bundles of cut flowers in her arms. As the casket left for the crematorium, a group of young servers in dark suits brought out trays of sandwiches and vegetables on cue and placed them quietly on side tables. Jimmy sat down and rested his elbows on his knees. He whistled out a slow sigh. A girl with brown hair tied tight in an austere ponytail bent toward him with a tray of frothy punch drinks, and he plucked a plastic cup with gnarled fingers and murmured an acknowledgment. He felt weary with years and wanted to go home. He wished he had a mickey of vodka to spike his drink, or one of those tiny airline bottles.

Rix sidled over, free of his newly attached partner, and took a seat beside him with a plastic cup in one hand and an egg salad sandwich in the other. "You going to be okay?"

"Sure." Jimmy felt a bristle of anger at his vulnerability. He didn't need some punk kid offering him pity. "Finally lose your sidekick?"

Rix sipped his punch. "She had to pee. She's afraid of you."

"Where'd you find her? Under an oak leaf?"

"She came into the ERI one day. Fresh off the bus."

"Ahh." Jimmy nodded. "So if you get the virus as a child, you just stay a baby forever?"

"No, you still grow up," Rix said. "You reach an optimum age."

"What is she, fifteen?"

"No, more like eighteen. She's street legal."

Jimmy scrutinized the young punk. "Street legal? What are you, a porn king?"

Rix frowned, pink at the cheeks. "No, she's mature, that's all."

"You're not doing her, are you?"

"No," Rix said. "'Course not." He ducked his head and swallowed with obvious difficulty. So, he had thought about it, for sure. His father had been like that, randy as the day was long.

"She looks fragile," Jimmy said, "like she might break in the winds of change."

"She's stronger than you think. We've been living on the run since the tower."

"You've always been on the run, Rix. That's your natural state."

Rix sighed and rose to his feet. He took a few steps away as though to end the conversation, but turned to study him. "A lot has happened, Jimmy."

"I know," he said. "Too much."

"The Beast has fallen. The ERI has burned to the ground. The world is in ruins."

"Sure." Jimmy shrugged and hung his head. What else was new? "If you say so."

"My grandfather's not dead."

A dread chill seeped between them, a ghost from the past. "That may be true."

"I'm wondering how much you're responsible for."

Jimmy looked up, measuring what Rix might know, how much was safe to reveal. "Me too, but blame will get us nowhere."

Rix nodded, shifting his weight from side to side, arms hanging loose at his sides like a hoodlum ready for action. "Have you met Philomena?"

Jimmy sighed. So the kid was surfing concave in the loop. Too bad. "Yeah. The pleasure was dubious at best."

"Is she really Phillip?"

"Philomena, Phillip, the Beast, they're all for one now. She's a sysop avatar, some kind of V-net goddess."

"She's turning V-space upside down," Rix said, "getting inside people's heads, bringing every thought into captivity."

"I know. Dangerous stuff, but V-space was never right side up to begin with."

"We've got to stop her."

Jimmy smiled at his audacity, a seed not far from his father's tree. "Do we now?"

"That's all that really matters."

"No, Rix," he said sadly. "You got it all wrong." Jimmy pointed backhand with his thumb to the public washroom. "That little wood nymph you're tracking around with is all that's important now. We're flesh and bone, you and I. We should stay where we belong. Zakariah learned that long ago. The V-net belongs to Philomena and her future ilk. She earned it fair and square."

"So you're giving up on V-space?"

"Our influence has passed away in that realm. The digital singularity came and went like a thief in the night and nobody even noticed."

Rix shook his head. "No way, man."

Jimmy shrugged. "Suit yourself."

Rix spread his palms with a grimace of supplication. "You gotta help me."

"Wish I could," Jimmy said as he rubbed his shiny pate, "but I've already sold my soul to that pixie. She sucks my code like a gargoyle, follows me like an evil twin. The Beast has it in for me now, some sort of permanent upload courtesy of the Soul Savers, all my trap-doors, all my loot. I've been promised like an offering to the queen."

"What, digital euthanasia?"

"Yeah, I guess so. Not much left for me here anyway."

"Have you gone senile, Jimmy? Look me in the eye and tell me, old man, 'cause I can hardly suss your shadow."

Jimmy looked up to face the young punk standing bold with effrontery before him. "You think you're tough, kid? You got the moxie to take on Philomena? Gonna change the future?"

"Yeah," Rix said, "you and me."

"I don't owe you anything," Jimmy said. "Every time I see you, it costs me time and money. When are you ever going to bring me good news?"

"This is it now, Jimmy. Good news."

Jimmy stared for a moment and burst out with a laugh. "You're worse than your father," he said with a grin, "a bad seed mixed with the blood of a martial arts master."

The kid's face turned stony at the memory of his mother, another good woman dead and lightly buried. They all still carried her essence like a candle flame that would never bow to the breeze. She lived inside them, everywhere and nowhere, mother Mia, speaking softly of a spirit guiding all Eternals, creating and sustaining the universe.

Jimmy shook his head, feeling oddly complacent with his twisted destiny. He had little to lose and nothing to gain, so why not throw the dice one more time? Why not take a chance on the next genera-tion? He chuckled and nodded, feeling a young fool again, a virgin slider bending the system grid for access up Prime. He could prob-ably ghost a new avatar if he worked at it, get back on the net clean and invisible, just another tourist in transit, marketing data in flux, maybe dodge Philomena for a day or two. He and Rix could check

STEVE STANTON

things out together, maybe storm Prime Eight for a fresh vantage point. What the hell, it might be fun.

"Why don't you bring Jovita over to my penthouse later, after the festivities, maybe stay a few days? I've got plenty of room and could use the company. We could tour the wineries of Niagara-on-the-Lake. They grow some of the best grapes in the world out on the flats."

"That would be great," Rix said.

"She's probably not old enough to drink the samples, but she could taste the grapes and mash at least. It's very educational for visitors. Where did you say she was from again?"

"Florida. She grew up in a trailer park."

"Ahh," Jimmy said, "hurricane country. Lots of oranges."

Rix nodded. "Something like that."

"Can't say I've ever been that far south."

"Me neither," Rix said, "but we're headed that way." His gaze darted past Jimmy and his eyebrows arched once in signal.

"Are you guys talking about me?" Jovita asked as she sidled alongside looking uncomfortable and forlorn.

"Yeah," Jimmy said. "The natural pleasures of Florida." She seemed tiny beside Rix, a stickpin girl with a big tuft of blond hair. Again he felt the urge to protect her, to make her feel at peace, but wasn't sure how to bridge the huge gap of culture. Any physical touch might be misconstrued, dirty old man that he was. "We were wondering if you might like to visit for a few days. I have a penthouse apartment with a view of the Falls."

Her eyes went wide with astonishment. "A penthouse?"

"I had some luck in business once," he said. "It's an investment." Why did he feel the need to apologize for spending money? That's what the damn stuff was for.

144

Jovita glanced at Rix for a signal. "Well, I guess that would be fine," she said. "We wouldn't want to be any trouble."

"No trouble," Jimmy said. "I want to hear all about your escape from the tower." He knew the full and horrible story, of course, but wanted to give Jovita the comfort of self-expression. That seemed to work well with most people.

"Sure," she said happily. "Thank you so much for the invitation. Rix certainly was right about you."

Niko pulled her worn backpack from a closet and shook out the cobwebs. It didn't look like much, the colour of dirt and scuffed with use, but she smiled at the sight of it. With this trusted accoutrement, she could turtle on a forest floor and be completely invisible, or wait blithely at a train station without showing obvious camouflage, her own private cloaking device. She dug out her trank gun from under the mattress and checked the clip. A few hundred loaded needles, not much. She should have taken a whole boxful when she left the ERI behind. It seemed like ages ago, a different life. Now the ERI had disappeared and Helena was dead, an apocalypse fulfilled.

She started a pile of travel items on her bed, necessities only, and began to rummage through her wardrobe. A change of pants and underwear, a good sports bra. Her hiking boots, in case she ended up off road, socks, gloves, a bug net for her head. A toothbrush and deodorant; Colin would appreciate that much at least, along with a handful of condoms.

And what about supplies for Sienna? She poked into her daughter's bedroom and looked around. A stuffed bunny gazed back from its perch on a pillow at the head of the empty bed. Ouch, the kid didn't even have her bedtime stuffy with her! How was she supposed to sleep at night without her bunny? Poor girl. A sickness of empathy welled up inside Niko. Her daughter was being held prisoner in a government institution somewhere, lost and alone, crying for her mommy in the darkness. Niko choked at the thought, felt a bubble of pain lodge in her sternum.

She forced herself to a wooden dresser and pulled out socks and underwear, a sweater and pants, a purple t-shirt printed with glittering butterflies. She grabbed the pink bunny and laid it carefully in the bottom of her backpack for luck. Niko had a list of possible targets from Colin7, district offices and foster houses, and a photo of Sienna to show round to staff and passersby. She would play it cool in the face of civil bureaucracy, bide her time with courtesy and grace . . . and shoot anyone who got in her way.

Colin7 showed up late at her door, empty-handed and underdressed. Something had gone terribly wrong. His face was tense, on the verge of confession, and she dared him with her eyes. "Where's your gear?"

He winced. "I can't go with you."

"What do you mean? I thought we had a plan." Niko studied him with suspicion. "What about the data you downloaded? We've got three district offices to check out. We've got to get busy."

Colin7 splayed his fingers and looked down at them as though they carried great import. "My father needs me," he said. "I have important work offplanet."

"Well, reschedule it, for God's sake. You can't leave now. We've got to rescue our daughter. Once the greysuits do a genscan, she won't be safe anywhere."

"My shuttle leaves in six hours," he said. "I would have told you earlier if I had known."

Niko huffed. "It's not the timing, Colin. It's a question of priorities." She cut the air with a swinging arm. "Let zombie Phillip handle his own problems. Sienna should be our number one concern, not your father, not the past. The future is what's important."

Colin7 shook his head with sad finality. "He's not my father, Niko. He's me. We share the same thoughts, the same motives. We're an exact DNA match. I can hardly refuse myself."

Niko curled a trembling lower lip under her teeth, seething with disgust. She sniffed a breath and summoned a steady voice. "So you clones just split up a single mind among the group, keep it all in the family. You're just parts of a whole, with no free will, no accountability. How can you hope to experience love, Colin, with no soul to call your own? Sienna is just a helpless little girl. Can't you see that? Our so-called fathers don't deserve a shred of allegiance. They sold our daughter into slavery and then abandoned her like a bad lab experiment, a spoiled petri dish. It's up to us to protect her now."

"She'll be fine for a few days," Colin7 said evenly. "I'll be back shortly."

"How do you know she'll be fine? We don't even know where she is. Vampires could have her by now, or government scientists. She could be in serious trouble!"

Colin7 reached his arms for her with a sad smirk of appeasement, but Niko pulled away from his pathetic token of comfort, such a sad act of condescension. If that was the best he could do, she had been completely mistaken. Had he played her for a fool all along?

"Go, then," she said. "Get out of here."

"Niko."

"No, Colin. Forget it."

His conciliatory eyes hooded with grim solemnity. He nodded to himself in acknowledgment and frowned, the bastard. Colin7 could not resist the trumpet call of his evil twin. He was dumping her and abandoning their daughter, and he knew it full well. He had no guts, no balls and no spine, the weak-wristed leprechaun. Good riddance.

Niko turned away and stalked to the door, flung it open. "Get out," she said, "and don't come back."

His face folded. Oh, now he was going to cry, the big baby. She steeled herself against any infiltration of sympathy. "Get out," she repeated and offered no pity in her glare.

Colin7 bucked up with a hesitant gasp of manhood, straightened firm shoulders, and stepped dutifully by her and down the hall. He glanced back once and hesitated as though considering a parting word, but turned away with regret and pressed for the elevator.

Niko stood in the doorway breathing hard against a cosmic vacuum fluctuation as time stood still between them. The distance down the hall came sharply into focus, an expanding universe, a widening celestial gap between bodies accelerating in opposite directions. She could feel her life fragmenting, falling apart so easily like a dream upon waking. She was all alone again and felt trembling in her knees at the realization. Another boyfriend down the drain, and this one with an actual DNA connection, the father of her test-tube baby. This would be the last boyfriend. She leaned against the doorframe as Colin7 stepped into the elevator and disappeared from her life. Oh God.

Where was Sienna? How could she ever find her now? Could she reverse-engineer a psi effect to pinpoint her location? Some residual telepathy between mother and child? Was that even possible? She should have tagged the kid with a GPS chip when she had the chance. She never should have bowed her head to the armed service workers from Child Services. She should have fought to the death for her maternal rights. In a vision she saw herself pulling her weapon and tranking the hired goons by the door, turning to plug Hiromi Lee point-blank, and fleeing with Sienna into pristine wilderness far away, safe with her young daughter in the bloom of innocence, building a new family, building a better future for all posthumans. Soon Niko was on her knees, hanging on to a sweaty doorknob for support, clinging to shards of promise.

NINE

"Which is more precious, Daddy," the little girl asked, "the future we cannot touch, or the past that lies within our control?"

Phillip smiled down at her. "In asking the question, you have fashioned your own reply. Now reach out your fingers and grasp the truth."

For Colin7, the thrill of blasting into Earth orbit was vastly overshadowed by the vertigo of apogee. During launch acceleration, his guts felt compressed by a thousand hammers, squeezed and distorted as the shuttle rumbled skyward in a violent war against gravity, but once the booster tanks gave up their last gasp of fumes and the rockets went black, his stomach seemed to balloon with nausea in the ensuing buoyancy. It took all his effort to keep from voiding himself at both ends.

There was no space in space. Every centimetre was cramped and confined, every gram of mass measured and surcharged. Payload passengers were squeezed into seats like toothpaste into tubes, hypnotized by colourful viewscreens that offered news and events at the touch of a fingertip, distracted from danger. No first-class creature comforts for the chosen few, no food, no washroom facilities. Colin7 counted eight passengers on this shuttle at a million dollars a pop. Easy money.

"New Freedom Transit Authority requests that all travellers remain buckled in their flight seats and secure all loose items," a male baritone voice announced smoothly over the speaker system. "We will begin docking deceleration in ninety seconds. Gravitational experience will approach 1.7 g for several minutes. Thank you for your care and attention."

Holding his hands to his growling abdomen, still struggling to keep his breakfast in stasis, Colin7 checked out the porthole view for a glimpse of the space station that housed the Macpherson Doorway. It was not a large facility. Most of the bulk was taken up by the antimatter generator that provided the raw power necessary to bend the fabric of spacetime into higher dimensions. The wormhole itself was quite small, a subatomic wrinkle enlarged by brute force to a diameter of just over a metre, superstrings vibrating under intense gravitational forces locked in tight parameters. Colin7 knew exactly how it worked—his progenitor had invented the damn thing in a past life—but the notion of engineering it from pure theory seemed a daunting task to him now. His DNA twin had pulled it off somehow, the Original architect, so he must surely be capable of such masterful discovery, but the possibility seemed remote. Perhaps something had been lost in the cloning process after all this time, perhaps he lacked the hybrid vigour necessary for higher schematic thought. His father had been a pioneer among enthusiastic provocateurs, a subspace explorer riding an expanding wave of ingenuity, standing on the shoulders of titans. Einstein himself struggled unsuccessfully with graviton field theory for the last decades of his life, having laid the eureka foundations of relativistic science early in his career. They'd all still be grubbing in the dirt without Einstein.

How could he hope to measure up to the achievements of his father, whose dreams stretched back to the big bang and beyond, a man whose vision elucidated the cosmos? No, Colin7 was just a menial grunt, a chess pawn in someone else's game. His paltry efforts to understand the psychic manifestations of the collective conscious-ness were laughable in comparison, the computations of a primi-tive intelligence. Colin Macpherson had died once, long ago, and now his cybernetic soul was facing death again, an ultimate oblit-eration unless his young clone could arrange a data upload across time and space. Colin7 picked at his upper lip with nimble fingers as he analyzed his predicament. Should he try to transport the deli-cate equipment to Earth, the neural helmet and resonance scanners? Should he try to bring Phillip's failing body into orbit and through the Macpherson Doorway to the Soul Savers Institute? Both options seemed risky, prone to failure. Colin5 would know what to do, his older brother, the acting patriarch on Cromeus Signa.

The space station came into view, a hodgepodge of extraneous planning around a cylindrical core, docking tunnels and barracks added without thought to symmetry, cubes and cones appended at strange angles. No up or down. No gravity, except for contained turbulence deep within the wormhole. An inverse funnel like an antique gramophone pointed outward to nowhere, nonspace, a log-ical absurdity.

A deceleration burn punched Colin7 in the gut again as the shuttle braked for rendezvous, and he gagged at the taste of bile in the back of his throat. He was not fit for space travel. He was infirm, inbred, a weakling genius dressed in borrowed shoes. Blind duty held him up, pushed him on; he wore an exoskeleton of family responsi-bility. The shuttle bumped into the docking orifice with a shudder of misalignment and a squeal of protestation as the flexible housing repositioned for entry.

"New Freedom Transit Authority requests that all travellers

remain buckled in their flight seats until airlock has been confirmed," the intercom resounded. "Magnetic treadways on Macpherson Station are marked in bright yellow paint. All passengers must orient themselves to the public treadway in order to be quickly processed past inspection and launch points. Please have palm verification ready for the attendant on duty. For your security and safety, passengers are not allowed any carry-on bags or accessories. All registered luggage must be packed in appropriate launch tubes. Have a safe and pleasant journey."

Stale, sweaty air wafted into the cabin as the shuttle pressurized with the station. Colin7 felt strain in his eardrums and swallowed several times to clear the discomfort. He tasted the familiar bouquet of recycled air, a perpetual hint of urine and methane. There was a limited amount of oxygen available and only so much the scrubbers could do to manage impurities. An old roughneck joke came to mind, recycled as many times as the tasteless diatomic gas: fresh air was an oxymoron.

Colin7 pulled himself along the ceiling handrail to exit the shuttle headfirst into a docking tunnel like a tight ovipositor. He wriggled forward using his elbows for purchase, following the boots of a shadowy figure in front, and swam out into an expansive landing bay where he could stand upright on his magnetic soles and stretch with languor. Sound echoed around him in the domelike enclosure, bouncing off metal ductwork and conduits. The scrubbers made a discontinuous chugging sound in the background, a faint pulse of pressure against the hungry vacuum just beyond the wall. A single hole, a fractured breach, and the precious envelope of air would quickly disperse. Life was a fragile, foreign bubble here, an uncertain extension beyond the exosphere of Earth.

Colin7 had the privilege of Macpherson kingship in this place, but he didn't care to lord it over the duty staff. He was just a clone, after all, though his face was featured in every physics text on the net. He was a humble working boy with his head down, just doing his job. Attendants hovering on jet-packs smiled with recognition and pulled him to the front of the line. They called him "sir" as they ushered him through x-ray scanners and settled him in a transport capsule. A nurse checked his pulse with diligence and murmured concern at his rising blood pressure. She rubbed his cramping muscles, patted him for comfort, and cooed through a convincing list of safety regulations by rote to assuage any fear. The lid closed with a pneumatic hiss, and cold air whispered against his nostrils. Just close your eyes, just rest awhile, the little death takes only a moment.

Twelve million years through space and time, according to the best guess from measurements of the background microwave radiation, a single heartbeat away through the Macpherson Doorway, the modern miracle of superstring field theory, Colin7 felt a tremor of movement as his capsule shunted forward and slipped through nowhere. A slice of his life too brief for conscious registry was theoretically removed from his chemical brainspace.

The lid opened above him to bright fluorescence.

"Welcome home," said a familiar voice, his own voice, and he looked up into the eyes of Colin5, his own eyes two generations older.

"Thanks," he said as he sat up in weightless space. "What season is it?"

"First summer," the elder said. "The desert is in bloom."

Colin7 smiled. "Nice." He always loved to see the cactus flowers rising from the dust, the natural dichotomy of resplendence in the arid barrens, a paradox of hope renewed each year. He would surely get a foil umbrella and a breather and go out for a walk along the dunes. "And how's the young boy?"

"A strapping youth, five years old now and testing out to genius levels. A child prodigy in mathematics, of course. Colin8 will carry the genome to heights not yet imagined."

"It will be good to spend some time with him," Colin7 said, "but I have business to attend to first."

"I got your missive," Colin5 said with concern. "We'll plug up for a family meeting after you get settled in your apartment." He checked his wristband and took a moment to tap in a text. "It's just past thirteen Signa now. Eighteen sound okay for a group conference?"

"Perfect," Colin7 said, feeling disjointed and dizzy at the rush of events. "I'm surprised you came into orbit to greet me in person. You must be tightly scheduled as always."

"Never too busy for a brother," Colin5 said. Big ears, big smile, infectious eyes, and familiar pointed chin, his own face in a looking glass of time. Colin5 clasped a forearm and pulled Colin7 up from his transport capsule with a hug on the shoulder, a slap on the back, fellow bondservants to the fraternity. "How is the interface on Earth holding up?"

"Phillip is not well," Colin7 said as they hovered together. "The synthetic virus has failed."

The elder frowned and nodded. "So I heard."

"We've got to get Father out of there and back to safe storage," Colin7 said.

"Eighteen Signa. We'll talk." Colin5 thumped him again on the shoulder. "Great to see you again with such vigour and purpose. I've got your favourite shuttle waiting for a good pilot, if you're feeling up to it, the silver shadow with the turbo boost. We'll have six passengers in the midship cabin for the trip down to New Jerusalem."

Colin7 straightened with a renewal of responsibility and brushed at his clothes to shake off the dust of a distant world. Germs and other sins, guilt and other sacrifices, he sloughed them all away like a second skin, home again where he was a prince among men. Confidence returned like an old friend as he boarded the tiny corporate shuttle for a quick hop to the surface. He had piloted this craft many times, both on and off the service record, and he took his rightful place at the controls as Colin5 sat in the co-pilot couch and the paying passengers made themselves comfortable in coach.

He went through his checklist and signalled a countdown for the crowd before launching. He didn't feel sick at all with his fingers dancing on the familiar console, not even when they hit hard atmosphere and the nosecone burned cherry red. Perhaps it was all a question of control, a psychosomatic irregularity. As long as he was in charge and calling the trajectory, his stomach knew everything was okay, his brain need not worry. He banked against thick air and heard the turbine brakes whine. He grinned with exhilaration.

New Jerusalem came into view, a majestic city of glass and gold— the pleasant land of his artificial birth from a robotic surrogate into a sterile incubator. Ah, good memories. The spaceport was on the northern outskirts, and the landing sysop put his position on the grid and made subtle course corrections as they approached. No cowboy flyers were allowed this close. Every kite was on the map, every probability contained. "Well, that was fun," he said as he relinquished navigation to the computer.

Colin5 glanced up from his data tablet and nodded with working disinterest.

Colin7 looked back to the glorious city of his youth, where clusters of solar panels glittered like the jewels of royalty. The buildings were spread out flat to maximize exposure to the energy blessing from above. Most of the planet was actively volcanic, and most industrial systems ran on geothermal power in the absence of any underground carbon fuel. The sun was a electrochemical bonus when the clouds were clear, the noonday streets scorching, every metal surface hot enough to cook meat.

The shuttle landed smoothly on autopilot and the passengers disembarked with buoyant smiles in gravity lighter by a tithe. After parting from his brother, Colin7 took a tram to his efficiency apartment and hefted his travel pack through the entrance, home again to his empty cubicle downtown. Every amenity in the single room folded away when not in use, leaving nothing but a barren hallway to a single window at the end. On the left side, a table tipped down with bench attached, and a sleeping mat slid out from underneath. Further on, a single door pulled open to create a kitchen corner with cupboards and every modern convenience, and another door opened to a water closet with toilet drain and a full-length dressing mirror. The wall opposite was a media viewscreen with a fold-out launch couch and V-net cable to virtuality. No space was wasted in New Jerusalem, no comfort overlooked in a perfection of design.

Domestic familiarity washed over Colin7 like a balm as he inspected his personal belongings, his clothing neatly arranged in drawers, dried foodstuffs in the pantry, favourite movies loaded in the vidi, his launch couch finetuned to his V-net schematics. He stepped to the window and turned the blinds to see the smoke rising perpetually from distant Bashan, an active volcano to the east. Everything was still the same, and the passage of time seemed an illusion. He could imagine it being just a few weeks away on Earth, not two long years resurrecting his progenitor in a neuroscience laboratory, not a lifetime of new experience. Looking back now from the other side of the Doorway, his trip to Earth seemed like a whirlwind. He had fallen in and out of a sexual relationship in a frenzy of emotion. He'd been a father on a distant planet and never even knew it. He'd had a lover and a daughter and lost them both in no time at all. Nice place to visit.

Colin7 found some dehydrated chicken and brittle pasta and made himself a homecoming casserole while a synthesized orchestra played a calming cantata in the background. The music in the colonies was soothing compared to the jarring cacophonies of Earth, the pace slower, more relaxed. The water from the tap tasted tinny, something he'd never noticed before. He sampled his meal and chewed with little enjoyment. His spice palate had been altered on a foreign world. Home could never be home again, not in the simple sense of childhood lustre. Some veil had been taken away, some innocence impoverished. Colin7 began to notice everything anew. His steps were bouncy in the lighter gravity, his clothing too thick and cumbersome in the heat, and the food tasted funny. He stripped down to boxer shorts and parked in front of the vidi to watch the local news while he ate.

As his scheduled V-net appointment approached, Colin7 began to roleplay the meeting in his mind. Only one goal was important now, and all his effort had to be focused on his mission to rescue his father from Earth, to get him back home and safely uploaded in the colony he had founded. The whole resurrection misadventure had been a bad gamble with death, the foul experiment with the Eternal virus an unnecessary complication, but he would hold back his criticism for the sake of the family. The data was long past the gate and the damage done. Mistakes must be made right, the patriarchy restored to grandeur. His paramount responsibility was plain.

Colin7 plugged up on schedule to meet Colin5 in a sparse V-net vestibule, a back-end private corridor in the cyberworld they controlled. Colin5 looked younger in his avatar, a virtual duplicate of indeterminate age with pointed chin and ears like butterfly wings.

"We're hosting some friends in here," he said as he opened a public portal, and they stepped into a charming tableau of antique stone buildings and cobblestone walkways, a picturesque fantasy. Towering red-brick structures stretched up four stories high around them, with tall windows and sculpted cornices. Weathered gryphons looked down from on high, green with corrosion. A wrought-iron table had been set with a bouquet of flowers under a café-style awning, and Colin5 led the way toward it.

Colin7 followed dutifully. "Why the fancy scenery?"

Colin5 scanned the horizon and held his hands and eyebrows up in mock ridicule of such ostentation. "We have civilian visitors today, saved souls. They're accustomed to extravagance, living out the wildest dreams of their imaginations day after day." He shrugged his good humour.

A third Colin stepped out of a zoomtube doorway carrying a potent aura of digital power, a celestial hum of stable harmonics. He was an older version, larger, his hair balding with feathery tufts above his ears, the face from a thousand textbooks.

Colin5 bowed with due respect. "Hello, Father."

Colin7 gaped in alarm as uncertainty teased like a burrowing worm inside his brain. "You can't be real," he blurted.

"I am," assured the man, the Original, Colin Macpherson, architect of all.

"But . . ." Colin7 held up a hesitant finger as his mind reeled through possibilities. "But . . ."

"A copy," the man said with a flip of his fingers in dismissal. "A backup file put to strategic use. Each split persona assumes the personal heritage, of course. That's the way these things work."

Two copies of the Original mind, cleaved apart like particles in a hadron collider. Two different entities, two trajectories through spacetime. "But Phillip is dying," Colin7 said as he struggled with the revelation. "*You're* dying."

"Yes, that's an unfortunate byproduct of a risky experiment," Colin Macpherson said. "We owe no contractual obligation to Phillip's husk. We'll save what consciousness we can, of course, upload the remnant for posterity. Don't worry about the details. You've done well in difficult circumstance." He turned his attention aside and smiled with poise. "Ah, I see our visitors have arrived."

Colin7 whirled toward two new figures coming up the cobblestone walkway hand in hand, a genteel dignitary greying at the temples and dressed in a ceremonial cassock, and a middle-aged woman of wide recognition, Helena Sharp from Earth. She held up a hand and waved in greeting.

Colin7 rocked back with shock, felt his avatar fizzle with bubbly dissonance as the couple came near. "Helena?"

"Colin," she said with a slight nod of courtesy. "Seven, is it?" She glanced around at the trio. "A family reunion?"

"Come and have a seat, my friends," Colin5 piped up as the master of ceremonies. "Make yourselves comfortable."

Colin7 studied the two civilian avatars with suspicion. There was no need for comfort in digital space, of course. Muscles did not grow weary, nor hearts discontent, but the drama of familiarity provided order and a moment of reflection, a calming of minds in motion. Colin5 moved chairs into a circle and negotiated seating arrangements with quaint social etiquette until they were all settled under the café canopy with a red sun on the horizon casting a haze of pink magnificence in the sky.

"I'll have a mint jump-up," Helena said, and the digital drink appeared instantly on the table in front of her. She took a sip and peered at her companion with invitation, but he declined with a subtle nod and press of his lips, their non-verbal cues almost imperceptible yet rich with meaning, so well were they attuned.

"We bring news of your husk," Colin5 said.

Helena sat forward with interest. "I suspected as much."

"She's dead. The test virus proved ineffective in the end."

"Ah." Helena slouched back in her chair with casual ease. "Did she suffer?"

Colin5 looked to Colin7 and signalled his role with a tilt of his forehead. He was the expert on the ground, the cultural observer with all the answers. "Um," Colin7 said, "no, I suppose not unduly. She was suitably medicated and well cared for in a private hospice."

"Good," Helena said. "I'm glad. We owe our husks that much at least." Her partner reached for her hand and patted it with fond affection and deep appreciation for her words. They exchanged glances of mutual support, and she turned back to Colin7. "This is my husband, Ian Miller."

"Um, hi," Colin7 said. Husband?

"A pleasure." Ian smiled with well-mannered condescension. "I remember that husk as being a firebrand of passion." He looked to his wife with smug glee at some shared witticism.

"Indeed," Helena said, "she was a wonder."

Colin7 scrutinized her face. No sign of remorse, no prostration at the wailing wall. So this was death in digital nirvana, the relinquishment of a worn-out husk in a timely manner, no muss, no fuss.

"We wanted to thank you, dear Helena," the architect proclaimed as he probed for her attention, "for your volunteer efforts in the program. Unfortunately, the synthetic virus did not meet our clinical objectives."

"It was well worth the wager," she replied with a backhand flourish. "That husk would have died without it, in any case."

"Nevertheless," he said, "it was a brave move."

She bowed her head at his compliment. "Why, thank you, sir. I do believe all husks should be disposed of with dignity. Is there any news of Zakariah?"

The Original turned to his seventh incarnation with an eyebrow raised in query, and Colin7 was quickly the focus of periscope stares.

"Um," Colin7 said, not sure where to begin the runner's tragic story. Kidnapped, mindwiped, brain-burnt hacking the Beast? What good would it do to reveal the devious truth now, to admit culpability for damage long done? He cleared his throat to pause for time as he reeled through recent memory. "Zak's wife was killed, and he remarried. He's reported to be quite happy living as a recluse." Life seemed so stark at the final report, a distant echo, barely more than a poignant tombstone inscription.

"Wonderful," Ian Miller interjected. "Was it a royal wedding?"

"Uh, no, not really. Just a private affair."

"Aw, too bad," Ian said with good-natured charm. "I do love to do it up."

"Yes, you do," Helena said and pursed her lips at him, almost a kiss.

They coddled each other with their eyes, completely satiated by their digital dream, an indulgent, consistent, and perfect eternity. Who could ask for more?

"Helena didn't know about any of this," Colin7 said, feeling the need for some token of sympathy for her fate, some closure in his mind. "She thought that she was all alone."

Helena turned and frowned down her nose at the naming of her other persona, as though the mere mention was très gauche.

"Well, the truth would have compromised the experiment, of course," Colin5 said and glanced around the room with a nod at the obvious. "Her understanding was that she had chosen physical life instead of a saved soul."

Ian Miller and Helena huffed a courteous chorus of disbelief at such an outrageous and antiquated notion. Physical life was laughably passé to them now.

Colin5 clucked affably. "We manipulated the situation just a micron," he said to garner a few more chuckles from the crowd.

Colin7 levelled an accusatory gaze at his brother. "You deceived me and sent Helena to her death."

"I hardly think so," Helena interjected with distaste. "The husk acted on her own. Blind stubborn, she was, and foolish."

"Now, now," the Original declared with palms upraised for peace, "we won't quibble about increments in the immortal realm." He gave his young clone a glare of chastisement. "Helena made great sacrifices for science, in the flesh and in spirit, and she is to be well commended."

"That's our cue, honey," Ian Miller said as he rose to his feet. He offered a gallant arm, and Helena rose grandly to her feet and stepped away with him through a silvery portal to paradise.

"I can't believe it," Colin7 said in confusion.

"I know," Colin5 said with a nod of concurrence. "It's such a superficial existence, hardly life at all. Time speeds up for them, you know, as with all other saved souls in the collective. They've experienced centuries since their upload, and shared every memory a thousand times. It's hardly fair to speak of them as separate entities now. They're part of the soul cloud, a consortium of intellect. Did you notice the fuzziness of their avatars? They're ghosts now, communal vapours trending toward a baseline of intelligence. We can't expect them to care about dead husks from antiquity."

"I'll bid you two adieu and get back to work," the Original

pronounced and touched his brow with a forefinger in salute as he disappeared.

Colin7 stared after his father, floundering for balance, bereft of moral foundation in this curious paradox of digital life and physical death, chafing against the tangled webs of family responsibility. He wondered what Niko would do in such a strange situation.

Niko waved a wine bottle in greeting as the door opened to reveal her ex-boyfriend in cotton pyjamas and belted blue robe. He looked kind of cute with a hangdog jaw. "Hi, Andrew," she said.

"Oh, shit," he replied. "Are you on a bender?"

She looked at the bottle with a frown. "No, I haven't even opened it yet. Can't we be friends?"

Andrew studied her for a moment. "Sure," he said as he stepped back. "What happened?"

Niko breezed by him down the hall. "Do you have a corkscrew?"

"That bad, huh?"

"They stole my daughter," Niko said from the kitchen. She yanked out a drawer under the counter with a squeal of metal and a rustle of flatware. She peered down and poked among the utensils.

"Shit," Andrew said. He stepped up and reached above her head to take the corkscrew from an upper cabinet. He took the wine bottle and began working on the cork. "That sucks."

"At gunpoint," Niko said.

"No way!"

"Government gestapo."

"Shit," Andrew said again, his face white and tight with sudden fear. "In the building?"

"Child Services, they told me, but it was just a front. Sienna's been whisked away to a research facility. Somebody knew something about her special powers."

Andrew took two glasses from the cabinet and poured red wine. He took a big slug from one and passed the other with a shaky hand. "They must know everything," he said with sad certitude. "You just can't keep any secrets these days."

The glass stem snapped in Niko's fingers, and the goblet shattered on the floor as wine splashed in a crimson cloud. "Ohh," she exclaimed as she inspected her fingers.

"Jesus, Niko. Are you hurt? Are you bleeding?"

"No, sorry," she said, exasperated, "shit."

"Here, take this," Andrew said as he handed over his wine. "And be careful." He threw a dishtowel to the floor and dropped to his knees to mop up the mess. He pulled a dustpan from below the sink and scooped carnage into a wastebasket. "You sure you're okay?"

"Yeah, sorry." Niko took a sip to allay his concern.

Andrew pulled another glass from the cabinet and poured more wine. He gulped another slug. "You seem a bit tense."

Niko sighed at the understatement. "Can you help me, Andrew?"

"Sure. What have you got so far?"

"A bunch of government bull from the V-net. District federal offices and email. Nothing with Sienna's name on it. Maybe we could run the pavement, track something down."

"Sure, that's a start."

"Colin bailed on me, just so you know."

"Great," he said. "I mean, you know . . . whatever."

Niko shook her head. "This isn't going to be a rebound relation-ship, Andrew. That's not why I'm here."

"'Course not," he said and ducked his face away at the notion, perhaps a bit too quickly. "Colin's under a lot of pressure right now. There's a rumour of contagion, some alien plague. Phillip has gone into quarantine. It would probably be best if we cleared out for good while we still can."

Niko stared, aghast at the news. Had the whole world gone mad? "What's wrong with Phillip? Can I see him?"

"No, you can't *see* him," Andrew said. He took a gulp of red wine. "He's in strict quarantine. He's deathly ill."

"What happened?"

"Dunno." He slumped his shoulders at his impotence.

"So Colin's going back to Cromeus Signa to find a cure?"

"No one's supposed to know anything, but I've heard rumours about transporting him through the Doorway to higher technolog-ical care." Andrew walked to the living room and sat on the couch. Niko chose a chair opposite, sipped her wine.

"Do you have any money?" she asked.

"No, but I had a good résumé until recently." He shrugged. "I could get together a few thousand on short notice, enough to get somewhere."

"We've got to find Sienna," Niko said.

Andrew rotated his wine under his nose and took a sip as though to sample it for the first time. "You know, that kid always freaked me out." He held up a hand in apology. "Sorry to say."

"She's gifted, that's all," Niko said.

"She knows stuff in advance," Andrew said. "She reads minds."

"She doesn't read minds."

"Yes," Andrew said and sipped his drink. "She does. I've got data to prove it. Technically, Sienna has affective premonition, not precognition in the strict sense. She can't tell you the future, but she can feel it. She's eerie."

"Have you been testing her?"

He nodded. "Every chance I get. I'm inquisitive. That's what I do."

Niko smiled at him in affinity. "You creep," she said.

"So, it occurs to me to ask," Andrew said with a squinting stare, "what a clairvoyant might do if she knew she was going to be abducted to an unknown location."

"I'd take a GPS in my pocket."

"Good choice, but someone would find it in a standard scan and destroy it, or ship it to Siberia. Only low-level smartfibre would get through, commonplace items."

"Like what?"

"Well, all our lab coats are on smartfibre. All corporate supplies are tagged with our signature for inventory control. Heck, a toothbrush from the commissary might be enough to track short range." He smiled.

Niko felt hope bloom with a shiver of translocation in her mind. "You think Sienna would know enough to do that?"

He nodded upward. "The kid is freaky, Niko."

"Do you have a portable reader?"

"Yep, I can get a handheld, no problem."

"You're damn smart, Andrew."

"Yep," he said, "I know."

"So we just go through the resource list, start from the closest location and work a widening circle until we find her."

Andrew tipped up his glass in salute. "Just because they're federal doesn't mean they would move her out of state. They'll have to buy clothes in her size and leave a datatrail of purchase requisitions. Do you have any passwords?"

"Management keystroke," she said, "nothing high-level."

"That might be enough. Shoe size would narrow it down. Sienna's a ten, right? Tiny feet like you?"

Niko chewed on her lip as she studied her former boyfriend. Why had she left him in the first place? Just because he was a self-absorbed nerd with no social skills? So what? He was cute, and fastidious, and had a Ph.D. in neuroscience. What more did she need? "Can we keep this just business?" she said. "I mean, for now?"

"'Course," he said with an artful smile. He was likely planning more, but would bide his time as a gentleman. "I know you're probably feeling hurt," he said.

"I am. Thank you."

"Do you want to start charting maps, or get packing, or what?"

Niko moved to the couch and sat beside him. "Can we just sit together for a moment of silence? I need to process a few things."

"Sure," he said, "no problem." He draped an arm around her shoulders and settled deeper into the couch, closer toward her, balancing his wine glass like a magic elixir. "No problem at all."

TEN

"**W**e've got to kill Phillip," Rix said.

Jimmy eyed him carefully. The kid had gone crazy. "No," he said, "we don't." They were sitting outside on the balcony watching Niagara Falls, home again after a mid-afternoon winery tour. Jimmy sipped a beer and Rix a cola. Jovita was making sandwiches in the kitchen.

"It's the only way to get rid of his avatar, that priestess Philomena."

"You're speculating," Jimmy said. "Philomena may be the new logos on Main Street, but no one knows where she lives."

"She's inside Phillip," Rix said. "Somehow he's cooked up a supernatural avatar."

Jimmy shook his head. "Phillip is dead. This new girl is a pirate version, some kind of cybersoul upload.

"She's more dangerous that Phillip ever was," Rix said. "We've got to kill her."

Jimmy pointed a slender finger in accusation. "You're the dangerous one, Rix. You took retribution on a man in V-space, and now you think you can change the world. It's called egomania. It runs in your family."

Rix pouted in thought, looking hurt and betrayed. Good. About time. Punch some sense into the poor kid before he went completely over the edge. Jimmy scrutinized his face for a clue. A madman would never accept the truth of his own madness; that was the acid test.

"The murderer lived," Rix said. "He's still bedridden. I checked up on him after the incident."

A cold-blooded, carefully engineered execution, now just an *incident*, an excusable eccentricity. "He suffered a stroke," Jimmy said. "You delivered a brain burn, pure and simple; we both know that."

Rix stiffened with affront against any insinuation of guilt. "He killed my mother!"

"Sure, he did. I'm not saying I wouldn't have done the same," Jimmy said, "at your age."

The punk kid hardened his eyes with malice. "Vigilantes must rise to fill any vacuum of justice. No one would blame me."

"You got away with murder once, and now it's made you crazy. You want to kill your own grandfather. And for what? Politics?"

"Freedom from tyranny," Rix said. "Phillip has taken over the V-net. He controls all the encryption algorithms."

Jimmy waved an arm in dismissal. "Phillip is an old burn-out in a neuroscience lab. He hasn't got the wherewithal to be a criminal mastermind."

"Philomena is using his body as a base of operations."

"You don't know that."

"She must be. No consciousness can survive without a human brain."

"You don't know that either," Jimmy said. "You're jumping to conclusions without rational evidence. That's what crazy people do. You're fashioning your own reality as an excuse to kill a helpless cripple in a wheelchair. You should see a doctor."

Rix shook his head sadly. "You're backsliding downlevel, Jimmy.

You need to wake up before it's too late. Philomena is reading minds, instilling cognition with strange new powers. She'll take over the world if we don't stop her by killing Phillip."

Jimmy felt affliction at the truth of it all, but didn't dare show any weakness. "Phillip is already dead. Don't you think I would know if he had truly been resurrected?"

"Resurrected?" Jovita said with amazement. "You mean like Jesus?"

They both whirled to face her, and Jimmy wondered how long she had been standing there, what she might have heard. He was getting lax in his old age, mouthy. V-space was getting too crowded for him, too many demands, too much at stake. He had to get out of the maelstrom. Maybe he should just unplug and imagine the freedom like Zak, cut all the tangled threads and take his toys with him to the rumpus room.

"We were just talking about something in the virtual world," Rix said, "a new movement on the V-net."

"I think V-space is fascinating," Jovita said. "I can hardly wait to get the surgery myself. All the kids are doing it now, but the operation is so expensive." Her posture shrunk forward, class conscious, a country girl pining for the big city.

"There's an easy opening in market research," Jimmy said. "You can get the wetware installed for free if you sign up for a thirty-day watcher, a gargoyle, as Zak would say. They monitor your early movements and halting progress, tag along to suck your data. It's all about grassroots development, you know, building efficient organics."

Jovita frowned. "Would that be safe for Eternals? I mean, I'm sure the surgery is the same for everyone, but the question of personal privacy would be paramount for someone with secrecy issues."

Hmm, good question, and pleasantly elucidated. This girl obviously had some smarts, not just big hair and pretty lips. Jimmy shrugged. "Haven't played that angle, but I could check it out for you. See what's available."

Jovita eyes brightened with surprise. "Really? That would be awesome."

"Well, sure," Jimmy said. "Any friend of Rix is a friend of mine." He tossed a nod at his virtual grandkid with a social smile.

Rix seemed pensive. "I'm not sure it's a good time for a newbie to be cruising Main Street. There's a new AI, Philomena, trying to take over V-space, manipulating the masses. She's exercising powerful magic, trying to change things."

Jovita's face soured with dismay. She studied the two wireheads like a sad waif at the side of the road, the highway to the future suddenly blocked before her.

"I'm wrong," Rix said, slumping his shoulders at the sight of her crushed hope. "You should totally get hooked up, if Jimmy can make it happen. We can sort things out with Philomena later." He looked at Jimmy and tapped his V-net earring with a finger: *We'll take down the Beast!*

"Great," Jovita said with a winning smile. She turned an eager face to Jimmy. "Can I drop you a line when we get settled?"

Jimmy ducked his forehead in quick acquiescence. "Sure," he said. Poor kids. Philomena would chew them up like candy. The vestigial soul of psycho-Phillip would grant little mercy to Eternals. It must be tough to see the world go to hell and know you'll live long enough to see the final apocalypse. At least he had death waiting close by to take him out of the game, always a shadow hovering near in his imagination, keeping him sane. "So where are you two headed, now that the ERI has fallen?"

"We're going to see my mother in Florida," Jovita said. "She's probably worried sick."

"Taking the new boyfriend home for dinner," Jimmy said, tasting the anachronism like sweet fruit on his tongue. "That's nice."

Jovita actually blushed, God bless her. Jimmy studied her face with awe, wondering if she felt some guilty desire or was merely expressing an acute sense of social conscience.

"Well, we're not really . . ." She cast a furtive glance toward Rix. "Well, you know."

"'Course not," Jimmy said quickly. "I didn't mean anything. It sounds traditional to an old man, that's all."

Rix kept his face impassive, but Jimmy could almost hear the cogs turning. Every generation had to invent sex all over again, renew that ageless, stealthy discovery. It wouldn't take long for Rix to get his gonads in gear, and he needed a good distraction to keep him safe from all this business with Philomena, his Hitleresque fantasy. He was too close to the truth, too connected with the rare empathic gift of his father, following the same inevitable pathway to trouble.

Jovita appraised Jimmy anew, testing his years with her eyes. "Are you Eternal, Mr. Kay?"

"No," he said, and looked away from the subtle shade of pity that clouded her expression. *I'm dying, honey. Just mark me down in your playbook and get on with it.* Life was black and white to her now, immortality versus death. There wasn't much grey in between. "Not yet," he offered to quell her discomfort.

Jovita pressed her lips and nodded. She had nothing to offer, no worthy condolence. Only the aliens could mete out eternity. "You don't mind if we stay a few more days, do you?"

"He doesn't mind," Rix said with confidence. "Jimmy is like family to me."

Jimmy smiled with all the grace he could muster. "I knew Rix before he was born," he said, "when he was just a glinting neuron in his father's backbrain. Stay as long as you like. You're safer here than anywhere."

Jovita stepped forward, businesslike, and offered an outstretched hand. "Thank you so much for your hospitality, Mr. Kay," she said. "You've been a great help, but we've got a long journey ahead of us. My mother will be worried."

Jimmy raised a reflexive arm to seal her sentiment, but Jovita cradled his hand in both palms, caressing his arthritic knuckles, fondling his fissured skin, trying to express, what . . . love? His body galvanized at such attention from the young Eternal. Her gesture seemed openly erotic but so framed with innocence to be sexually innocuous. Her smile was unabashedly sincere, condescending in its simple transparency, a woman without artifice in a world of braggadocio. She exuded some inner spiritual confidence. She had hope in something he could not see, belief in something he could not fathom. His entire body seemed to vibrate with energy and shoot out through his fingers into hers, an intermingling of souls. He could not pull his hand away, nor tear his eyes from the magnet of her being. Funny what a simple touch can do.

Niko gazed up at the grey federal building with trepidation. It was four stories tall, stippled concrete with circular portholes evenly spaced along the street side. The windows stuck out from the front like convex bubbles, very strange architecture, some archaic experiment with postmodernism that didn't quite work. It looked like an aquarium with bulging fish eyes, or a submarine ready to explode with pent-up pressure. She glanced over at Andrew as he peered at his handheld scanner like an oracle. "Are you sure she's in there?"

Andrew looked up with a frown. "No, I'm not sure. I've got two hits similar to Phillip's inventory signature, but there's plenty of frequency overlap in this spectrum. We're not really close enough for an exact match. Do you want to snoop around the windows like tourists?"

Niko dialled up visual augmentation to spy through the plate-glass entrance. "Two guards sitting at a long desk," she said. "Looks like a standard metal scanner, pretty low-tech."

Andrew studied the street. "Anything sophisticated in this neighbourhood would draw a lot of attention. Maybe they're hiding in plain sight. The building used to be a courthouse, according to the civic record, but they've made recent acquisitions for medical equipment. This is my top pick from all the intel."

"Well, I can't just go waltzing in there with my gun under my bra."

Andrew grimaced at the reminder. "Guns are always a bad idea," he said. "Why don't we hide it in the bushes and try the front door like good citizens?"

"And lose the element of surprise?"

"Don't be ridiculous. We're not secret agents."

"Well, we should be," Niko said and pointed. "Look, there's a man going up the walkway. Let's just watch." She placed a hand on Andrew's arm to steady her telescopic vision. "No lock on the door, no palm registration," she said. "He's emptying his pockets into a plastic bin, taking off his shoes."

"Oh, yeah, the old switchblade in the boot trick," Andrew said with mock solemnity.

"Okay, he's going through the scanners. No pat-down. Any

composite weapon would pass easily. The guards barely looked up from their coffee."

"They're not expecting terrorists in this backwater," Andrew said. "There's probably a lot of routine traffic."

Niko pressed her lips and glanced around. "All right, we'll ditch the gun," she said. "And the scanner."

Andrew shook his head. "I'll keep the scanner. I'll say it's a medical device if they ask. A monitor for allergens. I have ID as a doctor."

"You're a neuroscientist, not a doctor."

"Close enough."

Niko tilted her head at him in query. What if the guards demanded to see the scanner in operation? What if they were strict in enforcement?

"Okay, I'll surrender it if they make a fuss," Andrew said. "Let's take a quick spin round the building at close range, just in case."

They meandered down a side street and hopped a fence to get behind the building.

"Not even webcam surveillance," Niko said as she buried the gun and shoulder holster under a scraggly bush.

"Those bulky cameras are just to keep the vagrants away. They probably have an unobtrusive system with pinpoint lenses."

Niko brushed dirt from her hands and wiped them on her dark slacks. "So we could already be compromised?"

"Will you just take it easy? We're not doing anything illegal."

"I'm feeling nervous without my weapon," Niko said, bouncy with energy.

"No kidding," Andrew drawled.

"I'm not used to working blind and naked. I usually have everything under control."

Andrew paused for a moment as though considering a salacious comeback, but she stilled him with a glare. "We're just doing reconnaissance," he said. "Let me do the talking. I'm a job applicant looking for the human resources department, if they ask. We're just sizing up the government market, strictly business. You're my research assistant."

"Fine."

Andrew swung his reader as they stepped over parking barriers and past a decrepit garden. They slowly made their way to the front of the building while he studied the readings. "It looks like we want to get upstairs," he said. "I've got a good hit on a lab jacket, and the other is a miscellaneous item. Why the hell would anyone bother to tag a miscellaneous item for inventory?"

"We should be thankful they did," Niko said as she pushed open the plate glass door at the entrance. The guards looked up from their seats but didn't rise to the occasion. The smell of fresh baking from a delicatessen down the hall barely overpowered a lingering disinfectant. Andrew emptied his pockets into a bucket for a cursory inspection, and stepped through the metal scanner with casual ease. On the other side, he gathered his belongings, pocketed his reader, and quickly walked away. Niko caused a loud beep and stood red-faced under the plastic arbour, trapped. Andrew whirled in alarm with a grimace like a boy with his fingers in a cookie jar.

One of the guards pushed reluctantly to his feet with an electronic wand and passed it over Niko's body until he located a metal source at her chest. He waved his wand back and forth with a buzzing woop-woop sound, his eyebrows raised in query as Niko blushed and fumed.

"Underwire bra," she murmured, and the guard nodded without comment and resumed his seat with disinterest. So much for an undetected entrance. Niko ducked her head and hurried forward to catch up with Andrew.

He studied her with incredulity as she approached. "You're wearing a push-up bra?"

"My good one's in the wash."

Andrew's gaze went from her face to her breasts and back again, twice. His eyes crinkled with mischief, probably imagining some sordid Security pat-down. Or worse.

Niko narrowed a stare at him, the pervert. She stabbed her hands on her hips and puffed up her stuff with a quick intake of breath. "Don't get your hopes up," she said.

Andrew raised his palms with mock innocence. "Who, me?"

They stopped at a small delicatessen where a dozen tables with free-standing chairs blocked the concourse. A woman in a purple hairnet worked behind the counter putting sandwiches in foam cartons for pickup. The door to the stairwell was locked.

"Elevator's down the hall," the woman said and pointed to her left. "Legal aid is up one level. You need advance clearance for anything above the second floor."

"Thanks," Andrew said, and turned to Niko with casual ease. "Do you want some lunch while we're here, honey?"

"No," she said and pasted a smile for the woman behind the counter to show no offense, "not right now."

They sauntered down the hallway and found a palm scanner on the wall beside the elevator. Niko stared at it with dismay. "Why do I have the feeling that klaxons will sound if I touch that thing?"

"Because you're paranoid," Andrew said. "You're neurotic about it."

She pushed her chin forward. "You do it, then."

"No problem." Andrew stepped up and placed his hand on the scanner. A green light glowed and the elevator door opened promptly. He smiled. "That wasn't so bad, was it?"

Niko stepped inside with caution. The walls were veiny grey

marble, the floor glossy with polish, like a stone crypt in an expensive mausoleum. Andrew punched the button numbered four.

"Fourth floor?" Niko asked.

Andrew shrugged. "I'm looking for a job," he said to any invisible microphone, "and I might as well start at the top if they'll let me."

They both studied the numerals above the door as the cage glided smoothly upward. A tone sounded as the second-floor light came on, then two more at the third and fourth. The doors slid open with barely a sound, and they peeked out into an empty vestibule, hardly daring to believe their good fortune. Andrew pulled out his hand-held and activated the scanner. "Bingo," he said as he strode forward. "This way."

Niko felt wariness dragging her back. She had expected danger, some confrontation. This was way too easy; it had to be a trap. Paranoia, her faithful friend in times of trouble, clawed at the back of her brain. She could feel disaster looming near like a crouching animal.

"This is perfect," Andrew said with glee as he pointed his scanner to a grey metal door. "I've got a sure hit on a lab coat from our facility. I told you Sienna was a spooky kid."

Niko eyed the door, feeling fear and promise mingled in an exotic electrochemical stew. "You think she's in there?" Or just a lab coat, a false trail, a decoy.

"Only one way to find out," Andrew said as he palmed the door sensor. The lock clicked with a dull thud of sturdy mechanics. Andrew pushed the door open with eyebrows arched wide at the sheer impossibility of events. Their gaze locked in a brief dance of disbelief but dropped in the face of predestination, for better or worse.

They entered the small laboratory to find a child strapped to a gurney with her head encased in a neural monitor from the nose upward. Niko wailed a guttural exclamation as she recognized Sienna. She jumped forward to touch her inert face. She scrabbled at the metal casing over her forehead. *No, no, no!*

"Don't touch the equipment!" Andrew said as he wrenched Niko away from the bedside. "This is a sterile lab!"

Niko stifled a scream with her fingers over her mouth.

"Keep calm," Andrew said. "Jesus." He turned to inspect Sienna. "She's had major surgery of some type, probably a brain implant. They may have done her eyes also."

"Oh, God," Niko wailed. *No, no, no!* She clutched the hair at her temples, trying to resist the urge to embrace her child. "Is she dead?" *Please, God, just grant me this one favour and I will believe in you forever.*

"She's in a forced coma," Andrew said with scientific detachment. "It takes the body four or five days to adjust to brain trauma of this nature." He stepped toward the control console. "We might as well boot up the monitors and check the data. There's no way we can move her."

"Andrew?"

"What?"

"Andrew, take a look at this." A white lab coat lay neatly folded on a chair in the corner, still wrapped in factory cellophane. He followed Niko's pointing finger and picked it up. His face drained of blood.

"Shit," he said. His name was neatly embroidered on the pocket: *Dr. Andrew Oaten.*

Niko sobbed as realization dawned. "It's Phillip!" she cried. She staggered to Sienna and bent to embrace her torso, blubbering and spilling tears like rain onto the starched linen blanket. "He killed his own daughter in some foul experiment, and now he's willing to sacrifice his granddaughter in the same way. He's a psychotic monster!"

The bioengineering equipment beeped to life behind her with muted, market-tested tones.

"She's stable," Andrew said. "She actually looks pretty good. Peptide levels normal, good patterns throughout the brain. Jesus, that's a lot of alloy."

"The best damn thing on the white market," Niko said with surety. "Phillip is insane. Money means nothing to him now that he's passed out of his body. We're all just mice running circles in his twisted maze."

"This is a federal building," Andrew said. "Could he be controlling the government?"

"Who can tell the difference anymore? The corps are intertwined like tree roots in a tropical rainforest. State boundaries have lost all meaning in the digital world. There's no hope for justice in V-space. There's no respect for life and no recourse against evil. We're on the eve of destruction as a species."

Andrew gripped her arm and shook her gently from her reverie of despair. "Don't panic," he said. "It can't be that bad. Sienna's going to be okay. All she needs is time to heal." He moved to the door and peered out into the quiet vestibule. "Do you want to make a break for it while we still can?"

Niko shivered her head and sniffed back a sob with new resolution as she stared at her sleeping daughter. "I can't leave Sienna."

Andrew closed the door with a gentle snick. "I didn't think so."

"You go if you want," Niko said without turning. "You've done more than enough."

"No," he said, "I guess there's no place to hide now. My name's already on the monogram." He stepped toward her and draped an arm of comfort around her shoulder.

Niko flinched. "Please don't touch me, Andrew."

He jolted his hand back. "Sorry," he said, "but I'll stay anyway, just as a friend." He turned to the bioengineering equipment and scrolled through charts on a flatscreen monitor. "Maybe I can help," he said as he began to tap on the keyboard. "This is what I do best."

Niko watched Andrew quietly working and felt a pang at being so abrupt with him. She just couldn't handle any more relationships with men. Everything always seemed to go sour in the end, and it was probably all her fault. Andrew was a great guy, really, a genius at the forefront of his specialty. His fingers danced on the complicated control panel like a spaceship captain at the helm. His eyes surveyed mysterious data with diligence. He was taking command. He was willing to fight for her daughter. "This is a scary implant system," he said. "It's wireless."

"What?"

He pointed to an electronic resonance image of Sienna's skull. "You see that octahedral array? Those are wi-fi nodes transmitting through open air to the V-net. I've seen this configuration in development papers that were supposed to be years down the pipe, but Sienna's already hooked up and running."

Niko stepped closer to inspect the arcane equipment. "She's in V-space permanently? No plug? No off switch?"

"In theory there's supposed to be cognitive triggers for the virtual data, and filters to separate the visual signals. The best of both worlds."

"No way." Niko said. "The user would be screaming in the streets in a matter of hours. V-space is too intense to be on all the time."

"No one knows what to expect," Andrew said. "It's been too controversial to speculate openly. No scientist wants to jump off a building to see if he can fly." He turned to study Sienna at rest in her hospital gurney. "She doesn't seem to be in any physical distress."

"She's probably caught in a nightmare. How could she understand the V-net at her age? Can't we turn it off? Cut the electricity?"

Andrew shook his head. "Absolutely not. Her system is too fragile. That's why wetware surgeons induce coma for the first few days, to let the brain rest and recover. We can't touch anything."

Niko reached her hand to touch the glowing image on the monitor. Her daughter's young brain laid bare, violated by cybernetic science. How could this fleshy receptacle possibly contain all the wonders of the V-net, a system that stretched throughout the world? A tiny, undeveloped bundle of virginal neurons in solution, electromagnetic patterns in delicate balance, dendrites growing like spring flowers, reaching filamental fingers for chemical conjoinment across the viscous abyss. And now this rape by the witch doctors of modern medicine, this sickening sacrilege. Sienna's brain would surely transmogrify as it raged in perpetual overclock. Her innocence had ended. "I'll have to confront Phillip," Niko said as she blinked away tears. "Is there a V-net plug in this mess?"

Andrew glanced at her with surprise. "Are you sure that's wise?"

"No." She took a breath and had second thoughts. "But we've come this far. We have to do something. We've got to stand up to Phillip before it's too late."

Andrew winced with indecision, shrugged, and sighed. "There's a hardwire plug right here." He pointed to a blinking silver box where a network of cables sprouted like spider webs. "Looks like an XB interface with elite filters. You won't need any special schematics for the lower Prime levels." He turned for eye contact, his face grim. "But you'll give away our location within seconds. Phillip will have this node on his watch list, for sure." He nodded toward Sienna asleep on the gurney. "This is a big investment for him." Last chance to run, his tone said, before a situational escalation.

"Oh, hell," she said, "we're already bumbling around like blind robots on a tether. Go ahead and plug me up. We might as well meet our maker."

Andrew brightened at her display of bravado. "Well, pull up a chair, space ranger," he said with a silly grin. "We'll fire our proton guns into the heart of the Death Star." He pointed with a flat palm of invitation to a vinyl chair in the corner.

"You're such a drama queen," she said, but his smile gave her a lift of hope. He was just as crazy as she was, feeding on disaster like a drug. Manic warriors they were, with dented shields and dull swords. Their breastplates of righteousness were corroded now, but maybe tough enough. Niko grabbed the simple chair and dragged it over. What a crappy launch couch it would make. She could topple over and hurt herself easily, twitching and careening through V-space without a shoulder harness. She sat down and tried to make herself comfortable. She rocked her body a bit to see if the chair would move. It seemed sturdy. What a desperate mess.

Andrew offered a slender cable forward, a serpent in the garden. "You ready?"

Niko pulled her hair back from her ear and tipped her head to expose her V-net plug hanging like an earring. "Do me," she said.

A rushing wind carried her as she closed her eyes, a perilous momentum. In an instant she was on Main Street with a keen electric choke in her throat. Home again and invincible. Pop-up billboards glared gaudy with fluorescence, morphing continually with the hourly fads of fashion. Lime green was the go-go colour of the day, and the air smelled of nutmeg. HAIL VICTORY, a placard pronounced over a zoomtube tunnel pointing uptown to the next rave. The face of Philomena was ubiquitous, a petulant pixie leering with revolutionary zeal.

Niko wore her black leather avatar by default, skin-tight and lustrous, a plain working uniform camouflaged by darkness. She tried to stay in the shadows as she made her way toward the portal, but the street was a bustle of activity, a jostling mix of bodies in motion. Everyone seemed busy, purposeful, the energy level high. A marketeer guarded the tunnel and tagged her with a turnstile reader. All privacy on Main Street had been lost long ago; perhaps it had been a delusion all along. She felt a burst of fresh anger at the infringement, but kept moving and stepped into the zoomtube without delay.

The coliseum was quiet and unadorned, a universe empty and free of form, still hours before the next scheduled show. A crowd of kids milled around the open doorway chatting together about the upcoming event like concert groupies lining up for e-tickets, rapture on their faces, expectation in their hearts. Philomena can give you the answer before you look for it, they whispered. She knows what you need before you ask. They longed to view the new magic, the supernatural made manifest—a generation seeking signs and wonders, a roiling discontent looking for an outlet, a squall front seething toward splendour. Niko remembered back to the rave where she had first seen Philomena, the falling bodies of worshipers near the altar, slain in the spirit at the feet of the demigoddess, embracing the blessing of utter relinquishment.

Niko lingered among the avatars to test the harmonics of the group. Did these people have homes in the real world? Did they ride bicycles and jog in the early morning? Did they dance with mirth in the warm summer rain? Of course they did. V-space could never replace the true essence of humanity. Artificial consciousness could not substitute for love and joy, the neurochemical standbys of history. Institutionalized pornography could never supplant physical sex, not in the long run. Philomena's hallucination was limited to that extent at least. Real people would continue to laugh and sing, get married and bask in the sunshine with their children. Niko could take Sienna to the beach, get away from the augmented digital life, raise her like a normal little girl.

Perhaps she could escape with her daughter, whisk her away to a northern wilderness where the V-net could never reach. They could settle down together with Colin7. A young girl needs a father, especially during the boisterous teenage years. Sienna's future stretched out before Niko like something infinitely pliable. She could build a home for her, watch her develop into a confident woman, a lady of grace. In the end she might grow old and die, while Niko stayed Eternally young, but that was okay. One day at a time was all Niko needed. It was all anyone could ask.

Defiance bloomed like a hard calcite crystal inside her, a diamond of promise for a better world, as Niko climbed boldly up onto the stage and peeked behind the pulpit. She searched through empty vestibules backstage. The air smelled pungent with ozone, a brewing storm.

"Are you in here, Phillip?" she shouted. "I know you can see me, you bastard!"

Philomena coalesced before her, larger than life and brilliant with phantasmic colour. Her childlike features were smooth, snub nose, nubile chest, her edges clean like a cartoon. She seemed magnificent at first glance, perfectly programmed to concise schematics, a soulless animatron composed of code. Philomena smiled. "I've been expecting you," she said.

"Why are you parading around like a psychedelic princess, Phillip? What are you trying to prove?"

"I'm fixing things for you, dear child." Her tone was ingratiatingly sweet with a subtle hint of disappointment.

"I renounce your lineage, you monster. Have you no shred of decency? No common concern for human welfare? How dare you steal my daughter for some foul experiment!"

Philomena shook her huge head with a tsk-tsk of the tongue. "You never would have agreed," she said.

"Of course not. She's too young!"

"You were the same age when you first went under the knife," Philomena reminded her with a casual smile. "There's no harm in starting early. You turned out just fine."

Niko huffed through her nose, fuming with exasperation. Her predecessor had not been so lucky, her primal namesake dead on the operating slab. She felt buzzy with emotional overload, but could summon no release of violence against this cartoon giant. The woman was not real, not worthy of vengeance, just a digital pattern in the cloud, a bodiless intelligence. Philomena was the next big thing in V-space, the worst thing, a potential shift from freedom to despotism, all in the guise of peace.

Niko turned away from the puppet, tried to visualize her father controlling the strings from far above. Was he really up there? "God, Phillip, you could at least have told me," she proclaimed to the ceiling. "Don't I mean anything to you after all those years running Prime?"

"You mean the world to me, child," her false father said, her chirpy Asian voice a singsong.

"I'm not a child," Niko said. "I'm a grown woman, and you treat me worse than a slave." She sucked a breath to calm her raging spirit. "I served you willingly at first because I thought you were my friend, my mentor. You were a powerful intelligence, worthy of respect." What child could distrust her own father, the tall tower of masculine support? "I regret every moment now," Niko proclaimed, but the lie tasted vile on her tongue. She did not regret her past, not really. She had done her utmost all along, working together for a greater good. How could everything have gone so wrong? She shook her head. "I don't understand. What do you want with Sienna? She's just a little girl."

Philomena tilted her head at Niko and targeted her eyes, and a vision flashed in Niko's mind from the woman, the edges sharp and detailed, an ordered and sanitary world, a unified consciousness, children playing without fear on Main Street, no crime, no brutality, a pure and perfect playground. A soft song moaned in the background with lullaby voices crooning a choral harmony alongside a gentle wind. This can be yours, the avatar said, to have and to hold like a bride.

Niko blinked to dispel the dream, but the fragrance lingered with a nuance of honey in the back of her brain. "You can't control everyone's mind," she said.

Philomena smiled and nodded but would not decline the possibility.

"People need to think for themselves," Niko persisted. "Young men need to push boundaries, to rebel against the status quo. That's what drives culture forward. Just look at your son, Zak. He showed us our true heritage, a risk-taker, a warrior. You can't deny that natural expression; you can't corral the future behind artificial barricades."

"Zakariah was useful in his day," Philomena said with care. He's gone now, she implied in her tone. Zak hadn't plugged up since his brain burn years ago. He did not exist in her reality.

"You're blind to the true nature of things," Niko said. "There are people out there, and animals and birds. Your programming is faulty. You don't have all the data." With desperate envisionment, Niko projected an image from the front of a canoe, a simple scene on a quiet river with the fog rising around her in wraithlike spirals, the smell of fresh foliage in the air, the rhythmic dip of her paddle in still morning waters. She contemplated the simple beauty of unadorned life in the wild. She remembered riding her motorcycle through fertile woodlands, climbing hills salted with daisies and peppered with black-eyes susans. It was a world this fake avatar could never understand, the real world. Philomena could never skinny-dip in a cool mountain stream on a sunny afternoon. She could never hear the loons sing like lonely ghosts heralding the spirit of Gaia.

"I'm not careless of the ecosystem," Philomena said in response. "I'm conscious of environmental reports moment by moment. I'm using computational design calculations far beyond the realm of fallible flesh, and my corporate teams are making progress toward terraforming the planet for the preservation of all species."

"You don't know the difference between a grey jay and a grey heron."

Philomena took less than a microsecond to mine the data. "Yes, I do."

"But you can't feel it," Niko said. "You can't *know* the truth."

Philomena shuttered her eyes once with a nod of affirmation. "You have answered your own question, my dear. Now you see why Sienna is so important to our plans. She will be my sensory apparatus, a vanguard extension of our global neurosystem. There is no reason to be afraid of the future. We mean no harm, only good. We could never do evil."

Oh, God. Realization hit Niko like a physical blow to her chest. Zombie Phillip was planning a cybernetic mingling with his own granddaughter, a fiendish invasion. *No, no, no!* Niko felt her body pixelate as she lost bandwidth traction. Her body crumpled forward with anguish, trapped in a netherworld between two disparate planes.

She felt herself falling out of her launch couch in a distant land where her daughter lay strapped on a hospital gurney. Was Sienna already part of the infernal mix, listening via her new wetware installation, the virgin defiled? *Sienna, I'm so sorry. I wanted only to protect you.*

Niko coalesced again on the floor behind the pulpit, felt hard tile on her cheek and smelled a burning decay of neurotransmitters. Her eyes focused on the shiny black boots of a giant cartoon avatar, a devil incarnate. She felt insignificant, a bug in a woven rug. A sense of failure held her down like an anvil weight. She bemoaned ever having trusted her father. She regretted ever having plugged up to run his errands in V-space, helping to build his wicked empire. She remembered her daughter's cherubic face framed with dark ringlets, a child incorruptible and pure. *Just one small thing, God. Was that too hard for you?*

Almond-shaped eyes stared down at her from on high, a golem gaze without empathy, without compassion. A fresh wave of helplessness rained down on Niko as she grovelled in her ruin, her tension unfulfilled, her anger unrequited. They were both puppets, pawns in Phillip's schizophrenic drama. They had both served Phillip in mindless duty, without question, never thinking to examine their assumptions, to break free from bondage.

"You've done well," Philomena said. "You've been reliable at every turn."

Niko choked to find her voice. "This is not what I worked for," she whispered.

"This is the culmination of our destiny, child. Colin Macpherson and I ran thousands of computer simulations on each DNA segment to find the genetic markers for psychic enhancement. We built Sienna for this one purpose, to harness the future with her precognitive powers, to streamline V-space for the good of all humanity. This is the inheritance of System Intelligence that I promised you long ago."

"I don't want to be a queen in V-space," Niko said. "I don't want to control the world."

"You can't spurn your heritage, not after the sacrifice another has made for you."

"What," she asked, "my progenitor? The first Niko that died during surgery?"

A haunting sigh rustled the air around her. It seemed to come from everywhere, from the digital fabric of the walls and floor. "She didn't die during surgery," Philomena said. "She was incapacitated, broken. We were peering in the dark with flashlights in those early days; it's hard to imagine now. We gambled and made some mistakes. I pushed her termination button myself on the day of your conception."

Niko hung her head with shame at the horror of her family history. So it was true. Phillip had killed his daughter with his own hands and built a Frankenstein clone in her place. He had been driven mad by guilt ever since, consumed by a voracious need to make restitution.

"You've gone too far," Niko said as she pushed up to her knees, panting for bandwidth breath. "If I had known . . ." A fresh wave of weakness overwhelmed her. What would she have done? Given up a second chance at life? Rebelled against her father? Resisted the ultimate power he had orchestrated?

"We're on the verge of a grand vista," Philomena said. "The rich will share with the poor, the lion lie down with the lamb."

Niko wanted to spit with disgust. *Oh, spare me the myths of history, the fables that fostered only tyranny through the ages.* A buoyancy of insolence rose again in her breast. Cloned as a slave, raised as a servant, and treated like shit. Enough was enough. She was better than this comic-book freak; she had a mind of her own grounded in the fertile soil of Earth, the soul of Gaia. She knew how to paddle a canoe and ride a motorcycle. She was more than a pattern of data in V-space, more than a test-tube concoction of DNA, and she was a damned good mother! The light seemed suddenly bright and acrid around Niko, a crystal-clear acuity. She would never give up.

Niko got shakily to her feet. She held up her hand to test the opacity of her palm. Robust signal strength, no technical problems. Could Phillip read her mind even now? Could he sense her burgeoning defiance? "Things could get worse if we're not careful," she said.

Philomena smiled with delight. "I'm being very careful." No sign of distrust, no hint of suspicion.

Niko hung her head in servility to her former master, the Antichrist resurrected. She would bide her time, hold her horror in abeyance. "With Sienna's help, you'll know the end before the beginning."

Philomena nodded. "Exactly so," she said with a rock-star grin. "And how cool is that?"

"You'll need someone to feed her, to teach her," Niko said.

"Are you willing to volunteer?"

Niko sighed with a show of capitulation. "I will."

"Good," Philomena said. "You and Dr. Oaten will take Sienna back to our private lab for stabilization. Andrew will head the development team. He'll find the frontier to his liking and his payroll upgrade has already been processed."

Niko rocked back on her heels in surprise. Was Philomena that quick and connected? Or had she prepared in advance for Niko's inevitable surrender? Both options seemed scary, and Niko could only nod with glum resignation. Andrew would surely play along with the dictum of circumstance, and Niko would win his confidence in stealth. Her pathway seemed so obvious now, her will to survive stronger than ever. She had the bloodlight in her veins.

"Will you stay for the concert?" Philomena asked, and her under-tone said that attendance was indeed mandatory at the upcoming event, the celebratory rave of the day, to show her allegiance, to bless her fellow workers in the movement.

Circumstance had stripped Niko of freedom and choice. Her young daughter lay unconscious in a clandestine laboratory with her skull encased in a bioengineering computer, gold filaments in her head and an incubus in her brain. No question, no doubt about it, Niko would prostitute her anus on a brazen altar, if she had to, for a single chance at redemption. She would whore herself out with the patience of a saint, if need be, for one opportunity to steal Sienna away to a secure haven, some sanctuary, anywhere apart from this digital monster.

Niko nodded and raised a flat palm in salute. "Hail victory."

ELEVEN

Colin7 and Colin5 sat together in a cozy restaurant high up the hill of New Jerusalem, eating real food in real bodies, looking out at an actual sun on the craggy horizon of an orbiting planet in measurable spacetime. No electronic intermediary separated them, no subroutine recorded their conversation—two physical souls, not saved, eating roasted chicken with metal cutlery from a rare menu reserved for the elite. "It's all very confusing," Colin7 admitted to his fellow clone. "Split copies of the Original. I'm struggling with questions of allegiance."

"To your own self be true," Colin5 said with a grin. He stabbed a slice of red pepper with a fork and held it up for inspection.

Colin7 bristled at his lack of sensitivity to their predicament. "Our father on Earth is counting on me to rescue him."

"And so you shall." Colin5 took a bite and closed his eyes while he savoured the taste.

"To what? Some digital obliteration? He's expecting a return to power, a coronation with renewed control of his empire."

Colin5 paused as though surprised by an innovative thought. "In one sense that's exactly what he will receive," he said. "Our shared destiny is to return our souls in service to the Original."

"He *is* the Original, or so he imagines. And who's to say he's not the Original? How can we tell which father is the real Colin Macpherson?"

Colin5 pushed food around his plate with diligence. "The copy at home has priority of placement."

Colin7 presented an upright palm to test a new idea. "Why don't we upload the Phillip copy as a separate consciousness, let the two of them hash it out together, cybersoul to cybersoul? Perhaps they will come to some shared agreement."

"No," Colin5 said with a quick shake of his head. "Our forefathers were all conjoined back to the Original. That's the way it must be. We can't have multiple personalities running around trying to rule by committee."

"Why not?"

"Because committees never get anything done. They're reactive instead of proactive, stale by definition." He took a bite of chicken to indicate his confident jurisprudence. "In any case, the Phillip copy has been contaminated by exposure to another human brain, a known psychopath by all accounts. A good argument could be made for quarantine under the circumstances, perhaps a full screening and segregation of memories."

Colin7 could see little sign of sympathy in the mirror face before him. Perhaps his own mind had been polluted by contact with Earth, befouled by raging diversity. How could he look Phillip in the eye and tell him his sorry doom to digital imprisonment? Could he resort to fabrication? Could he lie to his own father, to himself? "I suppose my duty is plain," he said.

Colin5 nodded as he chewed. "Just get him through the Doorway alive. We're preparing a special transport capsule, a modified unit with bio-controls and life support. We can put the body in stasis with a respirator and cardiac pacesetter for the trip. We'll salvage and archive what we can as an anecdotal curiosity and dispose of the husk. There's no point in losing sleep over the copy's grandiose expectations. He will find a perfect resting place among his ancestors, more than most humans would dare to dream. We have that special privilege. Our genome has the assurance of eternal afterlife, not some superstitious fantasy of winged glory on a rainbow, but real, hard-wired heaven. We should all be thankful for the miracles of digital science." He pointed with a swaying fork at the food before them. "Enjoy your meal and savour your blessings. You've served well and deserve every good reward. Let the wine linger on your tongue. Can I schedule you a concubine for later? You're old enough now to relish the creature comforts."

Colin7 twisted in his seat as his pulse trilled at the invitation. A random sexual encounter with a stranger? Carnal lust without love? "No, thank you," he said. "I'll get some rest." He checked his wrist-band dutifully. "My capsule leaves early."

"Suit yourself," Colin5 said with a wink. "I know you're a talented performer with the ladies."

Colin7 felt a pang of guilt and a blush of lost secrecy. What could Colin5 have heard about his dalliance with Niko on the other side of the Doorway? "You do?"

"Of course," Colin5 said playfully. "We're the same person in mind and body. Cell by cell, neuron by neuron." He tapped the side of his skull with a finger. "There's nothing you can do that might surprise me."

"Ahh." Colin7 stared in wonder at his fellow clone. Was this the sage advice of maturity? Could life be that easy? Just lose him-self in the vagaries of the flesh and forget about the future? "What about our research into the nature of the multiverse, carrying on our father's ultimate work in celestial physics? What about the Alpha and Omega program, the breakthrough into the time dimension? Everything we worked for with the runner Zakariah? Surely that's all that matters in the end."

Colin5 carved a thin slice of white meat from a chicken bone and sopped up fragrant juices from his plate. "The concept of time is a mathematical conundrum, to be sure, and your own research provides the best hope to advance the theoretical framework. From a practical standpoint, there's little hope of reversing the polarity." He bent forward over his plate to taste the dripping morsel.

"But the math is symmetrical in either direction," Colin7 said. "Time is a variable component of the digital substructure."

"Naturally," Colin5 said with a smile as he wagged his fork, "I can't argue the math. But time can't be separated out in the lab or isolated in the equation. Our conscious movement through the warp creates an invariant forward momentum along the two-dimensional brane of warp space. We manifest a sense of duration out of necessity for conscious experience, but it remains fundamentally subjective."

Colin7 shook his head. No, no, that was too easy. Elegance was often a reliable tool in the development of theory, but never an infallible guide. There had to be more. "But Zakariah encountered an alien consciousness in a timeless state, the so-called superlight contact with the Source. Surely that changes everything."

Colin5 nodded with complacence as he chewed and swallowed. "There's no scientific evidence to support some indulgent divine intelligence behind the scenes in the multiverse. The runner's documentation was filtered by his experience and expectations, and corroborated second-hand by Helena, so technical bias has already skewed the findings. Zakariah's consciousness was digitized to a photon stream during the procedure, and of course a photon in its pure state has zero time and zero mass, so any reported transition through warp space must therefore be a fallacy inferred by the observer, an experimental blemish, nothing more." Colin5 stared at him with concern, a collegial fascination. "The data was voluminous and valuable, but doesn't negate the polarity of time, nor authenticate the notion of an alien species."

"My research shows a fuzziness to time," Colin7 said, feeling close to something glorious in the mathematical headwaters, groping for a solid rock just out of reach in the rapids. "Random-number generators monitoring collective unconscious forces seem to indicate a precognitive effect."

"I'm familiar with some of your work and suitably intrigued," Colin5 said. "Psychic powers and subjective time dilation may indeed have a delicate balance." His eyes probed for more explanation as he took another bite, his face expectant, empathic with fraternal understanding. Could they have a mind meld across the DNA, a brotherly bond that transcended the limits of cerebral flesh? Surely any such effect would be first noticed by clones. They were identical patterns, separated only by a single variable, frameshifted through the warp of brane-space like a drawbridge across a foaming river.

"Each consciousness creates a unique thread of experience in the quantum realm," Colin7 said, "like a jet leaving an atmospheric contrail. It's not something that can be lost or erased, and it has symmetry forward and back. I'm studying the ways these threads intertwine in phase to create collective waves that can be measured objectively, mind over matter, peaks and valleys."

"A permanent record forward and back." Colin5 glanced aside as he tested the idea in his brilliant mind. "That certainly flies in the face of free will, not to mention death."

"I'm beginning to think free will is a misconception. Death I'm not sure about." Colin7 stared at his unfinished meal as his appetite slipped away. He felt subverted as a theoretician, a rank amateur fishing in the presence of elder professionals, his experiments a futile hope for a lucky catch. He had eaten too much, more than his usual regimen, and longed for a bed and pillow to rest his bloated body.

Colin5 continued to fork food to his mouth. He chewed and swallowed. "You're hoping to pinpoint prognostics?"

Colin7 winced inwardly at the notion. Was he just a fortune-teller hiding behind fancy hardware and convoluted mathematics? A circus magician pandering to the crowd? He shook his head. "No, nothing like that. I'd be happy to make any small contribution to the compendium of theory." As the words left his mouth he could see that he had failed in his quest to codify the collective psi consciousness. He had devoted his career to a statistical anomaly in the name of science, but the experimental research of his colleagues had already ruled out any possibility of triumph. The Alpha and Omega program had slammed a steel door in his face. Time was an ineffable mistress and would never do his bidding.

"Well, you've done good work," Colin5 said, "and I wish you the best of luck for the *future*." His brother's tone was benedictive, subtly ingratiating, as he reached for his wine and held it up for a toast. "Rise on the wings of success in the morning," he said and quaffed a long gulp.

Colin7 touched his glass and tapped the stem with a finger, wondering how he would measure success if he ever stumbled upon it in the fog. A peer-reviewed breakthrough in psi physics? A pisspot of gold beside his bed at night? A gorgeous young woman on his arm, under his covers, Niko? He pushed the thought away, that dangerous vision of liberty. All he had was mute obligation to his genome hemming him in, a tortuous progression of fate. He had been splintered under an electron microscope, a fraction of a whole destined to return to the egg. He had no free will, no myth of separation to mar his ingrained moral imperative.

In the privacy of slumber in his darkened cubicle, Colin7 dreamt of white skin like alabaster, fragrant and pure, a consecrated maiden on a downy altar of delight. He felt fear at such forbidden virtue, a hot flush of disgrace from a sinner unclean by birth. His dirty fingers moved to embrace the sacrosanct offering and left black scars like scorch marks at every touch. The vestal skin felt as smooth as velvet, as fragile as gossamer, but hardened at his furtive caress and fissured into craquelure like a dry and ancient funeral urn. Blackened crevices gaped open to expose a wriggling mass of red snakes below the surface, and each had a tiny gaping mouth to consume the flesh of innocents.

A caterwauling alarm sounded beside his head, forcing him from the nightmare apparition. He clawed at a bedside shelf for his wristband to silence the clamour, the morning still dark, his appointment with the Macpherson Doorway beckoning him to the other side of space and time. He never should have tasted the wine. Alcohol always brought out the worst from his subconscious, his hindbrain like a seething animal.

Colin7 groaned and rose to face the day, stumbled to the water closet for ablutions and hot geothermal steam. He dressed quickly and slid his mattress into the wall. A tepid cup of tea laced with multivitamins was all his stomach could take this early, just enough fuel to get to a public protein dispenser. He shut cupboards and folded the kitchen nook in on itself, tipped table and bench up to the ceiling, and made for the door with a small travel pack slung over his shoulder—on to the next world. He looked back to an empty expanse, clean and neat, nothing but engineered seams and a single window to starry heaven.

The tram station was crowded with commuters poking at their wristbands or data tablets, boisterous night-shift workers coming home from the mines, reticent early birds sipping caffeine from cardboard cups. Colin7 lined up for his free breakfast of spicy grey goop from a government pouch. No one could starve in the Cromeus colonies, and poverty was by choice alone. The architect had spawned a controlled and subservient society, managing aspirations to a common baseline, manipulating the natural inclinations of man toward cooperation and consensual subjugation, no bats in the belfry, no rats in the shadows. So far, so good, with an undercurrent of dissatisfaction finding suitable expression in the art forms of the day, multimedia graffiti and horror poetry, the blow-off exhaust of the degenerati.

On the space shuttle Colin7 was once again subject to recognition and special privilege, an extra pillow and a pouch of candied fruit, an autograph request, the face on a million textbooks. He smiled with the practised charm of his genome: just a clone, nothing special. Stephen Hawking never had it so good. Lift-off left him sick with worry, his colon tight .with spasm. He breathed deep through his nose and tried to summon stasis as his stomach burbled with anxiety. Niko was right: he was such a wimp. He had abandoned her when she needed him the most. And for what? Some cruel charade with his fellow clones, a failed and useless experiment. What a waste of resources and ambition.

The specially modified launch capsule had been delivered to the Doorway for him, a medical-support system that would keep his father alive long enough to return home to his ultimate death. Colin7 would have the honour of testing it, debugging the schematics, preparing the celestial coffin for higher use. One day he would join his father and fellow clones in his own final upload to the aggregate union. He was but a single facet in a hard and scintillant diamond, carefully cut and polished by a brilliant communal mind to serve and obey.

He gave the capsule a cursory examination to familiarize himself with the modifications. The interior was lined with a white synthetic material that looked like satin but felt like brushed velour. Medical sensors were appended like buttons on all sides, but the wires were hidden within cushioned padding, and an extra oxygen tank had been installed between the knees to allow for his father's transport time up from Earth. An array of bottles on a side wall held drugs for every contingency, tubed together to mix and match on demand into the IV line. The diagnostic monitors were unobtrusive, hardwired into the mainframe, and an external viewscreen provided instantaneous data at the touch of a finger. Colin7 settled himself gingerly inside and signalled a technician to lower the lid down on his luxurious crypt. A whisper of air tickled his nostrils as satiny foam pressed against his face, and he closed his eyes as a rumble of movement led him to the Doorway and beyond.

Rix stepped out of a zoomtube into Sublevel Zero and surveyed the terrain with a cautious eye. The street was shabby with disuse, an ancient strip mall of storefronts on a forgotten legacy server, the programming stale, the surfaces just out of focus, tentative. He was deep in the unregistered tunnels where the denizens had not honed the source code to the polish of Main Street high above, but even here in the catacombs he wondered if he was under surveillance. Were his actions being monitored by the Beast, his thoughts recorded by Philomena? V-space had become a spooky place, a bedlam haunted by phantoms.

Niko appeared on schedule, wearing her catgirl outfit, looking awesome. Rix brushed at his hair with his fingers.

"Well, if it isn't the silver surfer," she said as she approached and gave him a hug. "You're taking a chance to meet me here," Niko whispered into his ear. "Things are not as they seem."

Rix held onto her shoulder as they parted, feeling a sure connection, testing her harmonics for bad buzz. No watchers, no gargoyles; perhaps they still had a vestige of privacy here in Sublevel Zero. "It's been awhile," he said as his fingers massaged her collarbone. Much too long. A aura of unfulfilled energy emanated from her. They had never really settled things, never really said goodbye. "Great to see you."

Niko glanced at his hand with a playful smirk. "Are you still hot for me?"

He dropped his arm and slapped his thigh with nervous anxiety. "Not really, maybe a little."

"You're looking good," she said. "Nice avatar."

"Thanks. I'm using enhancements."

"I can see that," she said, teasing him with her eyes, still playing the older-cousin role after all these years. "Totally superhero."

"Thanks."

"And you remembered our secret access code. That's so romantic."

"I'm not looking for a handjob, Niko. I'm here to kill Phillip."

Niko ducked her head as though someone had clipped her with a rock behind the ear. "Are you nuts?"

"Is that a double entendre?"

"No, you idiot. Are you insane?"

"Depends on your definition."

Niko huffed and set her hands on her hips. "You know, I've really missed your endless banter, Rix. Are you trying to get us killed?"

"Has he grown that powerful?"

She looked from side to side with uneasy caution, working her lips like a frightened little girl. She sidled toward an uncoded grey alleyway beside a vacant storefront to hide from the Beast's sniffing nose. "Philomena is holding Sienna as a hostage in a research experiment," she whispered. "I can't say anything about it."

Rix galvanized with alarm. "Is Sienna okay?"

"I don't know," Niko murmured. "I guess not. Philomena is working inside her now, inside all of us, manipulating our thoughts, trying to control everything."

Rix shook his head. "No way. The parameters would be fearsome. No consciousness could stretch that far, not over a million minds."

"Philomena's building a new consciousness, a machine intelligence." Niko looked past him into foggy grey shadows and ducked her chin. "She's manufacturing omnipresence."

"She must be using Phillip's body as a base," Rix said. "We've got to take out Phillip at the source. Even Jimmy's on the payroll now."

"You're hanging out with that old smuggler again?" Niko blew a scoff through pursed lips. "He didn't offer us much protection last time."

Rix waved a lazy arm to allay her suspicion. "Sometimes you have to let your enemy know you, Niko. You can't win a cold war without the opportunity for misdirection. Don't worry about Jimmy. I'm feeding him what he needs to know. My girlfriend and I are staying at his place in Canada."

Niko gaped at him in awe. "You have a *girlfriend*?"

Had he really said that out loud? Why did the idea seem so

strange to both of them? "Just a travelling companion," he blurted, trying to backpedal away from the bold confession standing like a barrier between them.

Niko squinted at him as though to test his mettle, and he looked away from her penetrating gaze. "I'm totally not doing her," he said, recoiling inwardly as the confession left his mouth. Why did Niko always make him think about sex?

"Don't be so crude, Rix. I never suggested a thing. I'm happy for you, really. What's her name?"

"Jovita. She's Eternal."

"Wirehead?"

"No."

"But I'll bet she a cutie. Two out of three, right?" She arched her eyebrows with whimsy, toying with him again, same old Niko, capricious to a fault.

"Forget that," he said. "What about Phillip? Will you help me get to him?" Back to business. Time was short.

Niko's smile faltered. "Phillip is sick, Rix. He's in quarantine with some rare disease. Colin7 is planning to take him through the Macpherson Doorway to find a cure."

"We can't let him get away! He'll spread Philomena everywhere he goes. He could infect the colonies like a digital cancer."

"We can't stop Philomena," Niko said. "She's grown too powerful. You can't fight her, and Jimmy can't help you."

"You don't know that."

Niko's face clouded with fear. "I've seen her up close, Rix. There's nothing we can do." She shook her head sadly, her natural insouciance trampled by circumstance. "Just let it go."

"We can't surrender V-space, Niko. It has to be free for all." He probed for her with his eyes, drawing out the shared history between them like a golden thread of promise. "Give me your password keys up Prime. Let me have the access codes to Phillip's research facility, get me in the building at least. You owe me that much."

Niko frowned and wagged a downcast chin as she deliberated. "Jesus," she whispered, perhaps not in vain, but she held out her palm glowing with jewels, the keys to her kingdom. "It's a suicide mission, cousin."

Rix took her treasure and stuffed the passwords in deep pockets. "I'll take my chances," he said. "I'll erase this meeting. I'll use anonymity. You won't get in trouble."

Niko held the tips of her fingers to her forehead. "We've got to get moving," she said.

Rix felt it, too, in the core harmonics around them. A roving gargoyle sucking code like a vacuum cleaner. Damn, the watchers had found them even here in the catacombs. Anything they said might be recorded now, published against their will. Niko pressed her lips tight, and Rix could tell she was clenching her mind against the intrusion. He saw a moment of fury in her eyes, or perhaps only imagined it to give himself hope, some solace against an encroaching invincibility. He ducked and stepped away from her, wondering if this might be the last time. He stopped and turned to study the cat-girl's retreating form with longing, a last gasp from his heart across the digital chasm. "Goodbye," he said.

The ND world was coming alive in Jimmy's imagination as he worked the holodesk in his office with diligence, tinkering with the framework of wi-fi design space. One day wireless users would surround themselves with holograms of data, layer after infinite layer in their daily experience, rainbows of search results at the tips of their fingers, an uninhibited encyclopaedia of understanding. He might live to see that emergent virtuality, the amplification of consciousness, if he was lucky enough to push this weary body around a few more years.

Too bad he couldn't live forever like some of his Eternal friends, his best friends, who would enjoy future miracles in quick stride and perhaps reminisce about his work. But the virus was not for sale. It was given away for free and cost everything to possess. Alien technology. Jimmy had enough trouble with the technology he could hold in his hands, creating the ND future, the progression of human consciousness through the shared use of holographic media. Out there, but right here at the intersection of digital V-space.

A knock sounded twice on the open door as Rix entered Jimmy's office with his usual punk swagger. "We're leaving now," he said. "The shuttle is out front. Thanks for the travel bits."

"You're welcome," Jimmy said. He patted down his holodesk to hibernation mode and looked up with a smile. "The Florida weather will be glorious, by all reports."

Rix shifted his weight side to side as though struggling with some inner balance. "Are you working for Philomena?"

"No," Jimmy said, "not exactly. She'll keep me around as long as I prove useful."

"What do you have that's so important to her?"

"Not much, a few trinkets," Jimmy said, frowning with misgiving. "Sometimes I wonder if she just wants a final witness to crown her conquest."

"I was thinking an open-source bomb would do the trick," Rix said.

"That so?"

"You could booby-trap the delivery. Blow the whole system public to expose the heart of the Beast. Transparency should work both ways, don't you think?"

"I dunno," Jimmy said. "That's a tall one."

"I know you can rig it. A simple trojan on one of your back-door codes."

Jimmy winced at the trite show of confidence, surely a deliberate ingratiation. "It'll be a lot more complicated than that."

Rix nodded as though some tacit agreement had been reached, some conspiracy set in motion. The kid was crazy, but at least he had toned down his murderous intentions toward his zombie grandfather.

"There's a new intelligence coming, Rix, whether we like it or not. The days of pretense are gone. We can't hold back the Beast much longer."

"Don't give up, Jimmy," Rix said, his face darkening with concern. "We're counting on you. All of us." He pointed a finger forward with menace. "Would you dare preach that song to my father's face, try to shovel some namby-pamby servility down his throat in the name of progress?"

The question, of course, was rhetorical, but Jimmy felt the need to clear his conscience. He looked away in humility to quell the tide of rising emotion, tried to keep his declaration calm and sincere. "We thought we could outrun the Beast in the early days, your father and I, obliterate the keystroke behind us. Leave no trail: that was our mantra. But you can't outrun an omniscient AI. You can't hide when every secret is exposed. The Beast is plowing up the soil, ripping up the foundations of V-space. Mankind is trending toward an ecumenical flatline, tolerance for all, no sharp edges to cut down the underprivileged."

Rix shook his head with sad defiance. "No one's going to fight for freedom with Philomena looking over their shoulder, judging every thought and action, sucking their data into a universal algorithm. A culture without innovation will fail."

"The fight for freedom is just an excuse for greed," Jimmy said, "an opportunity to subjugate the weak. Politicians hold it up like bait on a hook."

"Better than one tyrant sucking code and dictating order!"

Jimmy studied the young punk and decided to call it quits. There was no point in arguing with an impetuous and inflexible mind. Maybe Rix was right. The enhanced collective could be decades in development, a distant dream. Perhaps Jimmy was confusing old age with optimism. "I'll see what I can do," he said.

Rix pressed his lips with a nod and seemed satisfied that a pact had been established, that the situation was in good hands. Jimmy slapped him on the back and walked him to the door, but Rix stopped at the threshold to set one last barb. "Jovita wants to get the surgery and plug up someday, Jimmy—a rank innocent at the altar. What kind of V-net do we want for her?"

The next generation, a plea for the children, and save the whales while you're at it. Jimmy smirked his common-sense surety. "Don't worry about Philomena, kid, but let me give you one piece of advice that will change your life forever."

Rix tilted his head with interest, his punk swagger intact, his gait wary. "What's that, *godfather?*"

Jimmy smiled at the family reference, the veiled offer of renewed camaraderie. "When you meet Jovita's mother for the first time, don't forget to tell her how young and pretty she looks." He lowered a sagacious brow for emphasis, guru wisdom from the cloud, playing the body language to the hilt.

Rix chuckled and shrugged off another layer of insolence, just enough. "You want me to hook you up, don't you?"

Jimmy grinned. "Well, I always like to keep my options open."

Rix sniffed and nodded as though content with familiarity again, a simple solace. "Okay," he said, "but you better work on your tan."

TWELVE

A moment of nonspace through the Macpherson Doorway and Colin7 was back in the NFTA station orbiting the alien blue planet of Earth. A hiss of breaking vacuum seal roused him from his musings, and he rose from his sarcophagus and blinked as his eyes adjusted to the harsh light in the arrival bay. The air smelled earthy even here, organic, a smell he associated with dirt and dung back home in the colonies, a malfunctioning sanitary system. His miracle coffin had performed flawlessly, a luxury of cushioned comfort fit for a king, the architect of all.

Colin7 hovered above the capsule and ran diagnostics on the medical equipment while the transport staff waited for his signal. He followed along to ensure careful handling as roughnecks packed his special cargo on the Earthbound shuttle. Some of the jury-rigged modifications might be fragile, and there was no sense forsaking vigilance in a time of crisis. He checked the security of the restraints and sealed the cargo hold with a personal code. He strode to the cockpit and introduced himself to the launch crew as they came aboard, young men and women in bright orange uniforms. Colin7 took a seat in the passenger cabin and tried to feign calm as the shuttle lurched into space on an acceleration curve toward the planet below.

As they reached inner Earth orbit and dropped below the satellite horizon, he checked his chats for recent news. Niko was still angry, but at least she was relaying messages. Sienna had been returned to Phillip's neuroscience laboratory, but trouble was brewing. The text messages seemed like hieroglyphics to Colin7, truncated language codes without affectation, so easy to misinterpret. Communicating emotion by email was a rare gift, and Niko did not have it. He wondered if he could patch their relationship together, gain forgiveness for his short abandonment, make everything up to her somehow. Why did he feel such a precarious connection to Niko? Was this love, some antiquated biological function? He always felt like a fool in her presence, a little boy with sweaty palms hoping for a kind word and a gentle touch. Their rare sexual encounters had released volcanoes of eroticism from within him, voyages of adventurous discovery. The image of her naked body had been burned like a circuit board into his cranium.

He began to roleplay possible scenarios of clemency as he disembarked at the space station and waited for his transport capsule to be loaded in a medical truck. Surely Niko could understand his professional obligations, after a few days to pause and reflect. She was a reasonable woman, sharp-witted and thoughtful. He had never deliberately disowned her or abandoned Sienna. His only sin was a predestination to duty, a gullibility to purpose. The short trip to Phillip's neuroscience building seemed like hours in the back of the truck with his introspective protestations. His skin felt clammy with fear, his stomach roiled with uncertainty.

"I came as soon as I could," Colin7 said as he entered the lab where his daughter was under observation. Andrew looked up from his work on the control console at her bedside. Niko strode forward and slapped him hard across the face.

"What do you know, you Judas?" she demanded.

Colin7 rubbed his throbbing cheek. "Not enough, apparently."

"You betrayed us into the hands of devils!"

A scream sounded from Sienna reclining under covers, a short but horrible shriek of terror. Colin7 jumped to inspect his daughter as she contorted in agony with her hands over her ears and eyes clenched tight. He turned to Andrew. "What's going on?"

"Not sure yet," Andrew said, calm and capable in the face of fury. "She screams whenever she gets close to waking consciousness. She's had brain surgery, satellite wi-fi. I think she's overloaded with bandwidth." He glanced at her and grimaced with concern. "It's experimental."

"You must have known," Niko said, her tone acid with accusation. "You conveniently disappeared at just the right time. Just long enough for zombie Phillip to mutilate your daughter's brain!"

Colin7 shook his head. "No."

"I don't believe you," Niko said.

"Really?"

Sienna screamed anew, an octave lower, a howl from deep in the diaphragm.

"We're going to have to drug her again," Andrew said. He stood up and reached for a clear plastic mask on the table beside Sienna. Colin7 noticed a sweetness in the air, possibly nitrous oxide. The neuroengineering monitors showed erratic brain activity, a chart off the rails.

Without warning, Niko launched herself at Colin7 and punched him hard on the chest. "I never should have trusted you," she shouted. "You're a ghoul, the clone of an evil genius. Mastery and deception are written into your DNA. How could I have expected anything else?" She hit him again with the base of her wrist, and Colin7 caught her other hand to thwart the next incoming blow. He wrestled with her in silence as Sienna groaned in the background.

Andrew turned a valve and pressed the mask to Sienna's face. Her rigid body relaxed and her moans trailed off.

"I didn't know," Colin7 said. "How could I have known? Phillip is dying. He's barely functioning. This is all a complete surprise."

Niko shirked his hands away and stepped back. "What am I to think, Colin? You vanish after the kidnapping and return with an ambulance parked out front. What the hell are you up to? How can I ever trust you again?"

Colin7 gesticulated a juggling motion with open palms. "I've secured a transport capsule with life-support modifications. I'm supposed to take Phillip back through the Doorway."

Niko squinted at him. "Have they found a cure?"

"No," he said sadly, "there's no cure."

Andrew looked over with interest as he hung the ventilator mask on an IV pole. "Is it contagious?"

Colin7 shook his head. "No, it's not a disease. Phillip's condition is caused by systemic breakdown, a failed experiment. An artificial virus was developed in the Cromeus colonies." He held up a flat hand in promise to Niko. "Completely unknown to me. It had all the regenerative hallmarks of the legitimate Eternal virus. It passed all orthodox testing at the ERI. But in the end, it collapsed."

"You're as nasty as my father ever was," Niko said. "You're all insane megalomaniacs."

"Phillip's mitochondria are dissolving," Andrew said, nodding as he pondered the ramifications of insight. "The protein gradients are screwy. I know I'm not supposed to know anything, but I took a peek at the data."

"I'm not trying to hide anything," Colin7 said. "I only want to help."

Niko sneered. "We've had enough of your help."

"Just give me a chance."

"No," she said, "forget it."

Colin7 took a deep breath to calm himself. What a terrible turn of events. Was he responsible for this as well? Had he lost Niko forever? Did he deserve any better? "Well, what are you going to do for Sienna? What's your plan?"

Niko paused to gather her wits, frowning in thought. She looked at Andrew with expectancy and prodded him with a forward gesture to come up with something.

Andrew rolled his eyes with dismay. "You guys kill me."

Colin7 approached his daughter and lifted her limp hand, so tiny and frail. She still wore the ring he had given her in a gentler time that seemed distant now. "She has digital receivers in her head?"

"An octahedral array," Andrew said with a shiver of affirmation. "Strategically positioned. A brain within a brain."

"The Beast has uploaded a tracker into her," Niko said, "or some type of parasite."

"We don't know that," Andrew said. "But we can be sure that her progress is being monitored with diligence from V-space, moment by moment."

Colin7 winced to see his daughter trapped in another foul experiment, an atrocity that might never end. How could Phillip have accomplished this without his knowledge? "And we can't turn her off?"

"No," Andrew said. "It's wireless. She's supposed to learn how to control it on her own with cognitive commands. The schematics have been in development for years, but it's still way out there beyond the pale. No reputable scientist would go this far this fast."

"She's too young," Niko said. "Her brain is not mature enough to handle the bandwidth. God only knows the nightmares going on in there."

"We could try building a Faraday shield around her," Andrew said. "An impenetrable barricade."

"Or get her into space," Colin7 offered, "up above the satellite grid."

"We could reverse the surgery," Niko said. "We find the brain wizards and put them back to work, pay them whatever they want. That's the best bet by far. We can't hide her in a box for the rest of her life."

Andrew and Colin7 nodded grimly at the risk of further surgery. Tamper with her brain yet again?

Niko's eyes probed from face to face. "Well?"

"The procedure would be hazardous, probably fatal," Andrew said. "It's too soon."

Niko straightened her shoulders to summon bravado. "Don't wimp out on me now, Andrew."

"She's not a machine," Andrew said. "She's flesh and water, neurons in a glial stew. The brain is a delicate flower." He pointed to the bioengineering equipment with invitation. "Take a look at these images," he said. "I've never seen so much alloy in a brain, all those cobweb filaments. I'm not sure there's any road back from here. It's a miracle she's still alive. Most of the human brain is used to maintain the physical systems of life. Cell division and neurochemical balance. Consciousness is just a byproduct, and this type of augmentation is a blasphemy."

Sienna began to lilt a keening song from a dream far away, a high-pitched tremolo. Colin7 felt her hand clench with spasm in his own. What night terror was she suffering? Vultures and pirates, a million minds in motion. V-space was intense enough in a trickle of data through a fiberoptic cable. What would it be like all at once, forever? "I've got a transport capsule," he said.

At first they both stared at him in stunned silence, and he wondered if he had truly spoken aloud. What was he thinking? Abandon his father to save his daughter?

"No," Niko whispered.

Andrew blinked at him, his jaw slack. "The Macpherson Doorway," he said as his expression warmed to the idea. "Satellite wi-fi could never reach her in the Cromeus colonies."

"No," Niko repeated, but a sense of wonder had slipped into her tone.

"She would be safe on the other side," Colin7 said. "Her sanity would be restored. Perhaps as an adult she might learn how to control her augmentation. At least she'd have a fighting chance."

"No," Niko said to deny him a third time.

Sienna screamed anew at some hidden torment as Colin7 cradled her fitful hand in his palms. "We've got to do something," he said.

Andrew reached for the ventilator mask. "Let's give her another hit," he said. "She must be waking up already."

"We can't keep conking her out with gas," Niko said. "Can't we let her sleep?"

Andrew put the mask to her nose, heedless of her complaint. "She can't sleep," he said. "She may never sleep again. Her brain is in overdrive, permanently hyperactive. The V-net is not going to turn off for her like magic. We'll have to put sedatives in her IV, experiment with antipsychotics. I'll work up a regime to get started as soon as we make a decision."

"She's my daughter," Niko said.

Andrew pulled the mask away and turned off the valve as a puff of sweetness tickled the air. "Whatever you say. I'm just the doctor." He looked at Colin7 for any signal of strength.

Colin7 felt a spotlight burst of paternal responsibility. He was the father, by documentation if not deed, but he was drowning in uncertainty. A moan from Sienna trailed away in silence, poor lamb. "I'll go upstairs and grill my father for information. Perhaps he knows what Phillip is planning."

"That bastard," Niko said with indignation. "You can't cooperate with the Antichrist!"

"One thing we haven't considered," Andrew said. He held up his hands as though to ward off a blow. "And I don't mean to cause trouble, but what happens if Sienna wakes up with Phillip inside her? What if he figures out how to operate the wi-fi network? What if he jumps from one dying body into a young fresh one?"

"The Beast would be resurrected anew," Niko said, and her posture slumped at the realization. "With Sienna's special powers, he would control everything." She hung her head and wagged dark tendrils of tangled hair. "All V-space would be lost."

"I'm just wondering," Andrew said, "if we should keep our options open. The Macpherson Doorway might look pretty good if all else fails."

Niko looked up to face him. "Do you have any children, Andrew? Would you sacrifice your only child to save the world?"

"No," he said with steely calm, "no children."

"I'm keeping Sienna," she said. "We're going to figure this out somehow."

Colin7 flinched as she glared at him with glassy eyes, her face contorted with anguish. She looked ugly in this guise, the wounded mother. He remembered back to their first night of intimacy long ago, entwined in bed and enraptured together. He had shared her body and she had challenged his mind. He owed her a debt of love. "Sienna doesn't belong to us, Niko. Not really. We provided some raw material against our will, and we did what we could for her in a difficult situation, but perhaps she has a greater destiny."

"No," Niko said, her eyes dark and face haggard with worry. "I won't give up my daughter."

"She will be greater than both of us if we let her go," Colin7 said. "Sienna is the next step in human evolution. We can't let that fail, or be subverted by evil. Her freedom is the best gift we could ever provide."

Sienna began to murmur a gentle cadence, and they stepped closer to investigate. Niko bent her head down. "What is she whispering?"

They stilled their breathing to hear Sienna's plaintive whimper: "Hail, victory, hail, victory, hail . . ."

"Nooo," Niko groaned with horror. She grabbed Sienna by the shoulders and shook her violently. "Get out of her, you monster! Get out of my daughter's brain!"

Andrew jumped to pull her back. "Niko. Niko!"

She shrugged him off and whirled to face him. "Philomena is trying to gain control! She'll use Sienna like a puppet. We've got to stop her!"

"There's nothing we can do," Andrew said. "We don't have cognitive access. We're watching through a mediated window." He gestured at the bioengineering equipment. "We're trapped behind this barrier of dark hardware."

Niko turned to Colin7, her haunted eyes desperate. "Do you really think she'll be safe in the Cromeus colonies?"

"The brothers will treat her like royalty," Colin7 said. "We all know her special gift to the genome. She's part of our DNA family. I would trust Colin5 with my own life and hers. We're not tyrants, Niko. We know when to admit our mistakes. My father upstairs has been contaminated by exposure to Phillip and will be sent into quarantine if I bring him home. The brothers have disowned him."

Niko sighed and slumped her shoulders in defeat. "God," she said.

Colin7 touched her arm with a gentle caress. "Please, Niko, give Sienna a fighting chance for sanity."

Andrew studied them for a few moments, his face impassive, then bent to the floor to unlock the wheels on the gurney. He began disconnecting sensors and unplugging cables.

"We'll never see her again," Niko said vacantly. "The Beast will be tracking us the rest of our days. Philomena will never rest until she finds her."

"Sienna will be well cared for in the Cromeus colonies," Colin7 said. "A princess guarded in a celestial palace."

Tears trickled down Niko's cheeks as Andrew wheeled Sienna to the door and palmed the wall sensor. "Let's make this quick and slick past the webcams," he said. "Pack up her stuff."

"We'll need some extra weight in the capsule," Colin7 said. "Something to approximate the mass of an adult."

Niko sniffed a ragged breath for composure and exhaled with a whoosh of resolution. "I'll grab her backpack from the apartment. Meet you downstairs."

Colin7 checked his wristband and scrolled through data. They could just make the next launch window. Only one chance of escape, one path through the wilderness, and no turning back. "Okay," he said. "Let's go."

They took Sienna down the private service elevator and out to the medical truck as she curled in a fetal position and murmured terror into her blankets. Her limbs seemed like brittle sticks as they lifted her into the transport capsule. A beautiful mind in such a frail and tiny wraith, the firstborn transhuman, spliced together under a microscope lens, succoured in an artificial womb, her brain now implanted with cybernetics. How far can one soul be stretched before it breaks?

Niko arrived and began packing luggage at Sienna's feet and pillows at her shoulders. She tucked a pink bunny rabbit in the crook of her arm, and paused to study her work. "Sienna can't sleep without her stuffy," she said.

Colin7 draped an arm around Niko's shoulder. "She'll be fine," he promised.

Niko laid a hand on her daughter's forehead in final benediction. "Don't be afraid, honey. Your stuffy will keep you safe, and you'll wake up in a glorious new world." She bent to kiss Sienna on the cheek and whisper in her ear.

"Phillip could still stop us," Colin7 said. "He'll shut down the spaceport when he finds out I've misappropriated his transport capsule."

Niko nodded grimly. "We'll take care of Phillip," she said as she turned to Andrew. "Both of us, right?"

Andrew studied the tiny waif in her high-tech coffin and the pink bunny standing guard, his face sombre, his eyes glassy with emotion. "Just do your best for Sienna, Colin," he said. "We'll handle our end."

"Thanks," Colin7 said and shook his hand in firm salute, "for everything." They exchanged a wary gaze, rivals at love, brothers in arms, a personal paradox. Colin7 tapped his wristband. "The next launch window closes in two hours."

"Will you come back, Colin?" Niko asked. "Will you try to find me?"

"Uh, I'm not sure," Colin7 said, suddenly realizing the implications of his mutiny. Was he a criminal now? A vessel corrupted by insurgence? "My situation is complicated. My duties to the family genome . . ."

Niko studied him with eyes like magnets as he faltered. How could any man resist her? "You don't have to be that terrible person, Colin. You don't have to be a blind servant to fate. Life is more than twisted strands of DNA. We make decisions. We change. You can create your own future."

He spread his hands, his fingers freshly stained with rebellion. "I'm doing the best I can, Niko."

A shadow passed between them, and Niko dropped her chin. "Okay, then," she said. "I can't ask for more than that."

They settled the top on the transport capsule with a solid thump and a hiss of vacuum seal. Colin7 bent to work on the control panel to set up the air and temperature regulators as Niko and Andrew exited the truck and closed the door behind them. Sienna wouldn't need the cardiac regulator or dialysis machine. She was healthy enough to travel without the life-support system. Only her brain was sick. Andrew shouted instructions to the driver and the truck pulled away with Colin7 in the back with Sienna. He looked out the rear window at Niko's glistening cheeks as she receded in the distance.

Niko and Andrew slipped quietly into a basement supply depot to gather tools for a final assault against zombie Phillip. The old man was dying, but not soon enough. Niko picked up a two-handed bolt cutter and tried the leverage on a scrap of coax cable. "This should do the trick," she said and pointed to the wall with her chin. "Grab that fire axe and let's get to work."

Andrew took the bright red axe down from a sturdy bracket and hefted the weight. It had one sharp edge and a heavy, blunt back like a sledgehammer. "Nice," he said.

Niko handed him the bolt cutter and pulled out her trank pistol.

"If we get killed," Andrew said as he juggled the tools in his arms, "I'd like to be cremated."

"You're telling me this now?"

"Well, it's not fair to the future to use up space in the ground in perpetuity."

Niko tilted her head at him. "Do you have this written down somewhere?"

"No, I just thought of it."

"Focus your attention, Andrew!"

He ducked his eyes. "Okay," he said, "sorry."

Niko shook her head with annoyance and headed down the hallway with her gun drawn. There were no guards on this level and only a handful of webcams, but she didn't like surprises and Andrew was making far too much noise clanking behind her like an Orc in battle dress. They made their way to the electrical room and cut the padlock on the door with a quick snip. The main power supply hummed inside a grey metal box with a big handle on the side like an antique slot machine. A red switch for the fire alarm stood on the wall nearby behind a tiny glass window. Niko took the bolt cutters and broke the glass with a quick thrust. She pulled the switch to unleash a whooping mechanical siren, and they cringed instinctively at the auditory assault in such close quarters.

"Send out a text to the staff on your wristband," Niko shouted. "Evacuate the building. Electrical malfunction in the basement. Tell them Colin7 has already escorted Phillip to safety." She counted ten seconds while Andrew tapped out the message. "Do you think that's long enough?"

"Quicker the better," Andrew said without looking up. "Security guards will be running by now."

Niko reached up to the breaker switch and yanked a blanket of darkness down around them. Emergency lights came on immediately and cast a faint greenish glow from the corners of the room. The alarm continued to wail with a vicious intensity.

"Take the sledge and bang this thing up a bit," she said. "We don't want anyone turning the power back on while I'm skulking around upstairs."

Andrew picked up the fire axe and gave the box a whack that sent sparks shooting up like fireworks with a buzz of high voltage.

"Just break the handle off," Niko said. "Don't electrocute yourself!"

Andrew grimaced at her with wry sarcasm and raised his weapon high. He gave the handle a good hit and bent it downward. Two more blows, and it broke and clattered to the floor.

"C'mon," Niko said as Andrew set the axe aside with a wheezing exhalation. "Bring the bolt cutters."

Niko paused at the doorway and held a palm up for quiet. Running footsteps. She dialled up optical zoom and peeked around the corner, recognized the figure in uniform but didn't dare recall his name. The faceless enemy. She pulled out her trank pistol and thumbed the safety off. From a crouching position she fired a shot to his left shoulder as soon as he got within range. He spun and slumped against the wall with a thud. "Showtime," she whispered.

They scampered down the hall to a side entrance and down five steps to another closed door. The power lock was open in failsafe emergency mode, but the blinking lights inside were fully active on thousands of servers stacked like pizza boxes in a cavernous enclosure. A frosty blast of air rained down from vents in the ceiling.

Andrew followed her downstairs with the bolt cutters at his side. "The computers have their own power supply?"

"They're hardwired," Niko said. "No fuses, no switches. The V-net never sleeps."

Andrew stepped forward to examine the oblong megaliths. There was barely enough room to slide sideways between the rows of servers in the stale, refrigerated air. A thin film of grit covered every exposed surface, and a forest of fiberoptic cables sprouted like tangled spaghetti from the back of each rack. "V-space is in here?"

"Not all of it," Niko said. "There are hundreds of these nodes across the country, each one with petabytes of data. This is where Phillip lives now. Prime Seven, Prime Eight, who knows how high he's built his ivory tower? We'll cut off his access to the neuroscience lab."

Andrew held up the bolt cutters as though seeing them for the first time. "There must be a thousand cables." He peered up at blinking servers stacked to the ceiling under frosty ductwork. "How am I supposed to climb up there?"

"Just do what you can," Niko said. "There's too much redundancy in the system to make any permanent damage. All we need is a smokescreen, a temporary disruption of communication. Just until Sienna is safely out of this solar system and free of Phillip's influence."

Andrew shrugged his resignation and nodded to the door for her to get on her way.

Niko paused for a moment and placed a soft hand on his shoulder. "If anyone comes in, just throw down your tools and put up your hands. Tell them everything." She poked her pistol into his abdomen. "Tell them I forced you at gunpoint to cooperate. You'll pass the galvanic detector now 'cause it's the absolute truth."

Andrew smiled at that. He winked goodbye as she lowered her weapon. Perhaps they would meet again, but she wasn't counting on it. Niko dashed to the door and down the hall as the siren keened around her in a perpetual agony of auditory augmentation that she dared not tone down. She wished she could disable the alarm battery, but it would probably kill the emergency lights as well. Another set of footsteps. Damn, she almost missed it with all the distraction. She ducked and got off a quick shot as a guard came running around the corner. He huffed as the nerve toxin paralyzed his body. He fell with a thump like a sack of dirt. Sleep well, little baby.

The sound of the alarm was muted in the stairwell, and Niko heard movement coming up from below, someone creeping with slow stealth, breathing regularly, in through the nose, out through the mouth. She could almost sense a quickened heartbeat. Sometimes the edge of her enhancement blurred with imagination, but she knew enough to trust every scrap of data. She braced her feet as she raised her weapon and pointed it to the base of the stairs. If a gun came round the corner, she would get first shot.

She tensed as a silhouette slunk around the edge, but held back her finger from the trigger. Some subliminal hint of recognition stilled her hand, something in the body stance, a male with wide shoulders and a pistol pointed to the floor, a hoodlum. The figure crept forward and finally noticed her in the dim light. He froze, and his weapon quavered in an amateur hand. He was not a trained shooter, just a kid with gun.

"Rix?"

"Niko?"

She lowered her weapon. "What the hell are you doing? I almost popped you one."

He rushed up the stairs to meet her, his face white with fear and his lips trembling. "I'm sure you know," he whispered, teetering near the edge of panic.

"I never thought you'd go through with it," she said. "How did you get here?"

"Jimmy supplied bus fare and travel documents."

"You told him your plan?"

"No, we're on our way to Florida."

Niko peered past his shoulder into the gloom. "Where's Jovita?"

Rix tossed his bangs in a failed attempt at aplomb. "In a coffee shop around the corner. She's nursing a mocha latte while I pick up my last paycheque."

"Are you kidding me?"

"Sometimes you have to keep the truth even from yourself."

Niko stared at her stepcousin in wonder, feeling a deeper convergence of empathy with a fellow warrior in a family of soldiers. "Join the club," she said.

"Do you know where Phillip is?"

She ducked a nod. "He's bedridden in his lab."

"Did you set the alarm and cut the power?"

She smiled. "Yeah. The building clears in four minutes and forty-five seconds in a standard drill. The fire trucks arrive in six flat." She checked her wristband. "Two more minutes."

"Damn, you're good."

"Andrew's in the basement gutting the V-space server farm for a distraction. This will be our only chance. Have you ever discharged your weapon?"

Rix stared down at the pistol in his palsied hand. "No, not exactly. I got it from Dimitri."

"Do you know how to unlock the safety?"

"Sure." Rix held the trank pistol forward for view. "This button here."

"Do it," Niko said.

"What, right now?"

"Yeah, take a shot at that light switch." She pointed to the target a few metres away.

"Are you serious?"

"Yes, Rix. Are you afraid?"

"No," he said, but his face said maybe a little. He raised his pistol and sighted down the barrel. "What if someone hears us?"

"Don't be a wimp, cousin."

The gun went off with a crack and a whistle as a dart of nerve toxin careened down the stairway. "Crap," Rix said at the faster-than-a-bullet recoil. All those years running Sublevel Zero and he still couldn't summon the decadence of language to say shit. Amazing. A play of emotion paraded across his face, a glimpse of relief, a moment of pride, and a return of apprehension. "Satisfied?" he said.

Niko nodded. "Recognizing your fear is the first step to controlling it. Put the safety back on, and stay right with me. Don't worry." She tapped her augmented ear with a finger. "No one can sneak up on us."

She motioned with her shoulder for him to follow and hurried up the stairs to the neuroscience lab. As they snuck down the darkened hallway, the siren went silent like a painful abscess finally removed from her jawbone. The fire department had arrived in the building. Time was short.

They quickened their pace and barged into Phillip's room to find Zakariah sitting quietly beside his father's bed, hands crossed in his lap. Emergency lights in the corner cast a pallid glow on the dormant medical equipment. "You can put away your guns," Zak said. "It's finished. You're too late."

Dozens of empty IV bags hung on a rack behind the bed with dregs of crimson residue inside, Phillip's supply of Eternal blood now exhausted. Another bag of clear liquid hung on a pole, and Niko followed the tubular trail to the stump of her father's arm. Phillip's eyes were sickly yellow, and a ghoulish trickle of black dribbled from his mouth.

"He'll be dead in a few minutes," Zak said. "I maxed out his morphine drip to quicken the inevitable end. It's a mercy killing in my mind." He passed an open palm sideways in a tantric gesture of erasure, a holy motion. "This is for Mia. You kids have no part in this. He's my father, and the duty falls to me. Let his sins rest on my shoulder for eternity's sake."

"Don't you know who I am?" Phillip said in a slow, medicated drawl. "I invented the Macpherson Doorway. My fame stretches across the universe."

"Your name is Phillip Davis," Niko said sternly, "and a lake of fire awaits your evil soul."

"No," he moaned, and his ochred eyes rolled up into his head as his eyelids shuttered. His body stiffened and convulsed in a rhythmic tremor. His forehead tipped up, and his chest rose as though summoning one last vestige of strength. His eyes opened anew, alert and vigorous. His face transformed with familiar arrogance. He smiled. "Niko, my faithful warrior," he said, his voice now clipped and concise, the old voice, the original Phillip, "I knew you would come to my rescue. Macpherson failed me with his artificial virus. Sienna's botched surgery was all his fault. I'm taking . . ." He paused and blinked with confusion. ". . . this body back for my personal use. Everything's . . ." Again he trembled as another server went dead in the basement. ". . . going to be all right now."

"Don't listen to him," Rix whispered beside her. "He can't be trusted."

Niko's gun felt like lead in her hand, the dead weight of decades of abuse. Anger coursed through her like hot acid. She glanced at Zak sitting calmly in vigil at the bedside.

"Let him be," Zak said. "The responsibility is all mine. You kids shouldn't have a burden like this on your conscience. Go now in peace. It's finished."

"Shoot him, Niko," Phillip shouted, his voice imperious. He coughed and spit a glob of black necrotic gore. "Kill the traitor now while you have the chance!"

"I'll take my share of guilt and hoist it like a crown," Niko said as she pointed her gun at her father. "It's a small price to pay for this triumph."

Phillip's eyes opened wide and turned toward Rix as his ghastly face contorted with panic. "Help me," he begged. "Grandson!"

Niko fired her weapon and lodged a tranquillizer dart into the withered neck of her tormenter. She hung her head in victory and felt a righteous mix of mortified vindication. Her pistol clattered to the floor. Another shot sounded beside her, and a second dart landed on target. She looked up in surprise to see Phillip's eyelids close with a final twitch as the nerve toxins paved his way to death.

Rix turned to Niko with a heartfelt gaze. "All for one," he said as he lowered his trembling weapon.

Thirteen

"Can we swim that far, Daddy?"

"We must," Phillip said, "There's no land-bridge back from here."

The child stared out at endless waves and frothy whitecaps. An ocean of light surrounded them in all directions, a chaos of dancing photons. She heard singing and laughing, a gentle consolation. "It looks a long way," she said.

"Yes, but perhaps not far. Come on," he said. "I'll race you."

Phillip took two steps and dove headfirst into the tide, his lithe body responding in perfect symmetry, in ultimate synchrony.

Philomena smiled happily and waded in to follow her father.

At the spaceport, the transition went smoothly, the name on the registry like magic: Colin Macpherson, the original architect. The staff physician arrived to offer formal courtesy and professional expertise, but Colin7 ushered him away from his clandestine cargo with furtive grace. He kept sweaty hands on the control console and nervous eyes on the monitor as roughnecks loaded the transport capsule on the shuttle with care. He would not hear Sienna screaming if she woke up while they were still under the satellite grid, but her heart and respiration indicated a resting mode. He buckled into a fold-down jumpseat in the cargo hold for launch, but quickly unstrapped again after the first acceleration burst and checked the

235

medical readouts on the capsule. Just a few more minutes and he could open her dark sarcophagus. He felt like an angel waiting at the tomb for a promised resurrection, biding time with eternity.

A warning beep sounded as Sienna's heartbeat went above threshold. Her respiration began to increase. Damn. How high up were they? Colin7 whirled to stare out the porthole. Just stars in the distance, no landmarks of man. Could the Beast reach grasping claws even at this altitude? Could Phillip try one last desperate upload to new virgin ground?

Colin7 unlocked the lid and lifted it easily in weightless space. Sienna opened her eyes and smiled with recognition, and his heart melted to see youthful animation in her unpained and innocent face.

"Hi, Daddy," she said as she inspected her strange biotech bed-chamber with wonder.

Colin7 pushed up and hovered over her, hanging by a handrail and grinning with relief. "Hello, Sienna. Are you feeling okay?"

"I didn't know you could fly," she said.

"We're in space, honey. There's no gravity to hold us down. Everyone can fly."

"Can I try?"

"Sure," he said. "I'll unstrap your belt. But be careful." He bent to help her with the single slide buckle at her waist and gently pulled her up. At first she flailed, but he coaxed her to relax, and soon she was floating freely, pushing gently from wall to wall.

"This is fun," she said. "We don't need wings."

Colin7 smiled with delight to see her so happy. "Wings would be nice. Some people use tanks of pressurized air to move around."

"Like rockets?"

"Yes, like jet packs strapped over their shoulders."

"Cool," she said with sure wisdom beyond her years. "Can I try?"

"Someday, but not right now. We're going on an adventure today."

She studied him for a moment, and he flinched self-consciously from her inspection. Could she read his mind? Did she really know the end from the beginning? "I had a bad dream, Daddy."

"Yes, I know," he said. "We had to get away."

"That bad woman doesn't like me."

"Philomena?"

"She's not real," Sienna said. "She's an *artifact*." She stressed the new, uncertain word.

"Philomena won't be coming with us," Colin7 said.

"Good. I don't like all those noisy voices she carries. They hurt my head. It's nice and quiet here." Sienna peered out a portal at the stars in space, the bright banner of the Milky Way, and craned her neck from side to side. She grew quickly bored and turned back to her transport capsule, picked up her pink stuffy bunny and hugged it with familiarity. "Is Mommy here?"

Colin7 shook his head. "Mommy's busy elsewhere, but she loves you very much. She wants you to have fun in your new home."

"Where are we going?"

"Through a wormhole called the Macpherson Doorway. It's like an elevator through a different dimension."

Sienna gazed at him with amazement. "Is it magic?"

"No, it's not magic," he said. "It's science. Imagine taking a piece of cloth and folding it so two edges that were far apart can touch each other. That's what the Doorway does."

"Will you be waiting for me on the other side?"

He felt an ache in his diaphragm, an involuntary shudder of melancholy as he made his final decision. "I will be, honey, but I'll be much older there, like a grandfather. I'll still love you just the same, and you'll meet my little brother to play with. He's five years old.

You'll have to teach him all the things that only a big sister knows. He has the same name as me, Colin."

"That's funny," she said with a laugh. "How can you have the same name?"

"It just worked out that way. I don't know why." He shrugged his shoulders, but recognized anew the inbred arrogance of his family genome, the pompous protest against the invincibility of death. His progenitor was a mad maniac with a boundless ego. Colin Macpherson had sacrificed his life to science and lost his humanity in return. "We're almost at the space station. We'll settle you in your bed and close the lid for just a few minutes. You won't be afraid, will you?"

"No," she said, "I'm going on an adventure."

"I love you, Sienna," he blurted, feeling a fresh bubble of concern for her.

"I know you do, Daddy," she said. "I can feel it."

"You have a special gift."

"Yes," she said, bright with complacency, "a birthday gift."

Created and not conceived, an engineered egg in a mechanical womb. She knew everything and understood too much. Poor little perfect girl. Colin7 put up a show of good humour for their last moments together. They embraced a final time, and Sienna made him kiss her princess ring for good luck, the ring he had given her long ago and far away. He sealed her capsule with a pneumatic hiss and checked the instrumentation as they docked at the spaceport. Cargo roughnecks came in and lifted Sienna like a fragile chalice, with all respect due the holy name on the transport registry, the one true name.

Support staff fawned over Colin7 as Sienna's capsule slid into the darkened orifice of the wormhole to safety on the other side of the

Macpherson Doorway. They offered him a courtesy capsule to accompany the famous host, but he waved them away with thanks. He had a better life waiting for him on a bold frontier, a burgeoning hope, perhaps a beautiful woman to share his own unique adventure. He gazed out a porthole view toward his new home, the water planet, a hotbed of competition and cooperation, of possibilities unimagined. The blue jewel of Earth had never looked so fabulous!

Jimmy reclined in his launch couch with a creaky feel of familiarity as he prepared to settle the score with Philomena. Reports had trickled in that she had disappeared onstage at her latest rave, fallen from the throne of media grace like a Hollywood icon laid low by drugs. Something had gone terribly wrong, and it was good to have Rix out of the way and occupied with Jovita, out of the curious mix. Jimmy had promised his dead mother that he would try to keep him safe from harm, and that counted for something even now at the final culmination.

Jimmy plugged up to Main Street with a new ghost avatar, an invisible white spirit with no reverberation, no perturbation. He slid sideways through the cavorting crowd, careful not to touch any fellow users, avoiding the nodes and sensors, evading the greysuits and thought-police with their gaudy, gargoyle streams of advertising. He activated a secret portal with a simple mnemonic and zoomed uplevel with a gut-wrenching acceleration into the lair of the Beast in Prime Eight. He had been this way only a few times, but he always logged his access codes for later use, kept his back doors open and his trapdoors handy. He stored most of his data in mnemonic code, converting numbers to language for quick reference. It was a lot easier to remember a nine-letter word than a random string of nine numerals, and it carried less space in his cranium. He had thousands of passwords committed to memory, but the Beast was not interested in his personal eccentricities. Philomena wanted the encryption algorithms he had collected in the early days, the deep resonances that wove through the foundations of V-space. He carried them now in the form of glowing embers on his fingertips, ancient access codes from the dinosaur days of the American corps, the first primitive internet and freenet. These were the precious gems he would offer at the foot of the throne, the crowns he would cast down before the almighty Beast. He could delay no longer.

The control chamber in Prime Eight hummed with harmonic potential, the lower levels nested within the digital architecture like Russian matryoshka dolls, and data moved in living streams around him, linear threads interwoven like glassy, undulating mesh, cause and effect, promise and destiny, justice and judgment. But no sign of the guardian, Philomena, the AI personification of his aging partner.

"Phillip," he said to the living waters. "Philomena?"

Jimmy wasn't sure what to expect at this final surrender. The dagger teeth of a giant bear to grind him to pieces? The Asian anime nymph to tickle his fancy? In what form would the Beast accept his offering of treasure?

Jimmy looked around at the huge depository of data, the system codes for V-space. He could change anything from here, rewrite history, perhaps change the future. He could see Phillip's hand in much of it now, a tendency toward symmetry, strictures of order. Perhaps he should mess around with it just to wake the Beast from slumber.

First thing, and simple enough, he switched the ownership title on his penthouse condominium to the name of Rix Davis, his only sensible heir. Next, he prepaid the expenses on the place in perpetuity from a corporate slush fund, technically illegal and easily reversed by the Beast, but perhaps the only way to prod the bear to action. Two automated cybertrackers appeared to review the alterations, but Jimmy deactivated them with a gentle touch. It would take more than that to thwart him. Where was the Beast?

Jimmy held up the glowing jewels on the tips of his fingers, his treasure trove of secrets. "Phillip?"

A whisper replied, a faint suggestion of sound: *In here, old friend.*

Jimmy's keen senses tracked the harmonic to a slender aperture in the wall behind a watershed of ribboned data. He slid through a narrow doorway and shielded his eyes from brightness. A huge glowing ball filled the expanse, a bundle of living filaments turning and twisting together. Threads of rotating light shot out from the globe and arced in splendour to quickly return to the whole, giving the surface an airy, frothy appearance above a dense inner core. The nexus of the Beast, the foundational hub of V-space condensed in an exabyte sphere.

What palace of hardware on the skin of the planet could house this magnificent configuration? It would take a city of servers, racks and racks of active nanocrystals in piggyback array, a forest of fiber-optic connections. Perhaps it did not exist in hard space at all. Could it be peer-to-peer mesh architecture, harvesting and amplifying the capacity of all V-net users? Could it be a huge quantum computer operating outside of the physical continuum, harnessing the mathematics of negative space?

Jimmy stared in awe at the globe of brilliance, his arms limp, the trinkets in his hands all but forgotten, primeval in comparison to such glory. What could the Beast want with his paltry access codes when the whole world was contained and controlled? He looked down at the glowing tips of his fingers, his pitiful offering. A flashlight beam casts little splendour in the noonday sun, and his gift would make no difference to the god of V-space, but Jimmy felt an absurd sense of duty, a promise unfulfilled. His harboured treasure seemed like a millstone that he wanted only to cast off, to leave at the altar. He stepped forward and thrust his hands into the glowing globe.

A screaming transcendence enveloped his mind, an overwhelming ecstasy of understanding, a sense of history and a promise of prophecy, a united consciousness. He closed his eyes against the onslaught, tried to focus his attention against infinity, but the source code sucked him in all directions at once, trying to force his mind apart into multiple affinities. A trillion eyes, a billion ears, an obliteration of self. Too much data, too many threads of purpose!

Jimmy gasped and pulled his arms free. He stumbled back and fell on his fat ass, stunned by his brief glimpse of the machine brain. Humans were cave animals in comparison, blind bedbugs. He stared at his empty hands, his secrets washed clean in the river of data. The AI Beast had no need of his petty passwords, no use for a partner. Why had Philomena driven him here?

"Are you in here, Phillip?" he shouted. "What do you want from me?"

But no sound returned from the machine soul, no harmonics of personality. Had Phillip's plans been thwarted? Had his consciousness dissipated, transformed into something infinitely more complex, taken up into the whirlwind cloud like Elijah of old?

Jimmy stood and faced the burning altar. Was this what they had dreamed and schemed for, the global kingdom of communication? Had the Beast fallen under its own weight, dispersed into the very network it had sought to control? Jimmy chuckled at the irony of it all. A hollow victory, for sure, after all those hard years running V-space and gaming the system like pirates. He felt like a party guest at an empty banquet table, a final witness to some cosmic absolution.

"If you can still hear me, Phillip, I wish you well," he said, a token resonance on the shores of heaven. There could be no enemies in this place, no guilt. "I'll check on the kids as best I can."

And with that final promise to his old partner, Jimmy turned from infinite splendour, eased his way back through the narrow gate, past the luminous threads of the data-storage complex and out of the lair of the Beast. He left the portal locked open behind him as he sauntered away, a wide open door into the nexus of V-space. He nudged a few bloggers and poked a few friends as he made his way out past the security maze, throwing a few bread crumbs along the path for good measure. The mountains were not high and the empire was not far away. The psycho-king and his anime-queen had been obliterated into the ether and left the palace unguarded. The Beast would soon fall, and all his angels would be dragged down to Sublevel Zero, the digital baseline where all men and women were equal, where sin never sleeps and hope abounds. That would be fun for an old man to watch.

Jimmy smiled as he sat up from his launch couch and powered down his system. He loved these strategic moments of change, had cultivated them throughout his career, always looking for the next twist of innovation, the next fork in the road when anything could happen and usually did. Now he was content to consign the future forward into the public domain. He had never aspired to fix the universe, to create a better world. Let the DNA roulette wheel continue to spin. Let the smart kids play their hand at the poker table like their predecessors, try and fail, struggle forward. That was the history of civilization. The posthumans would do no better, and machines could do no worse. Let them all duke it out together on a grand stage, accountable to every netizen with eyes to see and ears to hear. In the coming age of infinite access, the questions would be more important than the answers.

Jimmy was a businessman, not a philosopher. He was handsome for an old geek, in a rugged sort of way, and he still had a few good moves on the dance floor. What the hell, he might even get laid a few more times before he died. Retirement life was long and luxurious; no need to rush a girl to orgasm at his age. He stepped out onto his penthouse balcony to hear the thunder of Niagara Falls in the gorge below. It seemed louder at night, a perpetual crescendo. The air smelled sweet and full of future promise. He could almost hear the bling of the slots on the casino floor in the distance, the siren lure of fast action and easy money. Nice night for a walk, maybe check out the action on the verdant green of the craps table. He had no secrets to hide now, little to lose, and plenty of time to toss some dice into eternity.

At ECW Press, we want you to enjoy this book in whatever format you like, whenever you like. Leave your print book at home and take the eBook to go! Purchase the print edition and receive the eBook free. Just send an email to **ebook@ecwpress.com** and include:

- the book title
- the name of the store where you purchased it
- your receipt number
- your preference of file type: PDF or ePub?

A real person will respond to your email with your eBook attached. And thanks for supporting an independently owned Canadian publisher with your purchase!